AD Fiction Fantasy
Priest Chr

Priest, Christopher, 1943 —   Green
Sleepers, Book 1   9000924781

D0435596

9000924781

DISCARDED BY
MEAD PUBLIC LIBRARY

SLEEPERS · BOOK ONE

SLEEPERS · BOOK ONE

By Christopher J. Priest and Mike Baron

ibooks, inc.
new york
www.ibooks.net

DISTRIBUTED BY SIMON & SCHUSTER, INC.

Dedicated to my nephew, Kyle.
—MB

An Original Publication of ibooks, inc.

Copyright © 2004 DC Comics. All rights reserved.

Green Lantern and all related characters, names and elements are trademarks
of DC Comics © 2004. All rights reserved.

An ibooks, inc. Book

All rights reserved,
Including the right to reproduce this book Or portions thereof in any form
whatsoever.

Distributed by Simon & Schuster, Inc.
1230 Avenue of the Americas, New York, NY 10020

ibooks, inc.
24 West 25th Street
New York, NY 10010

The ibooks world Wide Web site address is:
http://www.ibooks.net

Visit DC Comics online at
www.dccomics.com
or at keyword DC Comics on America Online.

ISBN 0-7434-8724-9

First ibooks, inc. printing July 2004
10 9 8 7 6 5 4 3 2 1

Front jacket art by John Watson
Jacket design by Georg Brewer

Printed in the U.S.A.

0924781

SLEEPERS · BOOK ONE

CHAPTER

1

The Sun rose over the South Pacific on February 25, 1945, illuminating a scene of massive devastation. The beaches of Iwo Jima, a tiny atoll in the Japanese archipelago, were littered with the bodies of American soldiers, many missing limbs, some partially buried in the rich volcanic soil, stained everywhere with viscous blood, black in the daylight. Seagulls hopped among the corpses and fought over gobbets of flesh. The entire island, eight square miles, was completely denuded of flora. Not a speck of green remained. Located six hundred and fifty miles south of Tokyo, Iwo Jima was the farthest outpost of the nation of Japan itself, and its invasion and occupation by the Allies represented an important turning point in the war.

There were no Japanese soldiers within a hundred yards of the beach, for they had chosen to conceal themselves below ground, or in bunkers and pillboxes built into the side of Mt. Suribachi. Two days ago, American Marines had raised the American flag on top of the mountain, but fighting continued sporadically as Japanese defenders who had sworn personal fealty to the Emperor fought on.

By the twenty-fifth, American forces were in control of ninety percent of the island. They'd advanced day and night since the nineteenth against withering enemy fire. Medics were overwhelmed by thousands of casualties. Many died on the beaches and on the mountain's slopes. By the twenty-fifth, fighting had subsided sufficiently that medics could at last move through the hellish terrain and answer the pleas of the injured, many of whom had lain where they fell for days. The cry of "Medic!" issued feebly from scores of parched

1

throats. Off shore, troop transport ships tried to deal with the over-whelming number of casualties.

Surviving medics had each been assigned a quadrant and were working their way inland from the beaches, searching for wounded Marines. There were still Japanese snipers taking deadly aim from concealed holes near the top of Mt. Suribachi, and it would be many hours before the medics covered the two miles to the base of the mountain. The entire island smelled of death. Not even the strong sea breeze could scour away the smell.

On the skirt of the mountain lay an American soldier who was not dressed in the Marines' drab olive green. Prior to the battle, his uniform had consisted of a crimson shirt, green tights, and a purple cape. Now, he was indistinguishable from any other bone-weary grunt, his costume the same wretched gray as the island itself, ripped here and there, revealing jagged gashes in his flesh. He wore a black domino mask. He was known as the Green Lantern.

Green Lantern was among the handful of "mystery men" who had begun appearing prior to the war in Europe. Not a member of the armed forces, Alan Scott had nevertheless volunteered to serve his country in this, its darkest hour, for Scott *was* the Green Lantern. The masked, costumed hero possessed immense power, linked to the ring he wore, which was in turn linked to a green lantern. The lantern derived its power from a unique, incandescent body called the Star-heart, which was not of this Earth, and in fact did not even exist in this universe.

A crime reporter prior to the war, Alan Scott thought he'd already plumbed the depths of predatory savagery. He was soon to learn otherwise. Not only was humanity not alone in the cosmos, it was far from the worst of species. While Marines of the 4th Division threw themselves into the Japanese meat grinder, Green Lantern had fought a parallel battle, a ghost battle against alien forces that had aligned themselves with the Japanese. Only a handful of humans were even aware that civilization's greatest battle was being fought in the shadow of a vastly greater contest.

Green Lantern had survived, if not triumphed. Although he was human, the ring of power he wore imparted certain benefits. Thus, on the morning of February 25th, out of earshot of any other living human, Alan Scott, the Green Lantern, opened his eyes. The battle had been exhausting and cruel. His enemy had struck at him numerous times with bolts of destructive energy. Scott gingerly felt the places where he'd been hit. He was bruised and bleeding, but there did not appear to be any internal damage, and he had no broken bones. Slowly, he tested his extremities. His fingers tingled from lack of circulation, but at least he could move them, and feeling was returning.

As he lay on his back, thankful for the warmth of the morning sun, he exercised his will: his body rejected its layers of grime and dirt; his costume mended and cleaned itself. The battle stains hovered for an instant three inches from his skin like a tiny rain cloud before the breeze took it away. His shirt reasserted its crimson glory. His leggings turned an incongruous green. Now he was a Technicolor man in a black and white landscape.

"Green Lantern!" a voice cried inches from his ear. Startled, Scott looked around. He was alone, save for the dead and the scavenging seagulls. In the distance, a B-25 headed south from a bombing raid toward its base in the Marianas.

"Green Lantern!" a gull squawked, circling his head. Scott shielded his eyes with his hands and watched its gyre. The gull now hovered in the air, ten feet overhead, its wings outstretched, feathering the breeze perfectly to remain in place. "Are you all right?"

Scott beamed and gave a thumb's up. The gull dipped its wings and was gone.

A half-mile from Alan Scott, Medic Eddie Rochford looked up from administering the last of his morphine to a wounded soldier. He saw a lone seagull wheeling overhead, corkscrewing toward the sun. Rochford, or "Roach" to his friends, had been up for thirty-two straight hours. In the middle of the night, he could have sworn he saw fantastic figures in the sky dueling with some kind of Buck Rogers raybeams. Later, he thought he heard the Glenn Miller orchestra tuning up on the beach. Some who survived the night said they saw werewolves and vampires in Japanese uniforms. One soldier swore it was the Battle for Valhalla, replete with horned Vikings.

Eddie was among a handful of medics going from body to body, checking for any signs of life. It was discouraging work. Most of the fallen soldiers were dead, and most of the wounded were too far gone for help. The only thing Roach could do was try to ease their suffering When he'd begun the morning's crawl, he'd carried twenty-two pounds of water, almost three gallons. He was down to a half gallon. The dying were thirsty. And now he was out of morphine.

If he returned to the beach, there might or might not be morphine available. Although it was the sixth day following Dog Day, and the bulk of the fighting was over, supply lines were still FUBAR (fouled up beyond all recognition). As Roach debated, he heard a cough and looked around. He was surrounded by churned-up volcanic soil and body parts. He reached for an arm, which he thought might be connected to the cough, but when he pulled on it, it was detached, bone sticking out of the half-bicep like a freshly stripped wire. Roach dropped it.

He heard the cough again, followed by a feeble cry. "Medic."

He found the guy half buried in soil. Roach had to gently wipe the dirt away to find his dogtags. The Marine looked as if someone had tried to hack him in two. A fiendish cut lay from shoulder to hip, partially exposing his rib cage. He was a goner. Even if they could somehow close that gaping wound, infection had already set in.

Roach took the dying man's hand in his. "Hang in there, fella," he said. "Help is on the way. You made it this far, don't fade on me now. Hey pal, the worst is over, and here you are goldbrickin'. They're probably gonna send your ass back to Pearl, where Betty Grable's waitin' with nothing on but a filmy little black negligee. How you doin', pal? Talk to me. What's your name?"

The man reached over with his other arm. Roach didn't see how he could even move, so deeply did the slash penetrate. He grabbed Roach's wrist in a fierce grip. His eyes blazed bright blue in his battle-blackened face, like sapphires exposed in a subterranean vein. "The ring!" he hissed.

Eddie leaned down. He had no idea what the guy was talking about, but these were his last words and the medic didn't want to miss them. "Did you say ring?"

"This ring! Take it." Unbelievably, the dying Marine found the energy to shake Eddie's hand fiercely. Eddie looked down at the hand that gripped his wrist. The guy had a chunky yellow ring on his left hand. The ring was so big, it almost prevented the man from closing his fingers. Funny thing to wear into combat, Eddie thought. Eddie put his finger on the ring.

"This? Don't worry, pal. I'll see that they get it. You got a gal back home who this should go to?"

The man's grip tightened. He tried to raise his head, eyes blazing with an unholy fervor. "You, Medic—you take the ring!"

"Me?"

"Yeah. I want you to have it."

"Hey, come on, guy. You don't know me. What about your folks, or a brother or a sister?"

The dying Marine reached up and grabbed Eddie by the collar, half raising himself, half-pulling Eddie down to his level. "No. You, Medic. Take the ring!"

Eddie could see the light of life fade from the man's eyes. The man lowered himself to the ground like a deflating air mattress. Eddie felt for his tags, hidden beneath the grime.

Private First Class Charles Lawler. The name meant nothing. Eddie looked around. He could see some movement as his fellow medics searched for the still-living among the battlefield's dead. Eddie felt funny about taking the guy's ring. But the dying soldier had been adamant, and it had been his final wish. With a weird feeling that he was somehow being watched, Eddie worked the ring off Langford's hand and placed it in his pocket. He put the dogtags in another pocket, where they jingled with a dozen others.

Wearily, he stood and began searching for survivors. By the time he located one, he had already forgotten the ring.

CHAPTER

2

Colorado: 1992.

H al Jordan was the first to notice the smoke, about one hundred miles west of Boulder. He was among the four headed west in the '71 Chrysler New Yorker. Oliver Queen was at the wheel, with Dinah Lance and Ganthet in the back. The Rockies soared skyward on either side of the roadway, leaving little room for error. A rushing creek paralleled the road on the left, sheer rock escarpment on the right. They passed a yellow highway sign that said WATCH FOR FALLING ROCKS. They passed another a mile later that said, IN CASE OF FLOOD, CLIMB TO SAFETY.

"Is that smoke?" Jordan said, pointing to something at the one o'clock position. Queen peered over the wheel to see. The extreme terrain made line of sight difficult, at least from the road.

"I don't know. Why don't you go see?"

Jordan lowered the car's electric window. "Is that too cold for you guys?" he asked.

"Don't worry about it, Hal," Queen said. "I'll close it after you go."

Jordan dove out the window.

Before he hit the dirt road, he'd transformed to Green Lantern and used the power of his ring to soar effortlessly up the slope, inhaling the delicious pine air. The road they drove on was at seven thousand feet. By the time Green Lantern achieved an altitude of fifteen thousand, it was clear that he had indeed noticed smoke. It was coming from a forest fire burning two valleys away. Spreading his arms for balance, Green Lantern hurtled three miles through the air to the town of Pumpkin Grove, population three thousand five hundred.

Fire fighters throughout the western U.S. had been battling blazes all summer. Jordan and friends had been extremely fortunate not to have encountered any before. But heading through the matchstick dry Rockies, they were bound to hit one sooner or later. There was no way to get through Colorado without seeing forest fire smoke. Jordan looked down as two dozen volunteers tried to create a barrier, a firebreak, working with a pair of caterpillars to remove beetle-deadened trees and loose brush in a hundred-yard swath at the town's edge. Fierce winds and extreme terrain made their task difficult, if not impossible. Jordan could see a wall of flame descending the mountain, headed for the town. He could feel the blast of hot air—seemingly trying to shove him out of the sky. Flying sparks leaped from treetops to housetops.

The town didn't even have a pumper. A dozen men were out there with lawn hoses. Water pressure was nil.

Green Lantern concentrated, sending forth a bolus of green energy that expanded into a molecule-thin sheet, which kept growing. The sheet continued to spread, now in the shape of a giant soap bubble, until it completely engulfed the peninsula of flame creeping toward the heart of the village.

The bubble was a half-mile in diameter. The villagers spotted him. It was hard not to notice the iridescent green beam emanating from his clenched fist. Some cheered, some wept, others began dragging their hoses and equipment in another direction, as another tentacle of flame approached. At least a half-dozen fingers of fire reached toward the town like the outstretched hand of a malignant giant.

The pale green Chrysler emerged from a choking layer of smoke that had settled in the valley. Green Lantern could see one of two policemen shouting at Queen, pointing to the side of the road. Queen didn't wait to hear what the cop had to say before parking the car in an abrupt maneuver and bailing out. Black Canary spilled out the right side. Green Lantern could see the cop's jaw hanging slack. Show people. Mystery men.

Black Canary often had that effect on people. She looked up at GL.

He put a finger behind his ear and touched his JLA micro-transceiver.

"Hal, get me up there."

"Up here?" he asked, splitting his attention from maintaining the fire-suffocating bubble.

"I need altitude if I'm going to bring down some rain."

Green Lantern directed a hand of green energy to reach down, grabbing Black Canary beneath her arms and hoisting her skyward. Green Lantern hung between two green tendrils, one reaching down to contain the fire, the other reaching up so far that Black Canary was no longer visible, a female kite lost in the smoke.

"I see clouds," she said through the transmitter. "Can you take me five miles west?"

As this occurred, Queen, still dressed in flannel shirt and khakis, joined the volunteer fire fighters trying to build a break.

Green Lantern suddenly realized that the cubic mile of forest he'd enclosed had ceased burning. It had run out of air. He redirected the bubble at another approaching tendril of fire, but he was weaker this time, and could only encapsulate half the area as before. Black Canary weighed so little he was not afraid of dropping her.

Green Lantern floated to the roof of a church and stood in the belfry to preserve the ring's remaining energy, one hand extended to support Black Canary over the horizon. He could "feel" her weight at the end of his slim support, as an angler can feel a fish. It took all his concentration to maintain contact. The ring was close to depleted.

"Hurry," he willed.

He was about to reel her in when a thunderhead appeared over the edge of the mountain like the prow of the *Queen Mary*. Someone on the street shouted, "Look at that!" Heads swiveled. The sky had been cloudless momemts earlier. Now, seemingly out of nowhere, a towering, dark-gray mass of storm clouds had appeared. With a militant drum roll, the thunderhead burst, sending fat, cold slugs of rain at the parched ground. The slugs increased to a deluge. Villagers laughed and danced in the street, oblivious to the wet, gray ash that fell along with the rain.

Green Lantern brought back Black Canary as swiftly as he dared and set her down gently as he landed in front of the church. Her hair was wild from having been in the wind at twenty thousand feet. The church bell began ringing. The peal momentarily deafened him. Pumpkin Grove was celebrating its deliverance. Green Lantern had just enough energy left in the ring to create a pair of earplugs.

The kid who'd been ringing the bell almost swallowed his tongue when he saw Green Lantern. He let go and left the steeple and ran down the stairs, with a goofy grin on his face, to stood moments later in front of the hero. He had a pony tail, granny glasses and was skinny as a rake.

"Oh man," he said. "Oh mannnnnnn—you're Green Lantern, aren't you?"

Green Lantern stuck his hand out. "Yup. Who are you, and where are we?"

The kid gave GL the soul clasp. "Mannnnnnn. I'm Dexter Dowling and this is Pumpkin Grove, Colorado. Man, you guys showed up just in time!

I never thought I'd see members of the Justice League of America in Pumpkin Grove. What are you doing here, man?"

"Just passing through, Dexter."

The front door to the church jerked open. A stocky man in brown Coveralls, and a leather and wool cap with the earflaps tied up, marched down the aisle between pews with an expression of delight. His ruddy face would have been bland if not for the extravagant white mustache, curled up at the ends with wax. Behind him came the town constable in his tan uniform and Smoky the Bear hat.

"Mr. Green Lantern?" the local official beamed. "Mr. Green Lantern? Justice League of America?" Without waiting for GL to reply, the man began to pump his hands. "Hobart T. Hinkes, Mr. Green Lantern, Mayor of Pumpkin Grove, and I just have to say there could be no more welcome sight to these tired eyes than the arrival of you and your companions. Hemingway could not have written, nor John Singer Sargent painted a more inspirational picture. Yes sir, by God, when I wrote to the Justice League three years ago, everyone thought I was crazy! But all it would take, I said, was to get one of you men of mystery to visit our town, and just look at how things would take off. Just one. Of course I never dreamed you would choose so propitious a moment to arrive, and I did expect you to notify me beforehand, but believe you me, speaking on behalf of the entire population, you all are most welcome to Pumpkin Grove!"

While Hinkes gushed and pumped, others streamed into the church until it was filled to capacity. Upon the conclusion of the mayor's speech, the people cheered as if the local high school football team had scored a touchdown. Outside, thunder rumbled and rain fell. Black Canary appeared in the door, spotless and dry. People gave her room as if she wore a personal force field.

Queen and the Mayor congratulated each other on their mustaches. Green Lantern took Black Canary aside.

"How did you do that, Dinah?"

"The clouds were there," Dinah Lane—aka Black Canary— said modestly. " I used a frequency which caused the moisture to coalesce into larger drops, precipitating precipitation."

"You talk funny."

"Your Momma wears army boots. Think they'll feed us dinner?"

Dinner was the least of it. Mayor Hinkes declared Heroes' Day. They were given the finest rooms in town, at a Best Western. At six o'clock, the mayor hosted Queen, Jordan, Lance, and Ganthet at the Pig's Ear, Pumpkin Grove's finest restaurant. Everyone who was anyone was there. They'd set the dining room up banquet style, with one table against the back wall for the dignitaries, and the rest arranged at right angles.

Ganthet wore a three-piece suit, which Diane had purchased for him at a St. Vincent de Paul in Denver. Jordan introduced Ganthet as an anthropology professor, and did not bother to explain his purpose. "Classified," he replied with a wink when the mayor asked him. At the mayor's request they dined in costume.

The fare, overcooked beef and seven kinds of starch, was less than remarkable. Mayor Hinkes made a speech following dessert that would not go down in history. Two of the more spirited serving girls tried to gain Jordan's and Queen's attention. Dinah had to grab one of them by the wrist.

She nodded toward Oliver Queen and said, "He's with me, sweetie," she whispered in the girl's ear. Thereafter the young sirens confined their come-ons to the Green Lantern.

It was nine at night by the time they returned to the motel, having shaken hands with everyone in town. Ganthet and Jordan each had a room to themselves. Queen and Lance shared a room. Jordan, who'd brought his lantern in the car's trunk, kept it in the room with him overnight. He watched Charlie Rose for an hour before falling asleep.

They rose at dawn and slipped out of town.

CHAPTER

3

Hal Jordan had been a test pilot for the Ferris Aircraft Corporation when the alien being known as Abin Sur had given him the green power ring. There had been an Earth-sector Green Lantern previously but he'd long since retired. The Green Lantern Corps was the inspiration of the Guardians of the Universe, headquartered on the planet Oa, in the Celestial System, near the center of our galaxy. The Guardians were great thinkers and ethicists. Following millennia of debate, they'd decided to fight entropy and divide the known universe into 3600 sectors, each to be policed by a member of the Green Lantern Corps, each member chosen for outstanding character.

Hal Jordan fit the profile.

Why had these ancient thinkers take it upon themselves to impose order across time and space, frequently at odds with native species whose thought patterns were so alien as to drive the Oans mad? Was hubris at work here? Certainly. The Oans had no religion and hence no faith. They were supreme rationalists subject to the flaws of linear thinking.

The Oans felt a sense of obligation for having unleashed entropy in the first place. Four billion, four hundred thousand years ago, the Oan Krona released entropy, spawning an anti-matter universe. Or so they thought.

The contemporary scholar is likely to scoff at such a theory. Entropy, he will say, is the natural state of the universe. It is the same as time. Time unwinds at its steady pace and systems break down.

That's entropy. The notion that it was introduced by a living species will strike the contemporary scholar as absurd, if not insane. If entropy were not the natural order of things, no one would age. Nothing would get done. You can't make an omelet without breaking eggs. Life's a messy business. Death moreso. Whether there is any truth to the story is beyond our capacity to know. Nevertheless, this is what the Oans believed, and being a moral race, they elected to do something about it. It took billions of years for the Guardians to reach Earth, which is in the sector designated as 2814. In 1939 (as earthlings reckon time these days), Alan Scott found a glowing green meteorite from which he was compelled to fashion a lantern and a ring, becoming, by default, Earth's first Green Lantern. Years later, the alien Abin Sur passed his ring and lantern to Hal Jordan, making him Earth's first *official* Green Lantern.

Scott had retired, without relinquishing his powers. What were those powers? First and foremost, the power of the mind. The Green Lantern ring converts thoughts to matter. Anything the wearer can imagine will occur, if he has sufficient concentration. The ring itself is merely a tool. Bad men can do bad things with it, which is why the Oans have such a rigorous vetting process. Those chosen to wear the ring must be of the highest moral and intellectual caliber.

Ex-terran anthropologists will point out that comparing morality between two different alien races is futile. However, no one can dispute that the Oans and humanity have much in common, not the least of which are their carbon-based bipedal bodies. Indeed, humanity at this stage resembles Oan culture of three billion years ago. Ganthet's own studies, published after an extended stay on Earth, show numerous parallels. Were his book to be available on Earth it would provoke a firestorm of controversy, for Ganthet was not shy about comparing cultures and finding some superior to others. He was quite explicit that only the United States of America truly resembled Oan culture at that time, other earthly geo-political systems falling far behind.

Ganthet himself was humorless. Queen famously said that he did everything but wear a Steve Martin arrow through his head to coax a laugh from the gray-faced alien, without success. It was Ganthet's appearance on Earth that inspired Green Lantern, Oliver Queen—who doubled as the hero called Green Arrow—and Black Canary to drive cross-country. Like the slumming royal heir in *The Prince And The Pauper*, Ganthet wanted to know how normal Americans lived and worked.

The Oan was still asleep while the others suited up and prepared to depart Pumpkin Grove. Green Lantern picked Ganthet's lock with his ring. Inside, the gray-faced alien lay flat on his back emitting a whistling sound with each exhalation.

"Ganthet!" Green Arrow stage whispered. "They're getting up a lynch mob. We've got to get out of town."

The alien sat bolt upright in his bed. "What did you do to offend them?"

Green Arrow turned to Green Lantern, standing in the door. "Didn't I tell you he'd assume it was my fault?"

Only the gentle laughter coming from the two men revealed to their alien companion that he had just been the butt of a human joke.

Once roused, Ganthet moved swiftly. He did not engage in the usual morning ablutions, was never seen to brush his teeth or comb his hair, yet he cast no odor and never seemed to get dirty. Fifteen minutes later they were on a curving canyon road heading west. Green Arrow's compound bow rested between him and Green Lantern, protruding above the front seat. The Transit River trickled by on their right, waiting for fall rains that would turn it into a rushing torrent.

Green Arrow drove. "Man, I can still feel that pound cake sitting in my gut. Hal, did one of those waitresses make it by your crib last night?"

Dinah leaned forward and swatted Queen across the back of the head. "We would have heard."

"Not necessarily," Queen said. "He can be right sneaky when he wants."

"I wondered about that," Ganthet said from the back seat. He sounded like a radio announcer, smooth and mellow. "It seemed to me that those young females were vying for your attention."

"Seemed to us too," Queen said.

"As I understand it," Ganthet continued, "a healthy male in your society will do virtually anything to bed a healthy female. I would find it surprising if you did not act on such an opportunity."

Green Lantern kept his attention out the window during this exchange. "A gentleman doesn't discuss such things."

"Oh my stars and garters," Queen groused. "Now what?"

One hundred yards ahead, they encountered two sets of sawhorses set across the road, each bearing a sign. The first read, ROAD WASHED OUT. TAKE DETOUR. The second sign said DETOUR, with an arrow pointing to the right, up a dirt road that led into the mountains.

"The trouble with Colorado," Queen said, "is there are only two roads from A to B, and only one of them is paved."

"I don't mind," Dinah said from the back seat. "It's all so beautiful."

Queen turned the big Chrysler up the dirt road. They passed clusters of mailboxes and more rugged trails leading up into the trees. Soon they had left even these signs of civilization behind. There was nothing but the dirt road to remind them that man had ever been there.

The road flattened out into high mountain pasture. The patch of green was encircled on three Sides by barbed wire and on the fourth by a sheer rock face. There was a pond in the middle, and a half-dozen cattle lounging in the morning Sun.

Dinah leaned out the rear window, inhaling the fresh pine scent. "If we could bottle this air, we could sell it at Nieman-Marcus for twelve bucks a pint. Look at how the pond reflects dazzling yellow."

Green Lantern, who'd had his nose buried in a map, looked out the window. He looked up. He reached over and grabbed the steering wheel above Queen's hands and forced it abruptly to the left, causing the car to swerve off the road. They stopped with a head-snapping jolt against a massive boulder.

"Hal!" Black Canary said.

"Heads up!" GL shouted, leaping out the window. His feet never touched the ground. In that instant, a yellow mallet, ten feet in diameter, struck the road where the car had been with earthquake force. The edge of the mallet caught the Chrysler's rear bumper, tearing it off and causing the front end to lurch up.

As members of the Justice League of America, both Green Arrow and Black Canary were used to sudden assaults. Not only were they born with sharper-than-average reflexes, the super hero business had further refined their abilities. They were out of the car in less than one second. Black Canary reached back in and yanked Ganthet out as if he were a sack of laundry.

"Split up!" Green Lantern boomed from above. "Don't let him concentrate his power!"

GA already had an arrow notched, looking for a target. "Who we looking for, boss?"

A tiny green megaphone bloomed at his ear on the end of a hollow stalk so thin it was invisible to the naked eye. "Sinestro. Renegade Green Lantern. Yellow ring, yellow power battery. And—as you will remember—the energy frequency broadcast by yellow cannot be affected by the power waves of my ring."

"Yes, I get the picture," Green Arrow said. "What's Sinestro look like?"

"He's hard to miss. He's crimson, and very tall." The megaphone zipped away like a hummingbird. Green Lantern had engaged the enemy.

"Dinah!" GA hissed.

"Over here." She and Ganthet huddled among several monolithic blocks of grantie that had fallen from the cliff face, forming a natural arch.

"Hal says it's Sinestro, a rogue Green Lantern."

"Ah, Sinestro," Ganthet said in his NPR voice. "He will prove difficult to overcome, with his experience."

"Got any ideas?"

An effervescence of green sprayed from the top of the cliff, a thousand feet above, and disappeared like fireworks. A smattering of rocks followed.

"As he is impervious to the power ring it would behoove either or both of *you* to incapacitate Sinestro."

"Like I said, got any ideas?"

"I do," Black Canary said. "But first I have to get to the top of that cliff."

Streams of yellow energy spattered from above, dissipating quickly. The sky rumbled with alien thunder as the combatants' power beams split the air.

"Dinah! I got a grappling arrow."

She replied with a terse nod.

GA drew an arrow with an unusually thick shaft from his quiver and fitted it to the bow. Extending his left arm, he pulled the bow-string to his right cheek and released the arrow toward the top of the cliff.

It soared true, cleared the lip, and arced back down out of sight, leaving behind an all-but-invisible monofilament attached to the bow. Green Arrow ran toward Black Canary as shards clattered, striking the roof of the car in a series of explosive-sounding reports.

"The rental agency's going to have a cow when they see that car," Black Canary said.

"Tough tamales. Take the bow. There's a tungsten spring inside, should pull you right up the cliff face."

Black Canary took the bow. "I'll give him a headache."

Green Arrow cupped Black Canary by the back of the head and pulled her close for a lip-searing kiss. "Be careful, Pretty Bird. And don't lose the bow."

Black Canary positioned herself at the base of the cliff, one foot on the rock wall, held the bow with both hands over her head and tripped the trigger. The spring began to wind in the filament, pulling her up the sheer face. It looked as if she were walking straight up the side of the cliff.

Green Arrow immediately fitted another arrow, this one with an explosive warhead. "Come on, whatever you are," he muttered, drawing the string back and looking up the cliff. "Give me a shot."

But Sinestro was otherwise engaged. The crimson alien stood atop a natural cairn atop the cliff, above the treeline, engaged in a trial of wills with Hal Jordan, his most hated rival. Although his back was toward Black Canary as she climbed over the edge of the cliff, she didn't fool herself into thinking she could approach his blind Side. Sinestro was a master Green Lantern turned renegade. He automatic-ally maintained a forcefield that alerted him to the slightest incursion. An ant couldn't enter that field without his knowing about it. Black Canary sensed this, but did not know how far the field extended. She was approximately a hundred yards from Sinestro, who stood with feet planted and arms extended as he directed a beam of piercing yellow energy at Green Lantern.

Green Lantern hovered fifty feet in the air, avoiding contact with the earth so as not to grant Sinestro another medium with which to attack him. Sinestro was capable of sending a stealth beam through solid rock. It could strike like a phantom rattlesnake.

GL's energy beam was brilliant green. Sinestro's was the color of the Sun. Where the beams collided blazed a distortion field too fierce for the naked eye. The heat it shed was intense. Even where Black Canary stood, hundreds of feet away, she could feel it like a blast furnace. GL saw her but gave no sign, nothing to alert Sinestro. Canary had studied Sinestro's dossier, but this was the first time she'd actually encountered the fallen hero. If he was the Green Lanterns' Lucifer, Hal Jordan was their Michael.

Sinestro used to be a Green Lantern in good standing. Nothing illustrated the gaping holes in the Guardians' philosophy like Sinestro. They chose him because they believed him to be committed to and capable of order. How right they were. Sinestro's order proved extreme, leaving little room for individual thought. When he was finally cashiered of his position on his homeworld of Korugar, Sector 1417, he turned renegade, vowing revenge on the Guardians and all their noisome spawn. Hal Jordan especially.

Sinestro had once been Hal Jordan's teacher. The Guardians chose Jordan to oust Sinestro, which he did in an epic battle, consigning the renegade to the anti-matter universe of Qward. Big mistake. The disgraced and embittered Sinestro proved highly receptive to the Qwardians, sworn enemies of the Guardians. As above, so below. The Qwardians supplied Sinestro with his yellow power ring. Since anti-matter cannot coexist with matter, the Qwardians could not enter the matter universe to make war directly. They needed surrogates. Sinestro could make this transition because his entire body converted. In our universe, he was constructed of matter. In the Qwardian universe, he was made of anti-matter. His thoughts remained the same.

Sinestro had laid a clever trap, waiting until the Earth heroes' guard was down, catching them in the middle of nowhere. But if Black Canary had never laid eyes on Sinestro before, the reverse was also true. Sinestro had no way of knowing that she had the ability to project a sonic beam as tightly focused as a laser over a vast range of frequencies. She'd learned through experience that certain frequencies could cause bone itself to vibrate, creating excruciating head and body pain. Crouching behind a natural rock outcrop, peering through a slot like a sniper, Black Canary projected her silent scream at Sinestro.

At first there was no response. Black Canary could feel her aural scream encountering a barrier—Sinestro's personal force field. She projected more forcefully and pushed through. With the utmost delicacy, she touched Sinestro's skull with her voice. He didn't seem to notice. Neither Green Lantern nor he gave an inch. GL had settled on a rock a hundred feet from Sinestro so that both combatants were on the same plane. He may have been trying to sucker Sinestro into a stealth strike through the earth, which would have split his concentration and allowed Black Canary to strike. The green-yellow energy collision between them began to melt the rock underfoot, creating a lava pool that glowed dull red.

Then Black Canary found her pitch, causing Sinestro's inner ear chambers to vibrate. His hate was his undoing. Sinestro was easily capable of mounting both offense and defense, but in his blood lust he threw everything he had at Green Lantern, leaving nothing for defense. By the time he figured out that he was under serious attack from a second front, it was too late.

Sinestro put a hand to his head. Then both hands. He staggered. His energy beam evaporated. A green hand the size of a cow smacked him into the lava field where he lay hissing until the green hand picked him up by his legs and laid him out on the rock. The alien left a Sinestro-shaped depression in the cooling lava.

Black Canary, her own ears ringing from the effort, ran forward. Sinestro lay on his back; he was an enormous creature, at least seven and a half feet tall. His skin looked like magenta naugahyde in a third-rate strip club. It looked like a terminal case of sun poisoning. She knelt by his unconscious body and extended one finger to his cheek. It felt dry and cool.

"Don't," Green Lantern said. "You never know what *residual* thoughts are rushing around in there."

Black Canary pulled her hand back. Her eyes went to the ring on Sinestro's left hand. It was yellow, but it wasn't gold. It was too bright for gold. Green Lantern used his own ring to extend a green hand that removed Sinestro's ring. GL held the jumbo-sized ring in the air before him. Black Canary could have worn it as a bracelet.

"Dinah, will you call the JLA to come get this character? He's going to need special handling."

Sinestro opened his eyes and smiled. "What did you do to me?"

Green Arrow leaped in front of Dinah, arrow nocked. Sinestro held his hands up placatingly. "I'm down. You took my ring. I have no means of defense."

"Guys like you always have some trick," Green Arrow said.

Sinestro shrugged. "There is no trick. You have sown the seeds of your own destruction. I am but the farmer."

Green Arrow held the arrow's steel tip four inches from Sinestro's eye. "What does that mean?"

But Sinestro would not speak again.

They put jade shackles on him. They sealed him in a jade coffin and put it into orbit around Saturn. They put Sinestro's ring in a capsule made of super dense matter and gave it to Superman. And they did it all before nightfall.

CHAPTER

4

E dward Harrison Rocheford III, better known as "Roach" to friends and detractors, peddled home furiously on his banana bike, the white-cloth sack of the *Huntington Times and Clarion* flapping from his shoulder. Roach had blazed through his delivery route that evening like Reggie Jackson rounding third base. Nine-year-old Roach was on a mission: home in time for the six o'clock news.

Marty Vole had told him in Mrs. Baumgartner's Social Studies Class that Green Lantern was going to be on the news. Green Lantern! Just about the coolest guy who ever lived. Roach had been ga-ga for the green guy since he was five years old and had seen Green Lantern in action with the Justice League on television. Grandpa Eddie, with whom he lived, tolerated Roach's obsession with bemused disinterest.

Roach had been living with Grandpa Eddie since age seven, when both his parents had been killed in a car crash. Some punk in a stolen pick-up, hopped up on liquor and bennies, had crossed the centerline and hit them head on. Gramps' wife had died before Eddie had been born, so it was just the two Eddies leading the bachelor life in Gramps' run-down Victorian.

Chez Rocheford occupied a corner spot at the juncture of North 28th St. and LaGuardia Boulevard, and was notable mainly for its unkempt appearance. It was the type of house children singled out as haunted. With its weedy lawn, overgrown oak, and vines creeping up every outside surface, it radiated a sort of otherworldly menace, a little slice of Lovecraft in the New World.

Eddie the First barked at any children foolish enough to cut across his tangled yard. He'd put up barbed wire once, until the city forced him to take it down. He was too stingy to put up a regular fence, so the best he could do was sit on his porch, invisible in leafy shadow, chain-smoking Camels, drinking Smirnov from the bottle and yelling at anyone who set foot on Rocheford land.

Eddie the First's laissez-faire attitude was fine with Roach. The old man let him do pretty much as he wanted, so long as he didn't bring the cops or anyone else home. Eddie pumped his bike, backside rising and falling like an Oklahoma oil pump, as he cut across LaGuardia toward the cool shadow of the Rocheford house. He jerked up on his ape hanger bars to clear the curb, rear wheel smacking, pedaled right up to the front porch, dropped the bike and raced up the wooden steps. Eddie the First sat in his favorite rocker at the far end of the porch, holding a pint of Smirnov behind his thigh.

"Where's the fire?" By the time he asked, he was talking to the wind.

Roach flew into the house, zoomed through the kitchen, grabbed a can of soda and a stick of jerky, circled back to the living room, switched on the television and planted himself sixteen inches from the screen. He was just in time for the evening news. The lead-off was about a group of Arab terrorists who'd taken the Israeli Olympic team hostage in Munich and were slaughtering them.

Roach wondered why Green Lantern—or *somebody*—didn't go over there and bang their heads together. He figured maybe it was because the problem was not America's, but Roach couldn't help think that someday it would be. If he had the power, he'd use it to look into men's hearts. Get rid of the bad guys before they did something terrible.

Green Lantern was the lead story after the break. Green Lantern himself didn't appear. What a cheat! It was all about how Green Lantern and his companions Green Arrow and Black Canary had helped some little town in the Rockies survive a forest fire. A bunch of talking heads from Pumpkin Grove. The only footage they showed of Green Lantern was an old newsreel of him accepting an award at the White House along with a bunch of other super heroes, and a close-up of the ring.

The ring! If only Roach had a ring like that. He'd use it to get rid of all the bad guys and to search for adventure. He would use the ring to rub Steve Larson's face in the mud. Larson was an insufferable bully. He'd use the ring to give himself straight A's. Could he do that?

Bam! Just like that he remembered something. He remembered that Grandpa Eddie, Eddie the First, had once had a ring like Green Lantern's. Not exactly *like* Green Lantern's, but big and powerful in some way Roach didn't understand. Roach remembered Grandpa Eddie showing the ring once to his parents, when he was five. Eddie the First had brought the ring home with him from the war, and there was something eerie about it. Roach's father had told his grandfather to put the ring away or give it to the government. Eddie the First put the ring away and stopped talking about it.

But the ring was still there, somewhere in the house. And Roach thought he knew where. Leaving the television on, he raced up the wooden stairs to the second floor where he had his own bedroom. He went down the hall to the rope hanging from the trap door, leaped to catch it, and let his weight pull it down so that the ladder slid free.

The attic smelled of mold and dust. At the top of the steps Roach had to stand on a chest to reach the light string. He switched it on. A single sixty-watt bulb illuminated the cavernous attic with its soaring ceiling and ranks of old furniture like silent sentinels. Roach was pretty sure he knew where the ring was, in an olive drab steamer chest with the legend, "E.H. Rocheford, USMC" stenciled on the side in faded white letters. The chest lay against the wall behind a wooden dresser with a swiveling mirror, and beneath three cardboard boxes full of books. The dresser juddered across the plywood floor when Roach pushed. The book boxes were almost too heavy. He had to rock them to the edge of their perch then lower them swiftly to the floor where they thumped loudly despite his best efforts.

At last the sea chest lay unburdened. Roach pried the steel latch loose with a screwdriver. The chest did not want to give up its secrets. When it finally creaked open it released a cloud of dust redolent of mothballs and far-off jungles. It was dim behind the big dresser, but Roach could see well enough. On top lay what Roach presumed was Grandpa's WW II dress uniform, neatly pressed and folded. An old cigar box held a pound of insignias and medals including Paratrooper's wings.

A greater prize lay below—a bayonet in a metal sheath. Roach drew the rusty blade with awe, thrusting it through the air making a killing noise, a cross between gunfire and nails scraping on a blackboard. Reluctantly, he set the bayonet aside and reached deeper into the chest. An American flag, folded into triangles. A pair of black leather boots, still holding a dull shine. A photo album. Roach flipped through it. Grandpa with smiling south-sea islanders on a white sand beach. Impossibly young Grandpa with a bunch of other young jarheads on board a troop transport. Roach's grandmother, a beautiful, smiling young woman.

Finally, at the bottom, wrapped in a chamois, Grandpa's old canvas medic's bag. Roach knew the ring was in it the minute he pulled it out of the chest. He could tell by its intense mass, pulling on the segmented bag like an anchor. Hands trembling with excitement, Roach unsnapped the latches holding the bottom pocket.

"Eddie," his grandfather called.

Roach about fainted. He'd been so intent on treasure he hadn't even heard his grandfather ascend the creaky ladder. A flush of guilt on his cheeks, Roach turned, holding the medic kit. "I was just looking. I was gonna ask you about this stuff, Grandpa."

Grandpa's eyes went to the medic kit. He glared at his grandson, but there was a question there, too. How much had he seen? "Give it here."

Reluctantly, Roach handed over the med kit.

"You put everything back in that chest exactly how you found it. Then you put these boxes back."

"But Grandpa . . ."

"I don't go messing with your stuff, do I?"

"I was just . . ."

"You do as I say. Then come tell me about it."

Roach watched his grandfather walk back to the trap door, set the medical kit down at the edge, and slowly, carefully position himself to climb down. *Man, I hope I never get old,* Roach thought. To have to think where you were going to put each foot. Slowly, with a sort of grim-lipped determination, Eddie the First took a tentative step down.

Dazzling light spilled upward, an eruptive incandescence in the second floor hall.

"Oh!" Eddie the First exclaimed. The next instant, he was gone. Something snatched him the way Roach grabbed apples off Old Man MacDonald's tree. A high-pitched humming emanated from below, like a Con Ed transfer station. As silently as possible, Roach inched forward on his belly until he could peer down. It had happened so fast he didn't have time to be scared.

Someone, or something, was in the hall with his grandfather. Eddie the First sat on his bony butt, one hand behind him to prevent him from falling backwards, the other outstretched in front as if to trying to ward something off.

"Please! Don't!" he cried. Eddie the First had never been afraid of anything. But fear cracked his voice now and he sounded weak and pathetic.

Roach felt a sliver of fear drive itself through his gut. What could possibly frighten Eddie the First, who'd returned from the war with a Purple Heart and a Distinguished Service Cross? Nothing Roach could name. Nothing he wished to name.

He shinnied forward. He saw a pair of feet. They were enormous, clad in some kind of leather boots that shimmered like oil on water. Calves like Doric pillars sprouted from the boots. Something crackled in the giant's hand, filling the attic with the smell of ozone and something else, something wild and electric. The humming permeated the structure and Roach's young bones, masking any noise he made as he squirmed to get a better angle on the huge intruder. From his position, Roach could only take in the creature to mid-torso, which resembled his grandfather's steamer trunk. The creature was stooped. It couldn't stand upright in the nine-foot hall. Roach had to back off to catch even a glimpse of the face, and when he had, he wished he hadn't.

It was an inhuman mask. Slots for eyes. Gash for a mouth. Helmet like an artillery shell, long, winding horns protruding. A Wotan, a Colossus. As Roach watched, heart pumping, the thing extended a massive hand toward his grandfather, who gasped and tried to scramble backward.

"No! Please! You can have it!"

An arc of energy leaped from the giant's finger causing Eddie the First to vibrate like a paint mixer. He screamed. The smell of ozone and burning flesh rose upward. Roach shut his eyes and covered his ears with his hands but the screaming and the awful sizzling sound went on and on.

Five minutes after the thing cooked Eddie the First, Roach heard sirens through a fear-stained haze. Acrid smoke and the terrible smell of burning flesh filled the attic. Roach was dimly aware of the firemen's thumping progress through the house, the shouted orders, the heavy boots. It didn't take them long to reach the second floor.

"Jesus Christ! There's a body up here. O'Malley, call the cops."

"On their way."

"Look at it. Guy's been cooked from the inside out."

"I think I'm going to be sick."

"Do it outside."

Creaks and groans as the firefighter climbed the ladder to the attic. It didn't take long to find Roach curled behind the dresser clutching his grandfather's med kit.

"O'Malley! There's a kid up here!"

The firefighter knelt, shook Roach's shoulder gently with an asbestos-gloved hand. "Kid. Hey kid, can you hear me?"

Roach turned toward the fireman, eyes filled with tears. "It killed my Grandpa."

The fireman wore an orange jumpsuit and a hard hat with a plexiglass visor, which he set aside. A label on his chest said Burrick. "What's your name, kid?"

"Edward Harrison Rocheford III."

"Eddie, what happened to your grandfather?"

"It killed him."

"What killed him?"

"The giant." He was about to say it was after the ring, but why should he tell the cops? They'd only take it away from him, and it was his. It had been his grandfather's, and now it was his. If he gave it up, his grandfather would have died in vain. Somehow Roach knew

28

the ring was the key to tracking down and destroying the monster that had killed Eddie the First.

CHAPTER

5

Colorado: The present.

L udlow "Bulldog" Kramer was on his way from Moab to Grand Junction to hook up with the rest of the Bedouins Motorcycle Club for the ride to Four Corners. The Bedouins raised a little hell now and then, but they didn't peddle drugs and they didn't abuse women. They were basically decent, God-fearing, blue-collar guys who loved the Broncos and liked to ride motorcycles.

Ludlow stopped at an arid wayside to relieve himself. He had to walk a hundred meters to find a rock big enough to stand behind. It was hot! When he got back on his 2004 Fat Boy, the hog wouldn't start. Cursing, he got off. Gas, check. Spark, check. Dead man's switch, off. But when he pressed the starter, all he got was a thin whining, like a small creature trapped in the crankcase begging to be let out.

Bulldog was not a backyard mechanic. He was an accountant, although you'd never guess to look at him. Wearing a denim vest over a Sturgis T, he looked like a well-fed middle-aged biker, someone with whom you did *not* want to mess. His biceps were like powder kegs. His beard was suitable for Father Christmas. He stood utterly alone in the middle of a vast landscape, baking in ninety-degree heat, cursing the gods and futilely stabbing at his cell phone.

Great. Just great. The cell phone was dead. With an inchoate snarl, he hurled it into the desert. It soared fifty meters before smashing on the rocks.

"Trouble?"

The calm voice, coming from just behind Bulldog, caused him to leap six inches in the air. Not a small feat for such a large man. He whirled, ready to cold-cock the sneaky bastard. This was Indian country. Anything could happen. Bulldog may have been an accountant, but he wasn't afraid of a fight.

The tall, gaunt man in overcoat and wide-brimmed straw hat, like something your Aunt Petunia would wear in the garden, didn't blink. Bulldog immediately dropped his fist and stared. This guy looked like Jesus. He had that thousand-yard focus in his limpid brown eyes, and the long flowing hair, and the beard. But where had he come from? Bulldog hadn't seen him on the road, and the land didn't exactly provide cover.

Disarmed by the man's eerily calm demeanor, Bulldog stepped back. "Sorry. Didn't see you sneakin' up on me. My gawddamn hog won't start."

The tall man walked toward the bike. Bulldog followed, a little freaked. Strangers were usually more reticent about approaching him. And this guy could be a loony—who knew what he'd do to the bike? "I was heading toward Grand Junction to hook up with some buddies, stopped to take a leak, and now the POS won't start. Harley's losing a lotta good will right here. I thought we'd put this stuff behind us. I mean, I've had Harleys for twenty-five years and none of 'em worked right."

The man stooped to study the engine. He froze in what Bulldog thought was a damned awkward position and just stared at the metal for two minutes. He reached out with one hand and gently touched the cylinder head. A spark leaped between finger and bike. The man stood.

"Try it now," he said.

Yeah right, Bulldog thought. *Well, what the hell.* He stepped past the stranger, straddled the bike, hit the button, and it started right up. Bulldog killed it and started it again. Killed it, got off the bike with a big grin. He stuck out his spade-sized hand.

"Ludlow Kramer. Bulldog to my friends."

The man shook his hand. Not exactly cold fish, but like the guy's mind was elsewhere. "Hal Jordan."

"You need a lift, man? Where'd you come from, anyway?"

"No thanks. I'd rather walk." The stranger turned away and started to stride.

Bulldog couldn't believe it. "Man, you cured my hawg by the laying on of hands! Thanks, brother! Thank you! And use that power wisely!"

Jordan watched the motorcycle disappear in the shimmering heat. The engine had stopped due to vapor lock in the fuel injectors. Jordan, who had been able to feel the engine as an organic whole, simply withdrew energy in the form of heat from the fuel injector, thus freeing the flow.

Assisting the biker gave Jordan no pleasure. Indeed, nothing did, which was one reason he found himself in the middle of nowhere. The Sicilians had a word for it: *menefreghista*. He who literally does not give a fig. Jordan had seen too many things, been through too much. Nothing touched him. Not the greatest human tragedy, nor the funniest episode of *Seinfeld*. He was devoid of all human emotion except the one which was expressly forbidden by every major religion: despair. No human being was meant to see what he had seen. It had given him a perspective wildly out of proportion to his true station in life, among the lesser creatures.

He thought back. Had there ever been a time when he'd been filled with hope? Of course. His career as a test pilot had made him happy for a while. He and Carol had been in love. It was a dream come true, every red-blooded American's desire to become a jet jockey. Over time even the highest of highs paled. The thrill of breaking the sound barrier no longer excited him. He started drinking. He broke up with Carol, shunned his friends and stayed to himself except when he had to go to the liquor store. After his second DWI he was sentenced to ninety days in the county jail. And that's where Sinestro found him.

The Guardians sent Sinestro to train Hal Jordan, Earth's new Green Lantern. The power of the ring blew away his alcoholic haze like cigarette smoke in a gale.

He became a super hero. The dying alien Abin Sur entrusted Jordan with the stewardship of Earth, sector 2814. Hal Jordan passed from the ranks of mortals into the pantheon of gods. As Green Lantern, he was a founding member of the Justice League of America. He strode across the universe in his seven-league boots, experienced a hundred worlds, a thousand civilizations.

As Parallax, he had tried to remake the universe in his own image.

Suicide was easy. He'd already done it once.

As Parallax, he had thrown himself into the Sun to save Earth. That should have been the end of it. Jordan was dragged kicking and screaming back to life, reminded once again that he'd surrendered an essential part of his humanity in exchange for power. He no longer had the ability to say "Enough." He wondered what it would take to prevent him from being brought back. The complete destruction of his body? Wasn't it his right to die? Since when did the notion that he no longer had the right to end his own life gain currency? He was supposed to redeem himself. Wouldn't his death do that?

He'd thought about it, and was ready to test his theory—even though he knew he was almost certainly wasting his time. Railroad tracks ran parallel to the highway, carrying ore west and autos east. Freight trains passed every couple of hours. One was due shortly. He could feel its vibrations in the soles of his shoes. He walked toward the tracks across the parched red rock. In the distance, to the north and east, he saw the outline of the San Juan mountains, a ghostly purple in the haze. To the west, he glimpsed a shadow slithering between rocks. Coyote. Pickings must be miserable in the high country to drive a coyote down here, he thought.

He kicked a stray McDonald's wrapper. He couldn't remember the last time he'd eaten—the Spectre had no need for food—or shaved, or taken a shower, or slept in a bed. He came to the tracks, part of which lay on a berm built across a gully. Now he could hear the train in the distance, a faint choogling accompanied by the occasional toot. Jordan took off his coat, wadded it into a cushion, and laid it on the polished steel track. Then he lay down between the rails, head on one rail, feet on the other. He could feel the Northwest and Pacific approach even through the layers of cloth. He could hear it, too. The engineer released a piercing blast. Perhaps they saw him, but the train was at least eighty cars long and would take several miles to come to a complete halt, by which time Jordan's skull would be reduced to moist shards.

The other rail thrummed beneath his heels, a not unpleasant sensation. The conductor definitely saw him, as the hurtling locomotive

34

bellowed its rage. The train's horn was steam-powered, capable of generating in excess of one hundred and eighty decibels—louder than a Limp Bizkit concert. Jordan was at peace despite, or perhaps because of, the train's approaching fury. He stretched his arms overhead, anticipating the instant of sweet oblivion. He could hear the air brakes now, hundreds of iron wheels locking up and spitting sparks as the engineer desperately sought to avoid crushing him. God scraping His fingernails on a black board. Jordan imagined what the engineer might feel. Guilt? Certainly. Anger? Probably. Jordan himself no longer felt anything, except the desire to end it all.

The sound approached tornado levels. *Here it comes*, he thought. Something grabbed hold of his pant leg and tugged. It pulled with stunning force, yanking his head off its iron cushion a second before the thirty-ton locomotive rolled past. It pulled Jordan over the track like a Ken doll, down the crushed rock berm to the cracked valley floor.

A coyote. A grinning, mangy, yellow-eyed coyote had seized him by the pant leg and saved his life. Four feet from Jordan's head, the train hurtled past causing the earth to shake. Far ahead and growing farther, the engineer leaned out of the locomotive backward, red-faced and screaming, flipping Jordan the bird. Jordan waved at him. Howdy. The train rumbled past. The coyote let go of his leg and sat grinning, tongue lolling, as if waiting for the next one-liner. Fifteen minutes later the caboose went by, two guys on the poop deck hurtling empty beer bottles and likewise expressing their opinion of Jordan via the single digit. The conductor must have phoned them.

The train chugged on, its rumble becoming more distant, angry horn downshifting, until once again the valley lay hot and still beneath the big bake light. The coyote remained where it was, sitting and looking at Jordan, tongue lolling, panting.

"Thanks," Jordan said. "Thanks for nothing." He knew it wouldn't work. This was the fifteenth time he'd tried. An empty gesture to protest an empty life.

"Jordan," the coyote said. "We have to talk."

CHAPTER

6

Kyle Rayner, Freelance, opened his eyes and gazed upon the loveliest face in Greenwich Village, if not the world. The face was asleep. It was green with the faintest blush of rose in the cheeks, and lashes the color of emeralds. It was the face of Jenny-Lynn Haden, daughter of Alan Scott, the original Green Lantern. Kyle was the current Green Lantern. And Jenny-Lynn was Jade, connected via Starheart fragment to the Green Lanterns.

Kyle counted himself among the luckiest men alive to have landed this beauty, never mind her moods. They all had moods. Last night he'd cooked dinner and they'd eaten by candlelight and Rod Stewart. Everything had gone swimmingly until Kyle had once again popped the question, and Jen had once again put him off.

Oh, well, he thought. *As long as she's willing to live with me I can't complain.* Just looking at her Ferrari curves under the sheet put him in a romantic mood. He rose stealthily, went into the bathroom, performed his ablutions and brushed his teeth. He was just about to get back in bed when the pounding started—*bang bang bang* on the front door. Kyle's enthusiasm melted as he slipped into a terrycloth robe. He had a sinking sensation it wasn't going to be the Seventh Day Adventists or the landlord. He went down the narrow stairs to the front door of their townhouse on a tree-shaded block. Jen's cat Mauser crouched like a meatloaf near the front door staring at him. *Do something,* the cat seemed to say. Kyle looked through the peep hole. The stern visage of Alan Scott looked back.

The day was off to a rocky start.

Kyle swung the door open. "Good morning, Alan."

Alan Scott swept into the townhouse, brushing Kyle with his dark-gray worsted suit. His tie was the color of a stoplight. "My daughter awake?"

"No sir. Would you like a cup of coffee?"

"All right. Cream, no sugar."

Kyle went into his compact kitchen where Mr. Coffee had done his deed. He took the coffee into the dining room where Scott sat at the head of the table, unconsciously emulating his posture at Gotham Broadcasting board meetings. "I do not approve of my daughter shacking up with you."

"Sir, I understand. I've asked her to marry me on numerous occasions. It's her decision to avoid making our arrangement legal. I feel compelled to point out that we are both of age."

Scott snorted and took a sip of coffee. "I'm not so much concerned about her behavior as yours. I heard you were at a strip club last week with a young woman who is not my daughter."

Kyle goggled. Where'd the old man get that bit of intelligence? "Sir, you should know as well as anyone that looks can be deceiving. I'm a one-woman guy. That was just an acquaintance."

"I know very well that looks can be deceiving. I also know that perception is often reality. I don't want to have to read about you two, separately or together, singly or seriatim, in the tabloids. It's embarrassing."

"I understand. It won't happen again."

Scott grimaced into his cup. He obviously had more on his mind. He released a long sigh. "You'll have to excuse an old man. The way you young people live is just a little hard for me to take. Maybe I'm old-fashioned."

It took immense willpower for Kyle not to say *You said it!*

"I do hope you're using protection."

Kyle's ears burned and he wanted to shout *It's none of your damned business!* But he'd learned a measure of self-control since becoming a Green Lantern. "Sir, we're both adults and we take full responsibility for our actions." Protection! Some things were supposed to remain private.

"Adults? Jen's twenty-one. She's still a child."

"Sir, may I remind you that Jen was born without benefit of legal union."

Scott seemed to shrink a little at these words. "You're right. I'm asking you to do as I say, not as I did. Part of it was the times. Back then, women were a lot less eager to jump in the sack with any Tom, Dick, or Harry. But once I became a celebrity, well I don't have to tell you. Power is the ultimate aphrodisiac. We matured faster in those days. We had less time. Our life expectancy was shorter. Only reason I'm still hanging around is because of the *residual* power from the ring."

"And we're glad of it."

Scott put his hands on the edge of the table and got up. Five years ago he wouldn't have needed the physical support. "All right. I've said my piece. Please have Jen phone me when she gets a chance. What are you working on?" He went through the arched entry to the dining room/studio where Kyle's drawing board occupied a corner surrounded on all Sides by shelves, electronic apparatuses, Todd Toys, and artwork. Taped to the board was an illustration of a streamlined locomotive, smoke from its stack forming fat, psychedelic letters. MILK TRAIN LIVE AT AVALON. Scott peered at it. "I do hope you're not smoking marijuana."

This time Kyle did roll his eyes. "Why? Because I did that in the style of an old rock poster? It's what the promoter wanted. Sir, I'll be happy to submit to a urine test any time you like, and I'm not even an employee."

Scott took the hint. "Goodbye." He was out the door.

Kyle felt as if he'd just shucked a two-hundred-pound load. He really liked Alan, had always liked him, since long before dating Jen. But they were of two different eras and cultural clashes were inevitable.

Scott's visit had derailed Kyle's romantic notion. He looked at his locomotive, sleek and powerful in art deco style. He needed to finish the illustration. But first, he needed to get dressed. He bounced up the stairs two at a time, floated through the room looking for a clean T-shirt. Nada. Somebody had better attack the laundry soon or they would be asphyxiated in discarded clothes. Jen was always stealing his T-shirts. He went into her closet, reached up to the shelf where she kept row after row of neatly folded T-s, and grabbed what appeared to be his own J. Geils Band T-shirt. He pulled. It came free along with a little cardboard box that struck him on the crown of his head and tumbled onto the shirt he held in his hands. He stared at it.

It was the Little Pink Pregnancy Test. He dropped it as if it were radioactive and gave a little gasp like a Victorian lady about to swoon. He looked out of the closet. Jen was still fast asleep. In fact, she'd started to snore a little with an odd whistling noise. Kyle stooped and picked up the package. No mistake. A pregnancy testing kit. In his imagination it came complete with an iron chain connected to a massive block of concrete on which it said, This Is The Rest Of Your Life. Kyle burning the candle at both ends trying to support a family. Jen stuck nursing when she'd rather be off saving the universe.

Mortgages. Health insurance. Life insurance. Pre-school. The enormity staggered him. He fell to his knees, gasping for breath. He was having a panic attack. Floaters appeared at the edge of his vision. "I can't," he gasped, "I can't be a parent! I'm too young!"

He could easily have verified his fears by probing her body with the ring. But she would instantly know it and fly into a rage. He was permitted to probe her body with one thing only, and it wasn't his mind.

Jen mumbled something and stirred in her sleep. Kyle frantically racked his memory, trying to figure out when it had happened. As if that would do any good. The fact was he and Jen *didn't* use protection every time they made love. Like any red-blooded, over-eager American boy, Kyle was only too happy to take Jen's word that she wouldn't get pregnant. Why not?

"It's not that time of month," she'd said. Oh, okay. Wham, bam, thank you ma'am. Now that the trap had sprung, he could see his mistakes. Not a super hero after all. Just a mere mortal.

Wait a minute—Jen wasn't exactly a conniving female. She was far from helpless. In fact, with her powers she was capable of anything. She could easily abort the fetus with a thought. Problem: those precise ethicists, the Oans, numbered abortion among their no-nos. She did not seem all that eager to become a mother. The few times the subject came up, she'd laughed about what a terrible mother she would make, with her commitment to cosmic justice.

Kyle countered by pointing out she hadn't turned out badly. But he never dreamed that fatherhood would be thrust upon him so precipitously. *I'm not ready* he wanted to wail, but it sounded too much like a child. No whining. He loved Jen, planned to spend his life with her, so what was the big deal? In previous centuries, man and woman would marry as young as twelve. Of course, they only had life expectancies of twenty years. He'd failed to connect the dots. What did marriage have to do with parenthood?

"Kyle? What are you doing?"

He looked up. Jen was awake and peering at him through emerald eyes, drowsy, desirable, and bemused. Kyle sat cross-legged on the closet floor, staring at nothing.

"Huh? Oh. Good morning! I was just meditating."

"Are you all right? You look a little lost there."

Kyle couldn't admit he'd found the pregnancy test. Each of them had privacy issues, and now was not the right time to broach the subject.

"What are you doing in my closet?"

"Nothing. I was just looking for my J. Geils T-shirt."

"You gave me that shirt."

"Well can I borrow it?"

She looked at him suspiciously. "Okay. But next time, ask me, will you? I don't want you poking around in my closet."

Kyle got to his feet. "Sorry." He used his power ring to surreptitiously tuck the pregnancy test back on the upper shelf between a pair of shirts.

Jen went into the bathroom and shut the door. Kyle imagined her doing girl things, examining a pink test tube, applying some exotic lotion. He put on the J. Geils shirt, which now held the scent of Jen's perfume, Docker khakis, hush puppies. Mr. Preppy. His Green Lantern costume was in his ring. Manufactured from a single Oan molecule, the costume never got dirty. As long as he wore the ring, he would never be naked.

While Jen showered, Kyle had a bowl of twigs-and-nuts cereal Jen had found at some yuppified emporium. He turned on the radio and listened to a procession of slacker vocals. Jen came into the kitchen wearing Osh Kosh B'gosh coveralls and a white T, drying her green hair with a towel. She reached over to the radio and changed to the all-news station.

"Hope you don't mind."

Kyle did mind. He hated the news. Every time there was a tale of human tragedy he flagellated himself for not being there to prevent it. He wondered how Jen could listen with half a mind, as if it were background music. Why didn't she feel compelled to *do* something, as he did? The morning's litany of woe began with a twelve car pile-up on the New Jersey Expressway. He turned it off.

"Let's not have any radio."

Jenny-Lynn almost ripped the refrigerator door off its hinges. "What*ever*. Did you finish all the milk?"

Kyle reached guiltily for the quart container close at hand. Empty. Mauser rubbed against his legs, purring loudly.

"Yeah. Sorry."

"Are you going to make me go down to the store and get more?" Kyle felt a snappy retort bouncing on the tip of his tongue, but he swallowed hard and said, "No. I'll get you some." Anything to get out of there. He grabbed his wallet and keys and stuffed them into his front pocket. He slipped out of the condo, went down the hall to the back stairway, and up the stairs to the roof. The heavy roof door swung open on well-oiled hinges. From atop the five-story building, Kyle could see the high-rises down by the river and, over the treetops, the Manhattan skyline.

He had charged the ring last night. He leaped.

His feet never touched the ground.

CHAPTER

7

Since the dawn of humanity, people have looked to the sky with longing. Man also has the capacity to understand gravity and know that his physiology is particularly ill-suited to flight. Gravity eventually defeats all. And even if man could somehow hoist himself aloft on his skinny arms, how would he endure the extreme cold and rarefied air of the upper atmosphere? No, the poor fellow was clearly designed to crawl on four, walk on two, and hobble along on three.

Except for the super heroes. Except for that lucky .00000000023% of the population who through accident or design have acquired paranormal powers. Superman looks human but he is in fact an alien from a radically different world. The Flash's powers are the outcome of a freak accident. But Kyle Rayner had his powers handed to him on a silver platter; he was the winner of a cosmic lottery.

In the past, the Guardians had been reluctant to give power to humans. Our lives are too short, our viewpoint too limited. Ultimately, they recognized humanity as a kindred race, one that concerned itself with high matters as well as low. Earth culture changes at a dizzying pace compared to that of the planet Oa. The Guardians were initially slow to recognize our constant state of flux. When they finally forked over a third ring, they took human idiosyncrasies into account. All people were not alike. They should have learned that lesson with Sinestro, but the Guardians often let their convictions color their conclusions.

Alan Scott was steady as a church, square as a Salvation Army meal, and conservative as a banker. Hal Jordan was a free spirit, given to hyperbolic excess before he became Green Lantern. For years after taking the ring, he wandered the world and the galaxy searching for something. The meaning of life, a good nickel cigar, his parents. He was still searching.

Kyle Rayner burst on the scene as the new Green Lantern with no such agenda. His grandfather, Roderick "Snowy" Rayner, had been an adventurer, anthropologist and explorer who worked with the legendary Buck Wargo. Kyle's father Aaron Rayner was a CIA agent who disappeared in the jungles of Southeast Asia when Kyle was three years old. His mother Maura worked as a cleaning lady. When he was five, he woke from a nap to find their rented trailer ablaze. Kyle would have perished if not for the quick action of the local volunteer fire department, an event that would have a lasting affect on him. He internalized the message of duty and obligation that defined a hero, but it would be many years before he would embrace it.

Five years ago Kyle was at the Heretic Club in Los Angeles with his friend Tyler Hutchence. Kyle had been making the rounds of ad agencies looking for work, but mostly it was an excuse to see California. He and Tyler had left New York on a whim, driving straight through in Tyler's '87 Celica, taking turns sleeping. It took them thirty-two hours. They stumbled onto Santa Monica Beach at dawn and fell asleep on the sand.

It was nearly noon when they woke, the beach vibrant with tourists. As they made their way back toward Tyler's car, people edged away. Kyle and Tyler looked like bums. They needed a place to clean up. It took them a half hour to drag themselves away from the boardwalk. There were babes everywhere—skating, boarding, surfing, bopping and dipping. They took a room at the Gas Light Lodge—a dive on Sunset—cleaned up and prepared to explore the legendary Strip.

Kyle and Tyler both wanted to catch the Trash Hounds at the Heretic Club. It was supposed to be a great place to spot celebrities. Naively, the boys showed at eight and thus gained entrance, little realizing that it would be four hours before any music began. Tyler wasted no time in ordering a jumbo margarita. Kyle stuck to soda. He tried to warn Tyler after the third margarita. The joint filled up. It was before the smoking ban and Kyle was nauseous from secondhand smoke. He and Tyler clung to their barstools like drowning men to flotation devices. A deejay brayed incomprehensible jive between ear-shattering industrial thrash.

Shortly after ten, Tyler looked at Kyle with bleary eyes. "I think I'm going to be sick."

Kyle grabbed Tyler by the arm and half-dragged, half-carried him to the men's room. As soon as they vacated their stools, two pierced and tattooed girls with bared midriffs landed on them. Kyle somehow got Tyler into the black marble bathroom where Tyler sank to his knees and threw his margaritas into the toilet.

"Stay there, pal," Kyle told him. "I'll be right back."

Kyle needed air. He went through the warehouse in the rear, where two bartenders in muscle shirts discussed the merits of various tequilas, out the open steel door and into the alley. It was an unusually clear night for Los Angeles. Empty cardboard liquor boxes were stacked as high as Kyle. He looked up. A few powerful stars shined faintly. Los Angeles' crown of light overpowered the rest. Kyle scanned the heavens, seeing how many stars dared intrude on the City of Angels. A green streak appeared in the night sky. It blazed toward Los Angeles. It blazed toward Kyle. He was entranced, like a child watching a magic trick. The glowing green streak filled his vision and landed at his feet with an explosion of light and a soundless impact he could feel.

Momentarily blinded, he shook his head. When his vision cleared there was a little man with a high forehead lying on the crushed boxes. The little man wore a purple cloak and seemed dazed. Kyle's first thought was that it was some kind of space traveler and that he might be carrying a disease. He was half-right. Kyle steeled himself. Space debris or not, it was some kind of man.

"Hey mister. You okay? Where'd you come from?"

The little man lay still and Kyle feared he was dead. He had to be dead. No one could survive a fall from the sky like that. Then the little man had opened his eyes.

"You," he hissed. "What's your name?"

"Kyle Rayner. Where'd you come from? You need an ambulance?"

The stranger reached into his cloak, withdrew something and thrust it at Kyle. He opened his hand. It was a strangely familiar bulky green ring. "Take it!" he hissed.

Kyle eyed the ring. What if it were radioactive?

The little man surged off the cardboard, seized Kyle's wrist in a surprisingly strong grip, and pushed the ring into his hand. The ring was hot. Kyle fell back gasping but did not relinquish his grip.

The little man erupted in a green nova, blinding Kyle again. The next thing he knew he was lying on the flattened cardboard still gripping the ring. The little man had been Ganthet. That was how Kyle had become Green Lantern.

Enclosed in an iridescent green sphere, the hip-hop Green Lantern now arced toward the sky, arms stretched before him, hands clasped before him as if in prayer. He accelerated, knowing the thin air was turning red hot on the edge of his protective bubble. To the east he saw the sun rising over the curve of the earth. To the west, Manhattan's morning shadows withdrew into a vast mosaic. The earth receded. Space gained. Kyle knew the bonds of gravity were slipping away. Although the ring protected him from harsh conditions, he could always feel his surroundings.

Space was cold. Cosmic rays plastered Kyle's protective bubble from all directions. It felt through his green filter as if he were plowing through a hurricane at sea, cosmic winds pushing hither and yon. Kyle put Earth and Sun behind him, tracing a parabola that would eventually bring him around the far side of Saturn. Even at the speed of light, the trip to Saturn would take over an hour. Kyle was going to do it in minutes. He knew he was traveling at faster-than-light speed, and that it was theoretically impossible. It didn't feel as if he were traveling that fast: His mind seized on a destination and the ring took over.

Kyle was no physicist. Nevertheless, he believed the ring moved him forward in a series of jumps, wormhole to wormhole, covering vast distances in an instant, and slowing down as he approached his destination. These wormholes imploded with Kyle's passage, reappearing light years away. He was sampling space. It was the only explanation that didn't send Einstein spinning in his grave.

It was almost 900 million miles from the Sun to Saturn, slightly less from Earth. Because he was traveling faster than light, there was nothing to see. He felt as if he were traveling in a series of pulses, like a subway car in the dark. Each leap propelled him effortlessly forward. The energy bubble acted as a miniature atmosphere filtering out lethal cosmic rays. Earth to Mars, no sweat. A stroll in the park. Then came the damned asteroid belt, a boulder field in space. If Kyle willed himself in a straight line he would occasionally pop out in the space occupied by all or part of an asteroid. The ring protected him, but there were detonations, some of which could be quite powerful. Powerful enough to jar a rock loose and send it toward the sun. The odds that such a rock would enter earth's atmosphere were about a trillion to one. But Kyle couldn't take the chance. Because his actions were magnified by the power of the ring, he voyaged carefully.

He willed himself into a shallow parabola that took him over the vast, washer-shaped asteroid belt. He amused himself by scanning rocks with light waves. Kyle was no scholar, but through experimentation he had learned to identify several dozen basic elements, including iron and gold. There was plenty of the former, trace elements of the latter. Iron glowed back at him a dull brick red. Gold was an iridescent aquamarine. Nothing as they appeared on Earth. Jupiter and its gravity was not a problem because Jupiter was on the other side of the sun, approximately a trillion miles away. The heavens hung around him in all their glory.

Saturn grew from a marble to a tennis ball to a soccer ball to an agate boulder to a disc that filled the sky, fat lady twirling so fast her skirt spun straight out like a halo. He saw four of Saturn's nineteen known moons, tiny Pandora tagging along after giant Titan like a wayward child.

"Daddy!" a tiny voice nibbled in his ear, causing his heart to jump and his testicles to shrink.

I'm only twenty-six! I'm too young for heated formula and dirty diapers!

Kyle had no delusions. Caring for an infant was a full-time job. Certainly for the mother, and he doubted Jen was ready to drop her career and adventures and pick up the Huggies. She was like him in that respect. Once you became a super hero there was no turning back. Addiction to power was the strongest addiction of all. It had ruined his predecessor, Hal Jordan.

In accepting the ring, he'd accepted the responsibility. He had become a steward of the human race. And there was no end to human suffering. It was a 24/7 job. Only by consciously forcing himself to turn his back on humanity for a few hours a day was he capable of leading a halfway normal life. And even that required a willful ignorance. As the sewer inspector said to the mayor, it's best not to look too carefully.

Fatherhood. The very thought made his spine ripple like a suspension bridge in an earthquake. His life would no longer be his own. He would have a responsibility to that child that would transcend his responsibility toward humanity at large. He knew this instinctively. It was also common sense. It was the law of nature. Charity began at home. You looked out for your own first, then your friends and relatives, and finally, if you still had some juice, humanity at large. As for alien races, screw 'em. They had their own Green Lanterns.

The ring had reversed his responsibilities.

Responsibility, the curse of the super hero class.

Responsibility, without which there would be no civilization.

Abortion was out of the question. He wondered if Jen would be willing to put the child up for adoption.

Sure. Everybody wants a green kid.

And of course there *would* be people who'd want a green kid, for all the wrong reasons. It would be a tedious process, selecting the family to receive Baby Kyle. And what if the child manifested powers and the new parents freaked? Man, what a mess. He and Jade would have to raise the child themselves. And what if Jade opted out? That left him. Daddy Kyle.

Hey—the reason you are looping around the solar system is to get your mind off *earthly problems. Open your eyes.*

Kyle opened his eyes and saw the heavens. They were big. He saw himself. He was small. And he saw something else, down below, hovering in Saturn's soup. A trail of glitter, like a shattered mirror hanging in the sky catching the sun's faint rays and winking up at him.

Down he dove. Like the asteroid belt, debris swirled out from Saturn's equator in a plane. Sunlight cast a wide ring shadow on the outer layer of the planet's atmosphere. The atmosphere consisted mostly of ammonia snow, a noxious stew that only got thicker as you approached the center. Saturn was a gas giant where you had to penetrate almost to the core to find hard ground, and yet the rocky core of Saturn is approximately the same size and density as Earth. The core hovered around 15,000 K. The very center of the planet was actually cooler than the outer core, but by the time you reached it you were toast. The Justice League had discussed placing a station either on Titan or Calypso—for those who really wanted to get away.

Kyle swooped low, feeling minute ice particles scraping across his green bubble, which maintained gravity similar to that of Earth. If the bubble didn't modulate gravity, he would not have been able to travel. He reached the trail of glitter. It was metal. Numerous metals, some of which Kyle couldn't recognize. And particles of organic matter. People blown apart in some kind of horrendous mishap. A slow scan of the stratosphere revealed debris spread out over fifty miles. It had been there a long time to spread so far, like a series of cirrus clouds. Millennia. The largest pieces were obviously machined. Kyle encapsulated a cubic foot of debris and sent it back to Justice League HQ for analysis in a green bubble infused with memory like a homing pigeon.

All JLA members and affiliates were required to report evidence of extra-terrestrial life. It was possible these adventurers had been human, but if that were true, it was doubtful they had originated on Earth. At least not the Earth Kyle knew. And they would be "human" in the same sense that Superman was human. That is, cursory review would reveal they shared all the same body organs and traits, but differed substantially on a molecular level.

Curious, Kyle thought, aware he was procrastinating. Jen wanted milk. He wondered when she intended to tell him. If she intended to tell him. He looked out toward the distant Sun, no bigger than a pearl. He tried to spot his native planet. Fuggedaboudit.

Leaving the mystery below, Green Lantern rocketed toward the distant pearl.

While Kyle had been scanning trace residue, something had been scanning him. Recognizing the unique energy of the Starheart, it had waited discreetly, far below the scattered remains. Now it climbed, shrugging off gravity like a snake sheds its skin. It emerged soundlessly from Saturn's chaotic atmosphere and followed the super hero at a distance, lapping at his trace radiation like a rat following a trail of crumbs.

CHAPTER

8

J enny-Lynn had finished her shower, tied a towel around her head, and was in the process of choosing an outfit when the buzzer rang. She was about ask Kyle to answer it, then remembered he'd gone to the store. Slipping into an XXXL Warren Sapp jersey, she went down the steps to the foyer and peeked through the spyhole.

Some guy in an orange jumpsuit with a tank on his back and a nozzle in his hand. Jen didn't bother to set the chain. She opened the door.

"What?"

She had to give the guy credit. He didn't stare. He blinked and smiled. He had a nice smile. "Exterminator, ma'am. Today's the day."

"What day?"

"The day I visit every apartment and spray for roaches. Didn't you get the notice from the landlord?"

"Oh . . . probably. But you don't have to spray here. We don't have any."

"That's not going to work. If you don't have any now, you sure will when I gas the other units. I have to do every unit or it doesn't work."

Jen clucked in exasperation. There were no roaches because whenever either of them thought about it, she or Kyle launched a bubble that grew out of the center of their home expelling all insects. Jen felt a flush of guilt. Had they been dumping their roaches on their neighbors? Were they not carrying their fair load of vermin? Not everyone could draw on the Starheart.

"Is it dangerous? I have a cat."

"Nope. Only to roaches. Personally, if it were my building, I'd try to do it organically. If that didn't work, then I'd call an exterminator."

Jen went into the kitchen. "What do you mean organically? Would you like a cup of coffee?" The guy was actually kind of cute, and he didn't smell like a chemical plant. An oval label said "Eddie" on his uniform above the breast pocket. On the other side was the company logo: Terminator Too.

He followed her into the kitchen and sat at the butcher block table. "I'd love a cup of coffee. By organically, I mean without poison."

Jen poured hot java into two Gotham Ballet mugs. "Cream? Sugar? And how would you do it without poison?"

"Both, please."

Jen got the cream and sugar out and sat opposite him.

"One way is to sprinkle plaster of Paris along the baseboards and put out shallow pans of water. The roaches walk through the plaster, which sticks to their feet. So they lick it off. Then they get thirsty. The plaster sets in their stomachs, killing them. Another is to buy a gecko lizard."

"Really," Jen said. She'd love to see the look on his face if she displayed her own unique method of pest control. "You know, you could launch a holistic extermination service."

"I've thought about it. Only, no one would hire me to get rid of raccoons and things like that if I planned to kill them. I'd have to trap them and return them to the wild."

Jade stuck her hand out. "Jenny-Lynn."

The exterminator met her halfway. "Edward Hamilton Rocheford III. But you can call me Roach." He smiled ironically. He really had lovely brown eyes. She couldn't help but notice the ring on his left hand. The kind of thing Mr. T would wear.

"Good name for an exterminator. You don't seem very surprised that I'm green."

"I've seen some strange things. *Besides.* Everybody knows you live here. *New York* magazine did a feature about supermodel pads."

"Is this the first supermodel pad you've gassed?"

"Will be."

"Will be what?" said a voice from behind them.

Jen and Eddie turned toward the door. There stood Kyle, in Dockers and J. Geils shirt, clutching a quart of skim milk. *He can do that*, Jen thought. He can just sneak right up on you like that. She felt a frisson of resentment. Now she would have to explain herself, as if there were anything to explain. Because that's the way he was: jealous.

"Kyle, Eddie. Eddie, Kyle. Eddie has come to spray our apartment, dear. It seems all the other units have cockroaches, so we must have them too."

"We don't have any roaches, Eddie. Thanks for asking, though." Kyle stared at the coffee mugs, then at Jen.

"I asked him to have coffee. Eddie is very un-exterminator like. He has interesting ideas."

"I'm sure he does. Here's your milk."

Eddie got up and retreated as gracefully as possible. "Y'know, folks, if you like, I can just come back later and do this when there's nobody here. The landlord will let me in. If that's all right with you."

Jen glared at Kyle as if to say, *See? He's more of a gentleman than you!* Which was undoubtedly true at that moment. Eddie let himself out the door and shut it with a soft click.

Jade shot green daggers. "Why did you have to be so rude?"

"Excuse me if I go to the corner store for a quart of milk and come back to find you chatting up the exterminator!"

"Oh, like I'm flirting with any service person who comes to the door?"

"If some gnarly dude with bad breath came to the door, you wouldn't give him the time."

"You've had a bee up your ass ever since you got up. If this is what meditation does, you'd better give it up."

What about the freakin' pregnancy test? Kyle wanted to shout. *When were you planning to tell me?* He had another thought that was less charitable.

The buzzer rang. They both looked relieved, like two fighters at the end of a grueling round. Kyle strode toward the door hoping it wasn't the exterminator. It wasn't.

GREEN LANTERN

It was Hal Jordan, looking like a man who'd spent the last six months on a desert island.

CHAPTER

9

E ddie headed out of the city, best pal by his side. Best pal was a mutt named Barkley, who looked to be part black lab and part wolf. Eddie had finished for the day, except for that one apartment. He knew perfectly well who lived there, and had deliberately saved the unit until last, hoping to meet the mysterious Jenny-Lynn.

He had her *Vanity Fair* cover framed on the wall. He had every clipping he could find, DVDs of her appearances at the MTV awards and talk shows. Having to spray her apartment was the excuse he'd been waiting for all his life. Not that he expected to blow her away with his exalted position. Since graduating from Huntington Community College with a degree in graphic arts, he was only qualified to join the vast pool of other overqualified job supplicants. There were eight thousand graphic arts freelancers in Manhattan alone.

He couldn't help but notice Kyle's table and illustration. He hated that Kyle was getting work and he wasn't. He hated that Kyle was a better artist.

Eddie's job with Terminator Too had him working in Lower Manhattan. He was one of T2's army of two dozen, fanned out across the tight-packed island to battle the vermin hordes. New York City's cockroach problem was legendary. There were approximately twenty thousand cockroaches for every human being in Manhattan. Cockroaches were instrumental in the spread of asthma, among other diseases.

Eddie fought them with a range of pesticides, necessarily limited by environmental concerns. He'd read about DDT. Man, he'd love to get his hands on that stuff. He wondered why Superman or somebody hadn't figured out a way to get rid of the roaches. Put guys like him out of work. If he had super powers, that's what he'd do. Of course he wouldn't need the money from extermination work. He'd be famous, able to create wealth with his bare hands like Superman.

He'd love to get his hands on Jenny-Lynn, too. It was too much to expect her to be single, but why did the most beautiful women always go for pigs like Kyle? She was sweet, daring, tough, wry, beautiful and fascinating. He was rude and arrogant. The glimpse of art Eddie had seen looked slick and superficial. And where were the portraits of Jenny-Lynn? If Dork-man were any kind of artist and really loved her, he'd draw her. Eddie would love to spray Kyle with DDT like a giant roach. Just erase him.

Eddie and Barkley headed toward the Adirondacks, a favorite fishing hole since Eddie had been a toddler. His grandfather used to take him there. When the going got tough, the tough went fishing. Thank St. Orkin it was Friday. Eddie was off until Monday morning. His own squalid crib in Queens remained mostly bug free. He liked to think it was because of the plaster of Paris. More likely it was Barkley, who ate anything that moved.

Eddie scratched the grinning dog under his muzzle. "Y'know, Barkley, if more dogs ate cockroaches, it would empty animal shelters from coast to coast."

Barkley grinned and stuck his wedge-shaped head out the half-rolled passenger side window of the '94 Tacoma. Knocking off work in the morning gave Eddie all day to get there and set-up his pup-tent, cooler, and gas stove. The highways were chock-a-block with families on the move, traveling salesmen, semi-tractor/trailers, double loads, triple loads; Eddie would not have been surprised to see two hundred trailers hooked up like a train weaving down the highway.

Although his closest companion was a dog, Eddie was happy enough considering the tragedy that had touched his life. He'd gone through college on a VFW scholarship because Eddie the First had been a war hero. His parents had left a substantial life insurance policy, which Eddie the First had invested for him. Not that Eddie was financially independent—far from it. He'd pretty much gone through the insurance money by the time he'd finished college. After Eddie the First's death, Eddie had gone to live with his Uncle Art. Art had been too young to fight in WW II, but had fought in Korea. Eddie had fond memories of growing up in Uncle Art and Aunt Isabel's chaotic household with three other kids, plus three dogs, two cats, and a Canadian goose named Gilbert who refused to leave and intimidated the mailman.

From the sixth grade on, when he'd moved in with Uncle Art and Aunt Edna, Eddies' life had been fairly normal. He got along well with his half-brothers and half-sister, joined the Boy Scouts, partici-pated in Little League. But there had always been something a little stand-offish about him, a dreamlike quality. His teachers noticed and sent notes home. Oddly, the one field in which Eddie never slacked off was mathematics, where he always managed to pull straight A's. Algebra, geometry, trig, it didn't matter. His half-brothers and half-sister counted themselves lucky to have such a savant in their midst.

It never occurred to him to become a scientist. Just didn't appeal. For as long as he could remember, Eddie had wanted to create some-thing. He just didn't know what. He'd gone through model cars, model planes, radio-controlled cars, radio-controlled planes and illustration. His figures were stiff and wooden. He'd never be more than a third-rate illustrator. He even formed a band—the Extermina-tors. They sucked. But he was a first-rate bug man.

By four, they were at North Hudson. Ever since that morning he'd been thinking about what he'd blurted to Jenny. He'd had those thoughts before, but never articulated them. It now occurred to him that an environmentally friendly exterminator might have a future.

"Barkley, would you be willing to eat cockroaches on a per-piece basis . . . or at an hourly rate?"

Barkley grinned and woofed. They turned off State Highway 28 and headed west on McKee Road. Little hills rolled back from the road, covered with pine, oak, elm. They turned off McKee onto Sandford, which wound through the hills passing small farms. Civil-ization loosed its iron grip. Every weekend, Eddie tried to get away. Living in New York was like living at the bottom of the sea. You felt the pressure from millions of your neighbors competing for oxygen. He recalled Green Lantern and Green Arrow's recently declassified sojourn on Malthus. He'd read about it in *The New York Times*.

Malthus was a planet where the population bomb had detonated. The surface of the planet was almost literally choked with people. They couldn't feed themselves and they couldn't control their reproduction.

It made his flesh crawl, all those people. Compared to Malthus, New York City was the country.

"Hell is other people, Barkley," Eddie told his dog.

It was dusk by the time Eddie had driven up the dirt road to Lake Agnes, his secret fishing hole in Adirondack Park. Lake Agnes only covered ten acres and was a well-kept secret. Eddie and Barkley had the place to themselves. The county had installed a little picnic area, a shelter, table, and grill. Eddie set up his pup tent, set the camp chair at the end of the little pier, brought down the ice chest and enjoyed a beer as he examined his tackle box for the appropriate lure. His portable radio softly played Otis Rush out of a college station in Syracuse.

Barkley explored the shore while Eddie hauled in a succession of worthless fish—crappies, carp, and tiny inedible bluegills—all of which he threw back. The sun sank behind the hills around eight, which was about the time Eddie realized dinner was not forthcoming. At least not from the lake.

"Fortunately for you," Eddie told his grinning dog, "I anticipated this situation." Inside the cooler was a sixpack of bratwurst, just in case. The truth was that Eddie wasn't crazy about freshwater fish. That was just an excuse to visit the lake. He was happier eating the brats, and so was Barkley. It was the solitude he craved. Sometimes he got so sick of other people he entertained fantasies of becoming a mountain man or moving to Australia's outback.

By nine-thirty, they'd eaten two brats apiece. Eddie had brought his camp chair back to his campsite on a grassy flat spot next to the little gravel parking lot. He'd set the chair like a recliner so that he could tilt back, sip his beer, and admire the stars. Here, far from the city lights, he could see thousands of stars that never penetrated Manhattan's glittering carapace of light. Barkley lay with his muzzle on his master's thigh.

Eddie rubbed the old dog's head. "What do you think, Barkley? Is she one hot mama, or what? Too bad she hooked up with that conceited fool. Did you see that *picture*? No, of course not. Take my word for it. He makes Peter Max look good."

Barkley growled deep in his throat.

"You like that, don't you? How'd you like to feel those green fingers ruffling through your fur? I know I would."

Barkley stood and looked at the sky.

"What's your problem?"

Barkley exploded in a paroxysm of barking, shattering the stillness of the night.

"Shut up!" Eddie said. He looked up to see what Barkley saw. It was a light, no a cluster of light—spinning in an odd formation and getting closer. As the lights spun, they mesmerized. Eddie couldn't take his eyes off them. They seemed to describe a complex molecule. Barkley stopped in mid-bark, whimpered once, sat, and wagged his tail. The lights swooped down so quickly, with such a sudden burst of acceleration, Eddie had the impression of an air bag going off in his face.

Something plopped down at the edge of the lake, crushing the ten-foot pier and sending a mini-tidal wave rushing up the beach to drench Eddie and his tent. He leaped to his feet, staring at the odd thing that lay at the water's edge. Its shape was indistinct. It was so hot that the water boiled around it, sending up sheets of steam. Gradually, the thing achieved some sort of equilibrium and the boiling stopped. Eddie took a tentative step forward and at last discerned its outline. It was twenty feet in diameter, and if the spindle beneath matched the spindle on top, at least ten feet high.

"Oh, come *onnnn!*" he wailed. "*Not* the old flying saucer routine!"

It looked like two ceramic breakfast bowls placed opening to opening. It was too dark to tell its true colors. The surface appeared smooth, but slightly irregular, as if it had been formed in a kiln. Lights continued to blink sporadically from what looked more like pores than machined holes.

When the hissing stopped, Eddie thought he could hear a deep hum issuing from somewhere inside the saucer. He got his flashlight out of the truck and approached the device cautiously. As he played the beam over its surface he could see that it was cracked like an eggshell. A pungent vapor escaped through the hole. It occurred to Eddie that he was risking inhaling an alien virus but curiosity got the better of him. Barkley began to growl again and slunk low with his tail between his legs and a ridge of fur between his shoulder blades.

"Hush." Eddie tentatively touched the object's outer shell. It was warm, but not hot. With a wrenching noise, a piece of the hull bulged outward where it was cracked. Eddie leaped back, nearly tripping over Barkley. Another blow from inside caused a shard to fall off. There was something inside struggling to get out, a hatchling casting off its shell. After the second blow, Eddie thought he heard labored breathing from within.

"Hello," he said, shining his light on the jagged hole. He rapped his knuckles on the surface. "Anyone in there?" He reached down and grabbed a rock.

"Edward Harrison Rocheford the Third," emanated from everywhere at once, in a voice so low it sounded like the grinding of the earth.

Eddie almost dropped the light. He did drop the rock. Barkley exploded. "What?"

"Is . . . it . . . you?" The voice was more normal, with less of the vibratory harmonics that seemed to shake every tree and bush for miles.

"It's me. What the hell are you?" *Man, I can't believe I'm having this conversation!* Eddie thought.

"Help me, Eddie." Now it sounded like his best friend. "I have searched the galaxy for you."

That didn't make any sense. Who was Eddie? Nobody. An exterminator. Of course he had the *ring*, but that didn't make him special.

"What do you want me to do?"

"The hatch is jammed. Do you have a wedge?"

"Okay, hang on a sec. I got to get some tools from the truck."

He jammed his wheel wrench into a fissure caused by the blows and exerted pressure. The outlines of a hexagonal hatch appeared. Abruptly, with a sucking noise, it popped out depositing Eddie on his seat in the sand. He looked at the hatch that lay next to him.

It appeared to be made like a sandwich, an outer layer of ceramic, a metal hull of some sort, and an inner layer of some soft, vinyl-like material.

"Excellent," the visitor said with satisfaction. Two sets of fingers fluttered out and gripped the rim of the opening. They were magenta. The crown of his head appeared, black and gleaming like freshly poured tar, reflecting the stars. He climbed out of the ship with dignity.

He was seven and a half feet tall with a bulb-shaped head and a pointed chin. His Snidely Whiplash mustache stretched over a fierce grin as he extended a shovel-sized hand. Eddie took it without thinking. The visitor's handshake was firm but not overpowering. Eddie let go, backed up and sat by his dog.

"Where you from?" he asked, an insane giggle lurking behind his teeth. Always nice to have company!

The creature made a gesture as if shooing away a fly. "No place of which you've heard. Another star. Another galaxy."

"You want a beer?"

"No thank you."

A well-spoken alien. Eddie chugged the bottle in one pull and popped another. If only he'd gotten drunk before the thing appeared he could accept it. "How is it you speak English, and what do you want with me?"

The creature shifted its narrow body to look at Eddie. Its eyes were surprisingly small and close-set in the big purple head. He had a widow's peak that looked like the business end of an arrow and wore a skintight costume that accentuated his long limbs. Instead of answering, the creature thrust his right fist forward. Purple power salute? Some sort of challenge?

"I don't get it."

"Your ring, Eddie! Touch it to mine."

For the first time, Eddie saw that the alien wore a ring on his third finger. A ring identical to Eddie's own. Something resonated deep within his soul.

"Touch your ring to mine and all your questions will be answered."

"You can't just tell me?"

"No time. Touch your ring to mine."

What the heck. If the thing had meant to kill him, it would have done so. Eddie formed a fist and leaned forward to meet the alien. The rings touched. Eddie's mind melted.

10

Dull pain, a soft wet rasp on his face. Insane knowledge. Concepts that inverted everything Eddie believed. Too much. Too much information, too much sensory input. *Go away and let me be. I just want to sleep.*

The soft wet rasp continued, seasoned by the crunch of tires on gravel. Eddie opened his eyes. It was mid-morning by the feel of the sun. Barkley sat next to him grinning broadly, taking credit for saving his master's life.

Agony and dizziness swirled in Eddie's skull as if someone were using it to pan for gold. He hadn't felt this bad since his final all-night drinking binge in college. Funny. He didn't remember drinking that much. He'd only brought one six-pack of beer, and only had three of them.

A shadow fell across his face. He looked up, beheld the backlit outline of a man wearing a Smoky the Bear hat. The man stooped. Eddie saw the badge.

"You all right, son?"

Eddie boosted himself to elbow height and immediately wished he hadn't. The world went tilt-a-whirl, and last night's bratwursts returned to plague him. The deputy hurriedly stepped back as Eddie leaned over and vomited. He paused on his hands and knees, panting like a dog.

"You been drinking, son?"

"I only had three beers last night, officer. Must have been the food I ate. Those brats were in my freezer for six months. I don't know, maybe they made me hallucinate. You can't arrest me for tripping on bad brats, can you? Did anyone report weird lights in the sky or something last night?"

"Yes sir, we did receive some phone calls last night around nine-thirty in the evening. You know anything about that?"

Way to go, Eddie told himself. He had enough sense to know that what happened last night made no sense and wasn't for the authorities. If it had indeed happened. The ring grew hot on his finger. *It happened all right.* Alien thoughts crowded his lips, itching to get out. He needed all his discipline to get by this cop. He needed time to sort through what he'd learned, figure out what it meant. Some little savage part of him said *You can take this guy, and nobody will ever know.* But how? How could he take a state trooper who outweighed him by fifty pounds, was in much better physical condition, and wore a pistol on his belt? Why would he want to?

You can do it, said the savage voice. *You have the power—the power of your mind. The power of the will.*

"Barkley and I were camping here last night. Those lights almost hit us. They swooped low over the lake." Eddie looked at the lake. The pier was flattened but there was no sign of an alien craft. No hexagonal hatch on the beach.

"It headed west. It was pretty spooky. I didn't know whether to croak or go blind."

"A-huh," the deputy replied. Eddie saw that he drove a New York State Highway Patrol cruiser. "What about the pier? You know anything about that?"

"No sir. It was like that when we arrived."

The trooper stared at the mashed pier, back at Eddie. There was no evidence Eddie had had anything to do with its destruction.

"May I see some identification?"

Eddie forked over his driver's license. The trooper returned to his car, sat, and called someone. Eddie went down to the lake, splashed water in his face, brushed his teeth with water from his canteen. The trooper returned.

"This park is closed from ten P.M. until six. Normally I'd issue you a ticket, but you seem like a nice enough fellow, and your dog isn't trying to chew my leg off, so I'll just let you off with a warning this time. Anything else you can tell me about those lights?"

"No, sir. Scared the crap out of us."

"People are jumpy these days. Probably kids playing with a radio-controlled device. You want to stay here tonight, get a permit."

"Yes sir."

The cop left. Eddie felt better, having purged himself. He felt different. It was the knowledge. Unbelievable, forbidden knowledge. The secret history of the universe. How the Qwardians brought the spark of life to Earth. How they nurtured humanity through its many trials, always there, unseen, behind the curtain. Man's religion, his science, his philosophy, all based on the Qwardian model. They were Prometheus and Pygmalion, gatekeepers and gardeners.

Into this Garden of Eden crept a snake in the person of the Green Lantern Corps, self-serving super beings chosen for their treachery. Service to the Corps was treason to humanity. Eddie understood from his newfound knowledge that the Green Lantern Corps spread toxic radiation, the residue of their miraculous "power." The radiation was partly responsible for lulling humanity into a false sense of trust. It was responsible for hundreds if not thousands of cases of child leukemia. And these were the mere indirect results of their actions.

The Green Lanterns routinely murdered their foes, or anyone they didn't like, hiding behind the mantle of super hero. They engaged in bestial practices, often with Third World minors. They were responsible for many of the problems plaguing humanity today, from the Middle East to SARS. They had their own agenda, which had nothing to do with human well-being. They were evil.

There were three such traitors on Earth: The traitor Alan Scott. The traitor Hal Jordan. And most odious of all, the traitor Kyle Rayner.

CHAPTER

11

Kyle and Hal Jordan went to the Starbucks down the street. Kyle got a pair of orange juices and took them to the rear of the building where Jordan had taken a booth. Jordan looked hard-traveled; his trench coat a filthy, ragged mess; desert island beard. He looked terrible. He smelled sour. Only when Kyle looked past the rags to the eyes did he get a sense that this was not just another bum. Jordan's eyes burned like lakes of fire. Kyle wanted to say something but Jordan was like an Old Testament prophet. It wasn't Kyle's place. Kyle had been in awe of the man long before he ever dreamed of becoming a super hero.

"You and Jen have a spat?"

Damn! The man just zeroed in on things. Kyle didn't know Jordan but felt at ease discussing his most intimate problems. "What do you know about our relationship?"

"Oh, I know a lot about many things. I'm sure it'll blow over."

Yeah, right, Kyle thought. "Thanks. So, what's this all about?" The man looked like he could use a shower and a decent meal. Why didn't he just make himself over with a thought? Lose the rags and whiskers, wear Armani. This wasn't like the man Kyle had heard so much about. That wasn't Jordan.

Jordan smiled and spoke as though he'd been reading Kyle's thoughts. "Yeah, I know. I was in the desert." His gaze wandered toward the ceiling.

"Uh—"

Jordan's eyes held a hint of amusement. "What?"

"But—you're the Spectre, right?"

Jordan nodded.

"Hasn't the Spectre always worn a costume—a hooded cloak . . . a mask?"

Jordan made a flicking motion with his hand. "The ego thing. Been there, done that. It's not about striking a pose or inspiring awe. It's a serious business, which requires humility. I dress like this to remind me who I am." He smiled. "And because I don't want to frighten barnyard animals."

"Fair enough," said Kyle. "So what's up?"

Jordan's gaze returned to the here and now. "I'm getting adumbrations of disaster."

Kyle did a quick rundown: Terrorist savages killing tourists, check. AIDS out of control, check. Mass starvation in the Sudan, check. "What kind of disaster?"

Jordan grimaced and looked to the sky. "Not your usual kind of disaster. Something from out there."

"Out where?"

Jordan pointed to the ceiling. "Out there."

Kyle flashed on the debris he'd found on Saturn, but it had been millions of years old. "Could you be a little more specific, sir?"

Jordan squinted, like a man trying to remember. "I was in the desert when I heard a voice. I believe it was a manifestation of the Starheart. It was a funny thing. I was just about to try to kill myself—again—when the coyote appeared." Jordan paused to sip.

Kyle couldn't believe his ears. "Excuse me? Did you say you were just about to kill yourself? Again?"

Jordan nodded.

Kyle felt as if he'd stepped on a rake. A super hero committing suicide? Would the ring even permit it? But Jordan no longer had the ring. Now he was the Spectre, the embodiment of God's redemption. God's redemption could not kill himself. The very idea was obscene.

"But you're the Spectre—why would you want to do that?" Kyle just had to ask.

Jordan gazed at him forlornly. "I was trying to stop the pain."

"What pain?"

Jordan stared at him until Kyle had to look away. "Loneliness. Uselessness. Styron put his finger on it in *Darkness Visible*."

"I've read it. It's supposed to ease your despair."

Jordan shrugged. "Maybe for some."

Kyle leaned forward and hissed urgently, "I don't know what you're talking about. If not for you, this planet would not even exist! You saved over four billion human beings! What's useless about that?"

Jordan shrugged again, like a bored teenager. "I'm glad I did it. I have no desire to cause anyone suffering. I just feel as if I've seen too much."

"Sir, that's nuts. There was a reason you were chosen, why you keep being chosen. For you to kill yourself would negate everything that we stand for. And whoever appointed you Spectre would feel pretty pissed."

Jordan sighed, coughing up the world. "I know. Don't worry. I'm not going to kill myself. I went to the edge and stared over. I even jumped. But an updraft caught me and deposited me back on these rocky shoals. Something like that happens every time. But I'm over it now. I wouldn't be here if I didn't recognize my responsibility."

Responsibility hung around their necks like yokes of stone. Kyle was tempted to tell Jordan about Jen, ask him for advice. But Jordan was the last guy to ask about relationships. The ultimate loner.

"Hal, do you believe in God?"

The million-mile stare. "Why do you ask?"

"I just think there has to be something behind all this, some unifying force in the universe. I mean, you look at the miracle of life, and you ask how could this happen by accident?"

"Sometimes we are guided by superior civilizations. Like the Oa."

"But who guides them, Hal? Answer the question."

"What am I, Mr. Natural?"

For the first time since leaving the house, Kyle smiled. Hal Jordan, the hippie super hero. "Speak, o wizened sage. God: yes or no?"

Jordan nodded. "Oh yeah, He's real. He spoke to me. He's the one who warned me that something bad was about to go down."

"If He's so bloody omniscient, why didn't He give you any details?"

Jordan shrugged. "He works in mysterious ways."

"Some people think *we're* gods. We're not, you know. We're among the lucky few who have been chosen to serve." The words tasted bitter in Kyle's mouth. The lucky few. His responsibilities were interfering with his love life! Or was it the other way around? But when he asked himself if he would be willing to renounce his powers, the answer was a resounding *no*. Power was the greatest addiction.

"No," Jordan answered after a pause. "We're not gods."

"You came to warn me about this incipient menace?"

"That's right."

"What about the JLA? Don't you think you ought to tell them?"

"I don't report to them anymore. You tell 'em."

"Well Jeez, Hal, it would help if you were a little more specific. All you know is, it's coming from out there." Kyle pointed up.

Hal pointed up. "That's right. And one other thing. This is not something new, but something old, very old. Something we've faced before."

"Is that all?"

"I'm afraid so."

One more pebble on his back. Kyle was weighing whether to bring this matter to the JLA's attention. It was like the domestic terrorism alerts. What good were they? They only made people apprehensive without increasing security. The JLA was already monitoring the spaceways, constantly sweeping for singularities that could be used to introduce anomalous elements.

Looking at the gaunt figure in the dirty trench coat, Kyle felt white-hot anger burst in his gut. *Thanks, pal. Thanks a lot. Thanks for dragging your ragged butt halfway across the country to lay this trip on me, as if I don't have enough on my plate.* Shocked at the vehemence of his own thoughts, Kyle felt ashamed. Jordan watched him as if he were a documentary, as the whole panoply of human emotions crossed his face. Kyle had never been good at hiding his feelings.

Still, Jordan said nothing. One thing about the guy—he was non-judgmental. "You going to stick around for a while? You need a place to stay?"

"No, I said what I had to say. Never liked this city. I don't like cities, generally. I don't like crowds. I don't know; maybe I don't like people."

"You need anything, couple bucks maybe?"

Jordan offered his Steve McQueen smile. "No thanks. I'm the Spectre. I don't need to eat. I don't need to sleep."

"Hate to argue with the God's Redeemer, but you look like you could use some rest."

"You're right about that, Kyle. I'm heading back to the empty spaces, get some rest."

"You're not going to try and off yourself. Again."

"No. Not that I really could, no matter how hard I tried. He wouldn't let me. No, I'm around for the long haul. What are you up to?"

Kyle almost spilled the beans. He needed to confide in someone, but it was just too personal. He was too confused. In his present state, Jordan could offer no insights. Kyle shrugged. "Down to Gotham City to beard the lion in his den."

"The lion?"

"Alan Scott."

CHAPTER

12

G otham Broadcasting's headquarters on Fifth Avenue in Gotham City was called Gray Rock for obvious reasons. Built during the Art Deco heyday of the Thirties, it resembled nothing so much as a stylized version of Gibraltar, a manmade cliff looming over manmade canyons. Three revolving and six conventional doors admitted visitors at street level. The ground floor contained a pharmacy and a restaurant on either side of the vast lobby. A blind man ran a magazine kiosk toward the back.

Several kiosks had been set up within the lobby itself, dispensing gourmet coffee, cinnamon rolls, the dailies, and, until recently, cigarettes and cigars. There were twenty-four elevators in the lobby, serving sixty-six floors. Half the elevators went express to the thirty-third floor as the first stop. Gotham Broadcasting occupied the building's top six floors.

Kyle lingered in the lobby reading *Entertainment*, one of the few magazines that didn't upset his stomach, and trying to work up the courage to go upstairs. Fact was Alan Scott had been more of a father to him than his own father, Aaron. Not that Kyle didn't love his dad. He did. But it was more the idea of a father that he loved than the actual man. Kyle had been three when Aaron disappeared on a mission in Cambodia. Whatever his father had done, it must have been secret because for years the government denied they'd ever employed him. It wasn't until his mother, Maura, filed a claim with the Freedom of Information Act that they learned the truth, and the government was forced to start paying a pension.

Kyle and Alan Scott had much in common. They were both members of an exclusive club. Alan was no square. He'd lived a little before and after taking the ring, and acknowledged as much. Jen was the unexpected dividend of celebrity, but once she made herself known, Alan had welcomed her with loving arms.

Alan deserved to know the truth, and to know that it wasn't Kyle who was behaving in an irresponsible manner.

But.

When you go to tell your girlfriend's father that she's pregnant, you must tread carefully. Kyle thought about another latte, but that was the last thing he needed. He looked out the floor to ceiling glass at the people and cars rushing by on Fifth Avenue. The whole world was racing off to work and he was dragging his heels in an office lobby.

Okay, Okay! he said to his superego. *I'm going.* Kyle joined a group of office drones at one of the express elevators. The only guy who looked happy was a bike messenger, filthy in once-white skin-tights, leather jacket, and scalloped fiberglass helmet, clutching a Federal Express package in gloved hands.

Kyle wore a jacket and tie. Nobody paid him any attention. He got off on the sixty-fifth floor, where Alan had his office. The first thing he saw when he got off the elevator was Mandy, the café-au-lait receptionist juggling phone calls behind her free-form desk. She acknowledged Kyle with a wave and a thumb, indicating that the Old Man was back there.

The security guard was new. Kyle produced his driver's license. The security guard gave him a shield to wear on a chain around his neck.

Kyle stepped through the metal detector and walked down a corridor lined on both sides with windowed offices outfitted with blinds. Some of the blinds were partially open, offering glimpses into more private spaces. Copy editors picked meticulously at the day's fare on their flat-screen monitors. The corridor debouched into the bullpen, where thirty-odd people labored at work stations. Tension hung in the air in place of the cigarette smoke of yore. People were hustling around with purpose, holding urgent conversations.

"Kyle! Over here, willya?" It was Karen Marks, the art director, a tall, thin drink of water with a withering and sarcastic manner. Kyle knew deep down inside she was a softie. He went over to where Karen was supervising a layout on a screen with a graphic designer.

"Jeez, look at this, will ya? What are you, trying out for Junior League? Where'd you get that tie? Is that one of those Rush Limbaugh power ties?"

"Come on, Karen. Don't bust my chops. I'm here to see Alan."

"Well I'll warn ya, he's in no mood to chat. Some gangbangers in a low rider cruised Jefferson Elementary School this morning and shot three kindergartners dead."

Kyle felt a chill settle on his skin. "You're joking."

"I wish I was. I'm not. The cops have got the bangers corralled in some old warehouse down by the river. We have three guys down there, trying to update the website every fifteen minutes. The old man thinks he's back at Iwo Jima."

Kyle froze. That would explain the frenzy of activity he'd noticed. He was torn between going ahead with his program, and changing to Green Lantern and cleaning up those gangbangers. The guilt returned like an eighty pound buzzard that liked to sit on his neck.

Stop it, Kyle. You can't be everywhere at once.

But he was in Gotham City. If he'd been at the school he could have prevented this tragedy, three kids shot dead.

If he'd known about it in advance.

Stop it, Kyle. You're not responsible for all the evil that men do.

Nevertheless, he felt responsible. He moved forward out of shock and inertia. The children were already dead. The cops had the bangers pinned down. They weren't going anywhere. Sure, he'd love to turn green and bolt. Anything to avoid talking about Jen's pregnancy with her father. He had enough difficulty talking about it with her!

Just when did she plan on telling him? It wasn't as if he didn't have a right to know. He recognized his anger with her. In a way, going to Alan was a betrayal of her trust.

Well, screw it. She should have trusted Kyle enough to tell him, not force him into this kabuki dance. Squaring his shoulders, he approached Alan's office. The blinds were drawn on the door and on the window. Holding his breath, he knocked.

"Come in," Alan called from inside.

Kyle let himself in and shut the door. Across the cocoa carpet, the president and CEO of Gotham Communications was holding one of those urgent conversations with his city editor, Rod Ault, a middle-aged sack of blasé cynicism. In his thirty years in journalism, Ault had seen a lot of things, and conveyed a certain world weariness with his eyelids. Ault nodded, but otherwise did not acknowledge Kyle. The two men went on talking.

"Find the parents. The killers' parents, and the victims' parents. I want interviews and pictures."

"You want me to send Sandford, I'm gonna have to pull her off that property tax story in Washara County."

"Do it."

"I already sent the chopper. She'll be here in half an hour."

Alan ran a hand through his long yellow hair with traces of gray at the roots. He snapped his fingers. "Well? What are you waiting for? An engraved invitation?"

Ault levered himself to his feet. He was built like Big Bird. "Cut some slack for mere mortals, will ya? Nice to see you, kid," he said to Kyle on the way out.

Alan began scanning copy on his desk. "Kyle, what a pleasant surprise. What can I do for you?" He did not look up.

"Sir, if this is a bad time . . ."

"Nonsense. You came all the way up from New York—what's on your mind? Walk with me, will you? I have to check on something." Alan stood and strode around the desk toward the door.

Kyle raced after him. "I heard about this drive-by. What a tragedy."

"You don't know the half of it. The mayor is reaming out the police commissioner even as we speak. As if there's anything the man could have done. Gotham has more than its share of random violence; the cops have it plenty tough. Psychos run rampant in our streets. These kids that got shot, naturally they come from the poorest of the poor. We're going to start a fund for the families."

They came to the art department. Alan went into a huddle with Karen. Every now and then one of them would come up for air and look his way. Alan motioned him over.

"Karen would like to use you for the cover of next Sunday's *Gotham Magazine*."

Kyle was thrilled and flattered. It was always nice to get recognition for the non-Green Lantern side of his personality. "What did you have in mind?"

"We have a story about gangs in development. I'll e-mail you a copy. A full-page illo that graphically illustrates the tragedy of gang violence."

A thousand horrific images ran through Kyle's head. "Are you sure you want to go that way? Could be a big turn-off."

"Kyle, let's you and me get together later this afternoon and discuss it. Can you meet me at three?"

"What about lunch?"

"That's my work-out time," she replied.

Kyle glanced at his watch. It was ten-thirty. This was his job. It was what he'd set out to do before the Guardians intervened. "Sure."

Alan had slipped away, and with him, the window of opportunity. No way could Kyle tell him about Jen under the present circumstances. Better to wait until things calmed down. Trouble was, when you held a hands-on position with a news company things never quieted down. At an age where other men had long-since retired, Alan continued to guide the organization he'd first joined after the war when it had been Radio Station WGBS. Alan had been on the job since before Walter Cronkite.

An intern with more facial piercings than Mr. Potato Head hurried over with some print-outs. "I got the dead kids," he said, laying the pictures down on a light table.

Kyle looked over Karen's shoulder. It was heartbreaking. Candids of two kids, a boy and a girl, at the peak of life. Laughing, wide-eyed, innocent.

"They're afraid they're gonna torch the warehouse. The commish has got seven stations on standby, so pray a fire doesn't break out anywhere else for the next couple of hours."

Kyle knew what he had to do. He turned and quickly walked away. The intern stared after him. "What? I say something?"

Kyle burned with impatience, desperate to get out of there. The elevator was taking its own sweet time and the building was sealed as tightly as Tutankhamen's tomb. He could have teleported but there were people around and it was the type of action that led to resentment. Alan had asked him not to do it in the building.

He had to wait. The elevator came. It seemed to take forever to move between floors. By the time they were down to the thirtieth floor, there were fifteen people crammed on board and everyone smelled of everyone else's cologne. When the elevator reached ground floor, Kyle found himself stuck in the back. He had a wild desire to savagely kick the backsides of all those who stood between him and freedom. When he finally got out, he nearly sprinted across the vast marble lobby, dodging irritated citizens like Ahman Green headed for sunlight.

Next door a Gotham Deliveries truck filled the narrow alley halfway back as two men wheeled crates down a ramp to a loading dock. Perfect. Kyle squeezed between the truck and the wall and made the change. His civvies disappeared. One of the men unloading the truck thought he saw something green rocket skyward—maybe one of the mystery men. His partner said, "Yeah right—more likely a giant frog." Most people who lived in Gotham had never seen a mystery man.

Kyle reached the waterfront in one minute. The warehouse where the bangers were holed up wasn't hard to find. It was six stories tall, made of red brick, with countless arched windows on the upper floors—a Gothic monster, encircled by law enforcement vehicles and a small army of cops. Kyle saw the blue of the Gotham Police, the black of the SWAT team, and the yellow of the fire department. He paused in the sky until he figured out who was in charge. You could always tell the guy in charge because he stood at the center. Everyone else was in motion around him, but he didn't move. A man standing behind a Crown Vic with flashing lights appeared to be the big kahuna. He wore a fedora and a brown trench coat. His posture conveyed confidence and irritation. Green Lantern landed next to him with a slight report.

Cop took one look and said, "Thanks, we don't want any."

"Green Lantern, officer."

"I know who you are."

"What's the problem? I can go in there and clean those guys out without a shot being fired."

The cop turned. His badge hung over his belt like a tongue. District Nine Chief Otis Strickland. He was black and built like a fireplug. "See that warehouse? It's scheduled to implode next week. It's a tinder box. Used to be a paint factory. If a spark goes off in there, that place will burn like last year's Christmas tree. They see you coming, they start shooting, bam." He snapped is fingers. "That's it. So, thanks but no thanks."

Green Lantern considered the problem. He could encase the entire structure in an airtight bubble, snuffing any flame. Unfortunately, that would also snuff the gangbangers. "How many are in there?"

"At least two cars' worth. Freakin' convoy. Probably eight, knowing the Murphy Street Shamrocks. They like to travel four to a car."

A black-suited SWAT guy came up, conferred in low tones with Strickland, hustled away. Strickland held a finger up and talked into his cellular. "Get somebody on the roof of the Pergament Building, maybe we can spot them from there." He turned toward GL. "The building's more or less gutted—they took out the interior walls, so we might be able to spot them from some angle. It's like a giant chunk of Swiss cheese."

"I could scan the building."

"What's that?"

"I can transmit a form of radiation that travels through inanimate objects and highlights animate objects."

For the first time Strickland looked at him with respect. "No fooling?"

Green Lantern rose one hundred feet in the air.

"Don't do that!" Strickland screamed. "You want to give them a target?"

Half the SWAT crew, sensing an opportunity, drew carefully on the building waiting for the tell-tale puff of smoke or snatch of flame. The warehouse stood silent. GL held his ring hand out in front of him and directed it to scan the building in search of warm bodies. An all-but-invisible green cone emanated, enclosing the building. GL shut his eyes. On the wrap-around screen with Dolby inside his head, he saw every level, every corridor, every closet. The only living things larger than microbes were rodents. Hundreds of rats inhabited the decrepit structure. Of living humans there was no sign, save for the faintest residue on the top floor, in the very center of the building, with no outside view.

GL flew toward the upper floor to get a better look.

GREEN LANTERN

"Hey!" Strickland shouted. He picked up a bullhorn. "*Green Lantern! Come back! Do not enter the—*"

Green Lantern entered the building.

13

G L knew right away the top floor was empty. It felt empty. The walls were covered with graffiti. Many layers. Most dominant were a series of shamrocks in iridescent green outlined in neon orange. *Murphy Street Shamrocks. Erin Go Bragh. Sinn Fein. Parnell Lives!* He floated toward the center of the building where he'd seen the strange glow. These had once been executive offices. An old Currier & Ives calendar hung on the wall open to April, 1989. The room from which the radiation sprang had once been a conference room. Remnants of the plush carpet still stuck to the floor. The radiation itself seemed to be coming out of a brick closet built into a cluster of brick pillars in the center of the floor. GL used the ring to pull the door open from a distance.

The inside of the closet looked like white noise, static on a television screen, a light riot devoid of meaning. As GL approached, he could hear the static. The sound increased exponentially within five feet of the closet, louder than a jet engine. The sound waves petered out within five feet as if they were being drawn back into the closet. Six feet away, nada. One foot away, you needed earplugs and headphones, and even then it would shake your fillings loose. The gate was obviously consuming incredible amounts of energy. Since the Gotham power grid remained intact, the energy had to be coming from the other Side.

Where could the Murphy Street Shamrocks have gone but through the gate? And that's what it was—an inter-dimensional gate. GL had encountered them before, from several civilizations. Each civilization offered its own style, but they all worked on essentially the same premise, a wormhole held in stasis via electromagnetic pulse. Only massive electro-magnetism could counteract the intense gravity. Graffiti indicated the gang had been using this gate for some time. There was a sort of crude timeline painted on a nearby wall.

A big arrow pointed toward the closet over the legend "Lough Ballyutogue—afore ye know it!" A series of green Shamrocks had been painted in a column, with names and dates beneath them. It took GL a minute to realize it was some kind of eulogy for fallen comrades. The memorial suggested they'd perished on the other side. There were notes, reminders to individual members to bring certain supplies: cylinders of oxygen, gas masks, tents, poles, rigging, food, liquor, drugs. Each of the notations was initialed by somebody. The most recent message was dated that morning: "Payback, big time! Then down the rabbit hole." Kyle wondered whom they were paying back. They'd succeeded in killing two toddlers. There was something about gang violence that tripped his trigger, a trait he shared with Batman. Human cruelty came in so many flavors, it was hard to pick a least favorite. Kyle had a zest for busting gangbangers due to growing up on Long Island. And he plain didn't like graffiti. He admired the designs and the craft, it was the canvas he hated. Private property represented the sweat of man's brow. It represented his time, and hence his life. It was only the sanctity of private property that stood between the individual and the tyranny of government. The right to be secure in your crib.

He stared into the howling void: Chaos in a closet. *Ring protect me*, he said to himself and stepped through the door.

The sensory assault was instantaneous and overwhelming. Blizzard conditions didn't begin to describe the savage forces threatening to uproot, blind, deafen, and destroy him. He had become a grainy black-and-white figure in a lousy broadcast circa 1956. Dangerous sonics sawed at his inner ear. He willed the ring to give him earplugs. Abruptly, the cacophony receded to a dull roar. The horizon twisted itself into knots. The earth heaved and buckled like a sheet in the wind. Gradually, as the ring absorbed data, his eyesight began to adjust and he could see the landscape, if you could call it that.

A rocky plain, stunted, denuded trees, hills in the distance, what might have been some kind of communications tower. None of it would stand still. As Kyle tried to focus on something it would begin to ooze and slither like a bad acid trip. It was all insane motion without rhyme or reason. When a gangbanger popped up from behind a rock like a whack-a-mole, Kyle first thought it was part of the scenery, an hallucination, a feature in an imaginary theme park. When two more gangbangers did it, he realized he was not alone.

He took a step into the air and fell on his face. Damn! The ring was having trouble adjusting. Every time he entered a new environment the ring took time to absorb the physics. He'd never seen a world like this; what if it lay outside the ring's abilities? How was he going to survive, much less return? He spun and breathed an enormous sigh of relief. The stargate hung a meter above the rocky plain revealing a distorted view of the abandoned factory. Tentatively GL stuck his hand forward until he just touched the plane. There was a tingling. As long as the gate remained, he'd have a means of escape. He hoped.

Question was, what was he doing here in the first place? Apparently the Shamrocks had learned how to travel back and forth between dimensions and were using this hellhole as a means of escape. No cop would ever put himself through a stargate. They'd count themselves lucky the bangers were gone and post a 24/7 guard on the other side. Maybe make it a top defense priority. Figure it out. Use it.

The Justice League could petition the government for control, and would probably get it. The advent of mystery men in general and the Justice League in particular had reinforced a certain "Let Superman do it" mentality at both Justice and State.

What was that? It sounded like a child's cry in his ear. He whirled. The landscape resembled a spaghetti Western in bad black and white as far as he could see. Some trick of acoustics. He had immediately envisioned the faces of the two kindergartners gunned down outside their school. Innocent children. *Like Baby Kyle.* Leave the Shamrocks, they'd pop back through the gate and do it again. Shut the gate, the Shamrocks would remain here. He didn't know how to shut the gate, but he was certain there would be a guard on it when he got back.

Part of him screamed *Get the hell out! Dive back through that gate before it closes up on you!* Apparently the gate had been open for some time. The Shamrocks put their faith in it. Of course the Shamrocks by definition had already given up on civil society. Who knew how many other gates to this nightmarish landscape existed? The Shamrocks might. Leaving them was not an option.

He turned and looked back toward the whack-a-mole. Three lead slugs tumbled toward him at a leisurely pace, slow as soap bubbles. He put out a hand and grabbed one.

Smack!

The impact spun him around and knocked him off his feet. His hand smarted. He looked down. It was a bullet. They were shooting at him. For some reason, the bullets only achieved firing velocity once they entered his force field. He looked up in amazement. Two Shamrocks were aiming at him with automatic weapons resting on rocks. They wore goggles and some kind of breathing apparatus. Orange flame bloomed from their muzzles in slow motion. GL could see the bullets coming like fat bumble bees. He had plenty of time to get out of the way, but found when he moved too fast, he got motion sickness.

GL shrank behind a rock and concentrated on his breathing. Nice and steady, in and out, from the diaphragm. Something Batman had taught him: "Breath is the flywheel of life."

Exhaling in a controlled stream he felt his pulse recede. He willed the ring to form optic fibers and a screen. It struggled like fingers groping toward each other in the dark. The screen slowly took shape, like a digital image. The ring was getting a handle on the environment.

The image was as distorted as the landscape, but he could at least see his enemy, crouching fifty meters away behind a series of jagged rocks. The rocks themselves were black, gray and white and appeared to be volcanic, but that was impossible, since nothing remotely resembling a volcano could be seen.

Kyle stared at his ring. What was wrong with it? He shook his fist impatiently, than banged his fist into his opposite palm. Used to work on his TV. When he willed the ring to form a perfect sphere, he got something like an oscillating pear. He could feel the ring struggling to absorb data—it hummed and clanged on his finger. Whatever this place was, he'd never been there, nor had any of the previous ring bearers. It could take weeks, months, years for the ring to master this new environment. Kyle didn't have the time. Who knew the time differential between this hellhole and Earth?

A ripple passed through his body and now things were clearer, as if someone had gone up on the roof and adjusted the antenna. The world was still out of whack, but he could see more clearly. The ring continued adjusting to the new environment. A couple of Shamrocks were trying to outflank him, one on the right and one on the left. As their firearms had proven useless, GL wondered what they intended to do. One thing was certain—they were infinitely more at home in this hostile environment than he was.

The ring was interfering with his perceptions. Without the ring, he could handle the environment. Or so he thought. He willed it to cease activity. Another phase shift. The world was still black and white, but sharper. In focus. Fierce winds peppered his face with grit, smelling of ammonia, ozone, and something that reminded him of fried insects.

His feet were jerked out from under him and he barely got a hand up in time to break his fall. Two hands seized his wrist. L-O-V-E was tattooed on the knuckles of one hand, H-A-T-E on the other. One hand ripped off his ring, but in his excitement the Shamrock lost control. When Green Lantern turned it off, the ring expanded slightly as if releasing him from its grip. It rolled across the rock and fell into a crevice. Two hundred and fifty pounds of shaved-skull Shamrock got on top of GL and began pounding on his head with a rock. The first blow nearly knocked him out and almost certainly gave him a concussion. As the Shamrock raised his rock for a second blow, time seemed to slow.

GL looked up into the face of rage, early twenties, small, close-set eyes, four day stubble, teeth like rotting stumps. A green shamrock tattooed on his forehead. *That's commitment*, GL thought. The rock reached apogee, ready to descend. GL instinctively threw up his left arm in a block. His arm seemed to move through varying degrees of resistance, like a layer cake, before it met the descending arm. Kyle was one tough cookie, even without the ring. He stopped the downward blow and with his other hand formed a beak, thrusting it hard into the Shamrock's Adam's apple and forcing him back. The thug loosed his grip and GL was free. He got to his feet first and drop-kicked the Shamrock's chin. The gangbanger flipped over and went to sleep.

A bullet tumbled lazily by, six inches from GL's head. Wild, he turned. A Shamrock was standing five yards away, shooting at him with a Heckler and Koch automatic pistol. The bullets tumbled toward him like a cloud of dopey horseflies. They looped and wiggled. GL stooped, seized the rock that had nearly brained him, and was about to hurtle it with the authority of a major league fastball. But he hesitated. Weird world. Inverse physics. He released the rock as gently as a soapbubble, gave it a little puff and sent it on its way.

The results were devastating. The rock flew from his hand at ninety miles an hour and struck the Shamrock in the solar plexus. The thug folded like a plastic ladder and sat down. Had the rock hit him in the head, it would have killed him. Maybe it had killed him.

Four other Shamrocks surrounded Kyle. All four were armed and all four appeared to be about to fire. There would be no way for him to escape the crossfire, even at the bullets' absurdly low speed. And he had no interest in discovering what would happen if a bullet actually reached him. He was naked without the ring. His head rang and he felt as if someone were tightening a metal band around his temples. He touched his goose egg. His fingers came away green. In this dimension blood looked green.

The bangers were talking to each other and to him, but their words got broken up, blown aside, slurred. He couldn't understand anything they said. He had an epiphany: this was it. Time's up. He was going to die on this nameless hellhole and leave his child without a father. Throwing it all away on some dream of cosmic justice, as if by pursuing the gangbangers here he could undo what they'd done. All he'd done was doom his child to life without a father. In his hubris. In his arrogance.

The wind went out of him and he sat down hard on the rock. He could feel its chill through the uniform, losing its insulating properties without the ring.

He put the heel of his palm to his head, astounded at his own callowness.

Oh, man. Jen, I am so sorry. The enormity of his crime settled in. A man's highest responsibility began at home, with his own family.

GL had reversed the natural order of things and was about to pay. He thought of everything he was going to miss. His wife-to-be, his children, his grandchildren, the future. He thought about his epitaph. Deserted His Loved Ones For Cosmic Justice. Threw His Life Away After Criminal Trash. Failed As Father, Husband, Lover. The Least Of All Green Lanterns. A Disappointment To Us All.

"Nobody will believe . . !" one of the gangbangers said before the wind snatched it away. The Shamrocks exchanged high-fives.

Nobody will believe these scum killed Green Lantern, GL finished in his head. *Unless they find the ring.* A strange lassitude had settled over him. It might have been the concussion.

The least he could do was die with his costume intact. He looked around for the ring. One of the Shamrocks pointed at him and said something. They leveled their guns at him. A green cone descended from overhead, enclosing GL in a translucent teepee. The bullets tumbled into the cone's surface and disappeared. Six spidery green hands descended on monofilaments, each hand seizing a Shamrock so securely they could not access their weapons. GL looked up fighting a spasm of pain from the blow he'd received.

Another Green Lantern hovered in the air, hanging onto his captives like the hub of a Maypole. Kyle put his hands to his head. Was he hallucinating? Was he in two places at once? Had this planet split him in two?

"One mo!" the mystery GL shouted at Kyle. The shout came through loud and clear with no interference. The newcomer began to rotate, slowly at first, then gathering speed. The hapless gangbangers, each secured at the end of a green line, began to rotate with him, like the spokes of a wheel. Faster and faster the newcomer spun. At the center he moved slowly compared to his satellites. The gangbangers flew through the air horizontally like the flying octopus that Kyle had ridden at the amusement park.

The gate hovered in the distance, a ghostly television screen showing snow, almost identical to its background, save for the variation in interference, which looked like a moiré pattern. A Zip-a-tone world. In rapid succession, the new GL released the gangbangers. One by one they soared toward the gate like torpedoes. Each disappeared into the gate. When the last one was through, the gate began to shrink.

GL got abruptly to his feet, fighting nausea. "Hey, man! Don't close the gate!"

He ran toward it but it got smaller and smaller, like the receding image in the center of an old picture tube shrinking until there was nothing but a little dot in the center of the screen. That, too, disappeared.

"Damn!" Kyle cried.

"S'okay," said the mystery man. Kyle whirled and sunk into a combat position. The newcomer was about Kyle's age, slightly taller and leaner. He held his right hand out. There were two rings: the one he wore, and the one he offered to Kyle. "Here's your ring."

CHAPTER

14

T he newcomer's outfit was different from Kyle's. His clothes were baggy, pants cinched at waist and ankle, shirt at wrists and neck. Eight pockets down one leg. The newcomer wore a green-tinted bubble visor. The coloring was the same as Kyle's, and he wore an identical ring. His thick black hair was brush cut short. There was no telling what year it was here in relation to Earth, or if the passage of time had any bearing. Kyle was in a different solar system, if not galaxy, if not universe, with no guarantee he would be able to return home.

Kyle took the proffered ring, put it back on his hand. "Kyle Rayner, GL sector 2814."

The other GL looked at him with a silly grin before shaking his hand. "Spire Raines, sector 2814."

"Where exactly are we?" Kyle asked.

"Right here," Raines replied.

"I meant in relation to Earth."

"I wouldn't know. I'm not an astrophysicist. No one's been to Earth in millennia. It disappeared long ago."

"Disappeared?"

Raines nodded. "Rogue singularity. Foul play is suspected. But what can you do? It's not there anymore."

"How can you be from sector 2814 and not know what happened to Earth?"

Spire shrugged. "I'm just a cog, Fud. Venus is my home."

"How far are we from Venus?"

Raines put his hands in his pants pockets and looked up. "Couldn't tell you. I access this place through a pylon in the Alpha system, which is more or less next door. I might be able to identify it if we could channel data to the CB, but that would take up too much energy, and for what? A place that makes Mars look good."

"Where are we now?"

"Right here."

"No, I mean what is the name of this place?"

Raines made a noise like a sucking drain. "That make any sense to you? Didn't think so. It's a way station, an anomaly that exists between two singularities that exert an equal and opposite attraction. It doesn't spin. The fabric of space here is unusually conducive to wormholes, which is why its relatively easy to set up a gate here, but certain quirks in the atmosphere can play hob with the settings. For example, we might set up a gate to Fard, but within minutes it will shift vectors and you could pop out in the middle of nowhere. We have to recalibrate constantly."

"What happened to the gate that was just here?"

Spire Raines shook his head. "Not one of ours. It's a spontaneous generation. Nobody comes here. Nobody important. We get an activity reading, we know it's the tribals. So some tribals are using it as a way station. No drag off our rotation. *You* add a new equation, which is why I'm here. Hard to ignore another ring in your sector." He had an infectious grin.

"How'm I going to get home?"

Spire Raines shrugged. "Just wait. That gate pops in and out at twelve hour intervals, always in this area."

"Twelve hours?" GL wailed thinking time spent here was analogous to his absence on Earth.

"More or less. It always comes back. Just don't let it catch you sleeping, Fud."

"Why do you call me Fud?"

Spire Raines snapped his fingers. "It's just friendly—Fud, Ax, Proly. Fellow Green well met. You don't know this stuff? Where you from?"

"Twenty-first century Earth."

Raines did a double-take. "Geezerlike!"

"How old are you?"

"Twenty-five."

"Well, I'm twenty-six."

Raines nodded. "That splains it. List, gotta go. You're still here when I get back, I'll bring you some food and my lantern so you can re-up."

"You're snowing me."

Raines made a quizzical expression.

"You're fooling me."

"I would never fool a fellow green, Fud. List, gotta go."

"Wait a minute! Tell me one thing. How come my ring doesn't work here?"

Raines made a face like, *What are you, stupid?* "It takes time to absorb the data. This is not an easy planet to absorb. Something happened here. The Qwardians tried to colonize the place. It was probably a beautiful planet before they did their thing. Don't waste your battery. Wait for the gate. The longer you wait, the more data the ring absorbs, the finer your control. List, gotta go."

Bam. Gonesville. There was a little pop as air rushed into the vacuum. Kyle was alone, more alone than he'd ever been in his life. True, he could breath the unlovely air, and the temperature was moderate, but everything else about the Zip-a-tone planet made his skin crawl. The black-and-white landscape, the black bugs which he could see out of the corner of his eye. Every time he turned to look at them, they vanished. Vicious gusts blew grit everywhere. Rocks rolled uphill. It was a place that oozed despair. How could those bangers stand it? Then again, if you were a gangbanger, your whole life probably oozed despair.

He started walking. Out of the corner of his eye he saw black beetles scuttling from rock to rock. Shortly he came across what appeared to be the remains of a stone wall. It rose above the ash-colored earth in a long low, undulating line, scoured by the winds to a rounded smoothness. It was unquestionably the work of a civilized race. In the distance he thought he made out the ruins of some great building on a ridge, but it may have been a trick of the atmosphere.

Kyle sat on a rock. Black bugs streamed over his foot. He could feel them on his instep, like light rain. When he looked down, they were gone. Twelve hours. How was he going to pass twelve hours in this terrible place? The Guardians told him that the Central Battery had mapped the entire known universe. If that were true, all Kyle had to do was envision Earth. The ring would grab the coordinates from the Battery and take it from there. Surely Raines was mistaken when he said Earth didn't exist in this spacetime. Perhaps Earth didn't exist in Raines' universe, but it must certainly still exist in Kyle's. He looked up.

The sky was a kinetic gray, like a television set that's been turned on but doesn't pick up any programs. It was possible that the atmosphere was interfering with the ring's ability to communicate with the Battery. Screw it. Kyle didn't have the patience or the time. He'd have to take a look for himself, outside the atmosphere. He pointed one finger toward the sky.

He soared away from the planet in fits and starts, maintaining a simple vector. The atmosphere felt like layers of loose fiberglass, the way it scratched and pulled at his green bubble. It began to thin substantially at twenty thousand feet, then he was through and out into space. Once free of the planet's influence, the ring performed smoothly. Kyle did a slow rotation, consciously scanning every prominent star, feeding the information to the ring.

Where are we?

Kyle was once at the Planetarium with Jen and saw one of their sky shows. This particular show took viewers on a tour of the galaxy. During the show, viewers were treated to different points of view around the Milky Way, such as: "And if you were on Arcturus, the night sky would look like this . . ."

Kyle needed the ring to match one of the sky projections he'd seen at the planetarium—an image he had in his memory. The ring had to move him around get a match. But once it had a match, it meant Kyle knew where he was in space, and consequently knew where Earth and the Sun were in relation to where he was now. Then the ring could take him back to Earth.

Green Lantern flickered across the galaxy, dashing from wormhole to wormhole like an FM radio on "sample," searching for a view that matched a memory from the sky show.

Time slipped away. Cosmic rays caromed against his protective barrier suggesting insane music. He'd learned at technical college that

Mahler had once written a symphony designed to drive listeners mad, that it had been performed once by the Stockhausen Philharmonic, that halfway through the performance the musicians fell out of sync, threw down their instruments, and turned on each other. It was never performed again. Until now. Radiation played on his protective carapace like a xylophone. The sound, he really couldn't call it music, made him nauseous. Yet he dare not divert the ring's power to give himself earplugs. He didn't know how much he had left.

It took a special type of courage to soar through space with nothing between you and the void but twelve inches of green glow. The vastness of space could crush sense of self like a fruit fly caught in a dictionary. Physical dangers aside, there was a far greater psychological danger. Most human beings would not have been able to handle it. The Corps chose its candidates carefully, despite Kyle's seemingly random selection.

Yeah. A random choice. That's what they'd told him. He knew it was nonsense. They'd seen the steel in his spine. Steel that had been tested when Kyle had become Ion, with the power of 3600 sectors flowing through his veins. As Ion, he'd experienced a superhuman omnipotence, a universe-spanning awareness. Only the human imagination was as large as the stars. All else was insignificant. The Guardians had chosen him for his imagination, but it was his experience as Ion that made him comfortable in space.

The problem was that Ion was everywhere at once. Ion was aware of a child's suffering in Calcutta, and of the erosion of pastureland on far distant planets. Ion was a god. Gods never slept. The universe kept on expanding, humanity grew larger, with its concomitant cargo of happiness and sorrow. Happiness took care of itself, but sorrow was Ion's job. Twenty-four/seven. No room for Kyle Rayner's minute concerns. Ion had felt Kyle Rayner slipping away like a childhood dream, behind an infinite army of more significant concerns. Ion was the ultimate obsessive-compulsive.

Ion had to choose between godhood and humanity. At the last instant, Ion chose humanity . . . and imploded. Kyle Rayner was reborn. Not one in a billion could have withstood that experience and come out sane, but Kyle was one in five billion, a unique human. Somehow, his imagination dealt with the never-ending data, the knowledge not only of man's inhumanity to man, but man's inhumanity to other species, and variations.

The tiny green speck of sentience approached a red-giant star. He could feel its radiation signature from a parsec away. Idly, he recalled that a parsec was a unit of astronomical length based on the distance from the sun that would result in a parallax of one second of arc as seen from Earth. This is equal to 3.2 light years. And "parsec" is derived from the two words *pa*rallax and *se*cond.

Parallax was the name Hal Jordan had taken when he'd absorbed the power of the Central Battery to rebuild Coast City. Kyle had been instrumental in bringing Jordan back from his terrible godhood.

They had both been terrible gods. Jordan, at least, was willing to try again. In his own way, the Spectre was as powerful as Parallax had been. And Ion. The Spectre had never fully tested his powers. Kyle hoped he never would.

Kyle was lost. Although the ring functioned well away from the Zip-a-tone planet, it recognized none of the millions of stars surrounding him. Its power was low. Kyle tried to access the knowledge he'd gained as Ion but nothing matched. He had no idea how long he'd been gone. Time was meaningless. Civilizations rose and fell. Rather than return to the Zip-a-tone planet, he had one last ploy.

Spire Raines was human. It was quite possible he'd returned to a planet in the home sector. He said he lived on Venus. In order to find Spire Raines, Kyle would have to transmit a spherical pulse that would reveal Raines' trace radiation. Who knew how long he'd been gone? And how could he find it amidst the riot of cosmic rays? Easier to find a single grain of black sand on Waikiki Beach.

Kyle folded his legs Indian style. "This is why they pay me the big bucks," he said, the sound of his voice reverberating in his skull.

He launched a pulse. A sphere of faintly iridescent green burst from the ring and expanded, growing fainter with each millisecond, becoming invisible within a yard. Finding the other Lantern's *residual* radiation required absolute concentration that itself was like a sphere, an unbroken, outward-sweeping consciousness attuned to the slightest variation. Each square inch of the sphere's rapidly expanding surface communicated back to the ring holder a cacophony of radiation, overwhelmingly incoherent, deafening, and useless. Sprinkled among the white noise were snippets of real transmissions, none of them human. The sphere expanded at greater than the speed of light, gobbling up countless wormholes. Because Raines' residual radiation would be linear and radial, there was little chance that the expanding sphere would miss it.

Some of the alien transmissions Kyle understood from knowledge gained as Ion. Some sought his attention bombastically, like advertising. Some were cries of raw emotion, but no emotion recognizable by man. Some were dry dispatches, bills of lading, reports of empire building, requests for assistance. Some were dialogues. Some were monologues. Some were screaming matches. They washed through his mind like fast moving water, nothing worth saving.

The sphere expanded, a thousand-parsec bubble, a ripple so slight only another Lantern would see it. The bubble began to pulse in the manner of a battery that is about to go dry. This was exactly true. Kyle had almost reached the limits of his power. He might be able to expand it by a few more parsecs, but soon it would be dry, and once it was dry it could not be rebooted except by exposure to a lantern or the Central Battery.

A blip. At the limits of its cohesion, the sphere encountered the faintest remnant of Lantern radiation. Kyle greedily sucked it in, like a man dying of dehydration who comes across a puddle. A vector. The trace radiation was stronger toward the destination. Kyle seized upon the vector and prayed to a greater God than any he knew that he had enough juice left to follow that faint trail back to the Sol system.

To conserve energy he reduced the number of wormholes, or samples, he used to attain destination, greatly increasing his risk of materializing inside his target or overshooting. The long minutes, hours, years of concentration had taken their toll. He felt dizzy, light-headed, thirsty, hungry, exhausted. He couldn't conjure provender out of cosmic dust. He couldn't draw on the ring for sustenance without flatlining. He had barely enough energy to bend space with the crudest targeting. The gaps between wormholes were so great he actually saw the constellations change, flickering in spurts into new arrangements.

The last wormhole spat him out in the orbit of Uranus, its look and radiation as familiar to him as his own home. He couldn't see Saturn—it must be on the opposite side of the Sun. The green vector here was strong, visible to GL's naked eye, arcing in toward the Sun. Kyle gasped with joy. His cheeks were wet. He touched them. He'd been holding his breath. Not so godlike after all.

Jen. Their child.

He'd found his way home. With his last trace of energy, he boosted himself to the green vector, put his ring to it, and it pulled him along. Through the asteroid belt. Past the orbit of Mars.

To nothing.

The trail ended where Earth should have been. Light from the sun was not as he knew it. The radiation spectra were all wrong, indicating the passage of many millennia. The Sun was in its final stage of expansion before explosively retracting into a red dwarf. He was billions of years in the future.

And there was no Earth.

"Fud, what'd I tell you?"

Kyle gasped and somersaulted involuntarily. Spire Raines was back.

CHAPTER

15

Spire Raines carried his power battery and a *Have Gun Will Travel* lunch box. "What'd I tell you, Fud? Sit your butt down and wait for the gate. What you doing here, Kyle Raines? Do you know how long I've been looking for you?"

Kyle eyed the lunch box hungrily. "How long?"

"Seven thousand, two hundred and twelve earth years. Five hundred and ninety Kro years."

"How far in the future are we?"

"We're not in the future, Fud. This is now."

"How far in the past was twenty-first century Earth?"

Spire Raines wrinkled his nose. "Oh fud, a long time. Maybe three billion years."

Kyle goggled. "How am I going to get back?"

"What'd I tell you, Fud? Sit your butt down and wait for the gate. Almost didn't find you. First, the ring." He proffered his lantern.

Kyle took it and held it in front of him. It was *his* lantern. The very one given him by the Guardians. It had the distinct scratches from a dozen battles. "Where did you get this? It's my old lantern."

"There are a limited number of lanterns. What, you think they destroy your lantern when you're dead? It gets recycled. Go on. Charge up. I brought a snack."

Kyle placed his ring hand in front of the lantern. There was a flash of green as power transferred from the lantern to Kyle's ring. Instantly, the nausea, weakness, dizziness, thirst and hunger disappeared. He still eyed that lunch box.

"What's in the box?"

"Lunch." With a wave of his hand, a checkered tablecloth appeared, pulled taut at the corners. Spire opened the lunchbox and began setting things on the cloth, where they stayed as if magnetized. The lunchbox was a tesseract, producing far more material that it appeared it could hold from the outside. Heavy crystal steins. A tall metal cylinder that was cool to the touch. Fine China with peculiar runes. Sterling silverware. Three plastic tureens held a platter of club sandwiches, a series of large, metallic aquamarine scarabs arranged in a salad, and a bowl of spiky fruit.

Spire picked up the metal cylinder and pushed a button. A stream of amber fluid arced unerringly into first Kyle's, then Spire's steins. Spire lifted his stein in a salute. Kyle followed suit. "The Corps."

They touched mugs and drank. Frigid, delicious beer.

Kyle wiped his mouth on his sleeve and took another swallow. "Where'd you get this?"

"We brew it."

Kyle saw a mountain of anthropology behind the simple answer and didn't pursue it. "Good stuff." He helped himself to the club sandwiches. Spire picked up one of the metallic scarabs and bit into it with a sound like glass shattering.

"What is that, a bug?"

"Baked sicilio. Try one."

"No thanks."

Spire shrugged and stuffed the rest of the bug into his mouth, chewing with several hairy legs protruding. He sounded like a trash compacter. "An excellent source of fiber."

Kyle tried the spiky fruit, which tasted both sweet and tart, texture like a ripe peach. An agreeable fruit, he decided. They ate in companionable silence.

"Spire," Kyle said, filling his stein for a second time. "Do you know what number you are in the succession for Sector 2814?"

"Numba seventy-five."

Kyle did a quick calculation. "You're not that far after me."

"Oh, you're legendary."

"You know me?"

"Were you not Ion?"

"Yeah."

"Then I guess I do. Dessert?"

"No thanks. I'd like to get back home."

"What'd I tell you, Fud? I'm going to take you back to where we met. All you have to do is . . . "

"I know. Sit my butt down and wait for the gate."

"Exactly. Shall we?"

The Zip-a-tone planet was easier to take the second time around. The ring had been processing during the long sojourn. The atmosphere looked less like an electronic blizzard and the winds had died down, but the place remained a desert. The last thing Raines said before he popped was, "You and me are going to have to have a serious sit-down one of these days."

Kyle sat his butt down and waited for the gate.

Several hours had passed on Earth since Kyle had gone to Gotham City to talk to Jen's father. All of a sudden Alan was on this morality kick, as if his own daughter hadn't been conceived out of wedlock. Jenny's father was reliving the entire Victorian Age through his actions. As a young man he'd been something of a rakehell. Now, at an age when most men were dead, he was a robust, disapproving, sanctimonious pain in the neck who thought she should get married in church. In church! As if she'd ever prayed in her life, other than to Hera. She believed in herself, and the other demi-gods. Most people called them super heroes. Bored and pissed-off, Jen saw only one course of action. She went shopping.

Gristedes on Bleecker Street was the kind of upscale grocer that featured eighty-seven different types of coffee, including a rare Sumatran blend that relied on the droppings of certain feral jungle cats for flavor. Yellow-fin tuna at twenty-two dollars a pound. The produce section was a riot of color from every continent, spritzed at regular intervals with misted water while Gene Kelly crooned "Singin' In The Rain."

Jen grabbed a basket and waded into the fray. One thing she liked about lower Manhattan, few gave her a second glance despite her green skin. Or perhaps because of it. New Yorkers were so blasé. She spotted Robert DeNiro in the next aisle, tossing oranges in his hand.

Jen liked her greens. She was examining a purple head of broccoli when a familiar voice said, "That's good for your skin."

She turned and there was Eddie the exterminator, smiling, radiating freshness and cleanliness, smelling of limes. You'd never guess he killed bugs for a living.

"Hi!" she said, smile blooming unbidden. "Eddie, right?" They shook hands. Jen noticed that the back of Eddie's right hand was covered with a purple splotch, like a birthmark.

"Call me Roach. Everybody does."

"I can't call you Roach! No way do you resemble a Roach. I'll call you Eddie."

"I guess I can live with that."

She looked down. Eddie wore unmatched shoes. His left foot was encased in a work boot. His right foot was in a tennis shoe with the toes cut out. A bandage rose out of the hole.

"What happened to your foot?"

"Bit by a rat."

Jade's mouth made a little o. "You're kidding me."

Eddie's grin was incandescent. "Yeah. I had a bunion removed."

Jade punched him in the arm. "Joker."

"Hey, you want to get a cup of coffee?"

"I'd love to."

They finished their shopping. Jen noticed that Eddie bought an expensive brand of dog food. The Chock Full O' Nuts on the corner had long ago been replaced by a Starbuck's. They snagged a window booth beneath a hanging fern while Eddie went to the counter, returning shortly with two steaming lattes and a couple of lemon bars. There was something about him, a new confidence she hadn't noticed before.

"Did you get your hair done?" she asked.

Eddie laughed. "I never have the same barber twice. I go to a barber college in Queens where the students cut your hair for seven bucks."

"It looks nice."

"Gosh, thanks. But look at you! Wow. I can't believe I'm actually sitting here talking to you. Celebrity photographer and a real Victoria's Secret Model . . ."

"Thanks for putting those in the right order."

"What are you doing these days? I haven't seen you on a magazine cover lately."

Jenny absent-mindedly touched a dangling fern. The tendril began to grow, unfolding as they watched. "I do a little modeling, and some research projects in biology. They say I have a green thumb." She winked. She couldn't decide if she was flirting or just showing off, but thought it best to change the subject. "What's the dog food for?"

"Barkley. Want to see?"

"Sure."

Eddie pulled out an enormous wallet fixed to his belt with a chain, held out a snapshot of the grinning mongrel.

"Oh, he's adorable!"

"Want to meet him?"

"I'd love to."

"Would you like to . . . no, that's probably not a good idea."

"What isn't?"

"I was going to ask you out. But, I mean, you live with a guy. So it's definitely a bad idea!"

"Not necessarily. Why don't you give it a try?"

Eddie leaned forward, shoulders hunched, hands folded. "Okay. How about having dinner with me? Tonight at LaScalia. Afterwards, we'll take Barkley for a walk in the park."

Her emerald eyes flashed hidden fire. "Seven o'clock."

"Won't Kyle mind?" He struggled to say the word without loathing.

Jen shrugged. "Kyle could have gone to Coney Island for all I know."

Eddie sprang to his feet. "Great! I'll meet you at seven, then. At LaScalia!"

"Looking forward to it." She watched with amusement as he half-lurched, half-levitated toward the door, did an exaggerated double-take, and came back, digging for the big black wallet. "Wow! I almost stuck you with the bill!"

Jen put her hand out, forcing his wallet closed. "My treat. You can pick up dinner."

This time, he made it out the door. There was something about the guy that appealed to her. Funny thing—when she'd met him the other day, he had an aw-shucks quality she'd found charming. Today, right up until the point he'd asked her out, he'd seemed smoother, sleeker, bolder. A different kind of charm. Still the same guy, but maybe in a different mood.

Smiling, she picked up the check.

CHAPTER

16

E ddie hobbled the two blocks to the parking lot in a daze. His foot itched so badly he had an insane desire to sit down on the concrete, rip his shoe off, and have at it with a rat-tail file. He fought the urge and ignored the itching. Maybe it was a bad idea to stick the ring on his toe, but when he saw what it had done to his hand, he got worried. Any more change and he wouldn't be able to go out in public, not without some sort of explanation.

Barkley was at the drool-streaked driver's window. Eddie unlocked the door, got in, pushed the big fool out of the way and went for the shoe. "Come on, Barkley. Give me some room. My foot is on fire."

He got the shoe off and ripped off the cotton batting, revealing the ring wrapped around his middle toe like a traffic boot. His foot was the color of a fresh beet. He pulled the ring off and began to massage the toe with his fingernails.

"*Ahhh,*" he sighed in relief. The trickle of knowledge momentarily ceased. It was the knowledge that made him itch. The ring told him things. Constantly. Rust never slept and neither did the ring. Eddie knew all about Alan Scott, Earth's first Green Lantern, and his brutal slaughter of innocent Qwardians. He knew all about Hal Jordan, the second Green Lantern, who'd gone through more changes than Madonna and was now the Spectre. And he knew far, far too much about Kyle Rayner, the present Green Lantern.

He knew that Kyle Rayner had a greatly inflated opinion of himself. He knew that Rayner drew, badly. And he knew that Rayner was living with the world's most beautiful woman. All his life, Eddie had seen the jocks get the girls. He'd always been one of those boys who got chosen last for basketball, who didn't have the nerve to ask a pretty girl for a date.

That had changed when he met the alien. Eddie had had the power all along, in his grandfather's ring. But it had taken the alien to activate it. It was as if subconsciously he had been preparing for this his whole life. He'd always known he was special. His grandfather told him so.

Ignoring the fire in his foot, Eddie whistled "Satin Doll" as he drove away.

In Gotham, Police Captain Otis Strickland had had enough. Not a peep from the warehouse in over an hour. Unlike most of his colleagues, Strickland had never been comfortable with the super heroes. If they wanted to do good, let them join the force and wear a uniform like regular cops. There was something a little too egotistical in the skin-tight costumes, the well-defined muscles, as if it were all about *them*. Batman was the exception, of course. Strickland had met the Dark Knight at a crime scene once. You didn't know he was there unless he wanted you to know.

This newest Green Lantern was a cocky punk. And now it seemed he'd gotten himself in trouble. Why else would he remain silent? With a sort of grim satisfaction, Strickland ordered his SWAT commander Jason Gertz to take the building. Strickland was right behind the black-clad Gertz as they approached the east entrance, the one through which Green Lantern had gone. Strickland wore a bullet-proof vest that made movement difficult. What the hell, he was fifty years old and set to retire in a month.

Two other SWAT squads approached the building from the west and the north, all linked by walkie-talkie.

"Squad Two here, chief. All clear. We're going in."

Gertz motioned his men into the building. From opposite Sides of the doorway, first one, then another criss-crossed to the inside. After they had secured the immediate area, Strickland followed. The interior of the warehouse was a gutted, vast expanse of dusty concrete punctuated by immense steel support pillars and red brick walls. It had been a paint factory, but the business had long since gone to

Taiwan. The mayor and the landlord had been squabbling over the bones ever since. Now Strickland wished they'd torn it down. For the past couple of years the warehouse, and others like it, had served as impromptu HQ and retreats for all manner of street gangs. Gotham's own Hole In The Wall.

Strickland's earpiece crackled. "We're getting . . . interference." The missing words were replaced with electronic cackle.

"Us too," reported Squad Three. "Seems to be getting worse as we head toward the center."

Strickland was worried. In his experience, there was nothing in these old factories that would cause electronic interference. Unless it was something new, outré, or other-worldly. Strickland hated other-worldly. He remembered when Killer Croc paralyzed the city for three weeks. People were afraid to go downtown. At night, the malls were like ghost towns. This crime scene was already contaminated by Green Lantern's presence. Strickland was seriously considering switching on the Bat-Signal, which he hated to do. No real cop preferred to sit back and let the mystery men handle business. Keeping order and apprehending criminals was police business. But in this day and age, even the most traditional cop had to step down when the threat was untraditional.

So far, they were dealing with the Shamrocks and Green Lantern. The Shamrocks were a highly organized gang of white boys with ties to the IRA, and a few token Latinos. The Shamrocks were bad enough. As gun dealers, they had access to a far wider range of weaponry than the police.

The three squads converged on the ground floor's center, which held a bank of abandoned elevators. They met in what had once been a lobby, its cracked tile floor beginning to buckle like an ice flow. An old poster behind filthy glass urged safety first. The walkie-talkies were useless, even in line of sight.

"Nothing on this floor, Chief," Gertz said.

Strickland nodded toward the stairs. "Okay, floor by floor."

There were five floors, but the squads worked quickly aided by the lack of clutter. Cautiously, they arrived on the top floor. Gertz switched his walkie on and off, on and off. He came over to Strickland.

"The interference is worse on this floor. You can track it by the crackle." He held his walkie out and depressed the button. Electric crackle spilled. He walked in one direction. The crackle grew fainter. He reversed direction. The crackle grew louder. Gertz held his hand in the air and made a circling motion, indicating that his men should gather round. He knelt in the center of fifteen heavily armed police officers.

"Okay, listen up. Whatever's causing transmission interference is on this floor. We can track it by using our walkies. When the crackle gets louder, you're getting hotter. Let's fan out to the perimeter and work our way inward, see where we end up."

"Sir." The cop's chest patch said Hooper.

"What is it, Mel?"

"Something funny—usually these old factories are crawling with rats. But we haven't seen any."

Gertz nodded. "You're right. It is funny. Comments?"

The men shrugged. They didn't know what to make of it. Someone said it would be a good building to turn into condos.

Fifteen minutes later, every cop in the building was arrayed around a steel door that looked for all the world like a janitorial stash. Gertz held his hand up.

"Turn off your walkie-talkies."

In an instant, there was silence. No, not silence: From outside, they could hear traffic whooshing by on the Gotham Freeway next to the river, the grunts of trucks in the alleys. They heard something else too—white noise from within the closet.

Gertz Sidled up to Strickland. Gertz was thirty, ex-Marine, gung-ho with a crew cut and intense blue eyes that held no room for doubt. "Chief, I'd like to get a bomb squad up here."

Strickland rolled his eyes. This he didn't need. Since 9/11, half the bomb squad had been on duty constantly at Gotham International. Same with the robots. The city only had four robots and they were in constant use. "Why?"

"You hear that crackling?"

"Lieutenant, bombs don't announce themselves. That sounds like a television with lousy reception."

"Sir, I don't want to risk any of my men opening that door. Do you?"

One of Gertz' men approached. "Sir, take a look at the door. It's not latched."

The men examined the door from ten feet away. It was true. The steel door did not sit flush in the frame, but jutted out a quarter of an inch.

"Okay, maybe we can just jerk it open on a rope," Gertz offered.

Strickland nodded. He sent a deputy back down for a rope and a video camera, to record whatever they would find behind the door. Just like Al Capone's vault. It took another fifteen minutes to rig the rope and deploy the men. Strickland sent all but five outside, just in case it was a bomb. Strickland, Gertz, and three men. Strickland had no desire to blow himself up, but he didn't think it was a bomb. Call it a hunch. On the other hand, no telling what lurked on the other side of the door. Strickland had seen the Joker and Two-Face in lock-up, so anything was possible.

Gertz deployed Strickland and his men behind cover. He took a position ten yards back, crouching behind a stout brick pillar. "Count of three," he warned, gripping the rope in both hands. "One, two, *three*." He yanked the rope.

The door swung open. An eerie gray television light spilled into the room, with a dark shadow across it. Gertz adjusted his position to see past the door, which was now open ninety degrees. A figure slumped against the back wall. The wall itself seemed to be transmitting the light, and presented a uniform surface very similar to a television tube switched to no station. The figure was a man, his feet spread in front of him, head tilted, arms at his side. He did not appear to be moving.

The figure was Green Lantern.

17

S trickland sighed like a semi laying on the air brakes. "I might
have known."

Gertz and one of his men approached the open closet, stepping carefully. The crackle flared momentarily, harsh light flattening
the cops' features. Then it fell silent; the wall behind Green Lantern
was just an old wall made of brick. Whatever it had been, it was no
longer.

Gertz nodded to his man. "Joe, you grab his right arm, I'll grab his
left."

They gingerly took hold of GL's arms, half expecting to receive an
electric jolt. There was nothing. Carefully, they pulled GL away from
the wall. Gertz reached down and cradled GL's head so it wouldn't
bang. He was like very heavy putty. They lowered him to the ground
so that he was flat on his back. He appeared to be breathing, but
unconscious.

"Get some medics up here with a stretcher," Gertz said.

Green Lantern opened his eyes and started. Gertz and Joe lurched
back.

"Whoah!" Joe shouted.

Gertz put a hand under Green Lantern's head. "Can you sit up?"

Green Lantern coughed. "I think so. What happened?"

Gertz grinned. "We were hoping you could tell us."

Green Lantern put a hand to his head. "Man, do I have a headache.
I guess I'm back, huh?"

"Green Lantern," Strickland said, striding out from behind cover. "What happened to the Shamrocks?"

Green Lantern looked around. "You didn't see them? We sent them back through the gate."

"Who's 'we' and where you been?" Strickland asked.

Green Lantern started to get up. He was still woozy. Gertz lent him a hand. "We are the other Green Lantern and I, and I don't know exactly where we were. There's an inter-dimensional gate that opens sporadically in this closet. The Shamrocks were using it as a hideout. They went through the gate into another universe."

Strickland twisted the brim of his hat. "I don't need this other universe horse puckey. I hate having to take a statement from you guys 'cause it makes no sense."

"What guys?" Green Lantern asked, ready for a fight.

"Super heroes. Men of mystery. You know—our physical and moral betters."

"Sir," Gertz said. "Wouldn't an inter-dimensional gate involve a wormhole?"

"Good question, Officer Gertz," Green Lantern replied. "The answer is yes, but I don't understand the technology. The other Green Lantern explained that singularities could be held in check through electromagnetic fields. That may account for the intense interference and radiation. I believe I was in the future."

Strickland threw his hands in the air. "Not time travel!"

"Sir," Gertz said to Green Lantern, "we're going to need to debrief you in detail. If you could come down to the station house with us it would go a lot smoother."

Green Lantern gave a wry little smile. "Officer Gertz, I could spend the next three weeks writing this up and it would still make no sense to you, nor assist you in the solving of any crimes, nor prevent any future crimes. Once I file my report with the JLA, I'll copy you."

Green Lantern flew out the window.

Strickland threw his hat on the floor. "I knew it!"

GL felt bad ducking out on the cops like that, but he'd pegged Strickland right off as a guy with a grudge against super heroes who would use every trick in his bureaucrat's bag to tie GL up. As if the

110

super heroes hadn't proved their value time and again. Like anti-Semitism, super hero haters would always be with us, he mused. Never underestimate the power of plain old human envy. It was envy masquerading as righteousness that made war on civilization. Green Lantern soared away from the earth on a parabola that would take him to Saturn. Still shaken from his recent ordeal, he needed to reassure himself that he was in the right universe. There was also something about the wreckage he'd discovered on Saturn that called to him, a frequency in sympathy with the Zip-a-tone world.

Never mind the cops' familiarity. In the multiverse, you could end up in a place that looked like home, smelled like home, and felt like home, but was not home. The curse of subjectivity. How could you prove to yourself that what you experienced was real and not a fever dream, or a chemically-induced hallucination, or an elaborate hoax perpetrated by some devious alien?

I could always cut myself. Blood and pain have a way of focusing the mind, GL thought.

Saturn was as he had left it, massive storms raging across the soupy atmosphere. A quick scan showed the remains of the alien spacecraft spread across many miles of the upper atmosphere. As GL approached the glittering silver cloud, he experienced a keening resonance with the atmosphere. He wondered how the JLA was doing with his sample. He would have contacted them, but this close to Saturn the electro-magnetic fields played hob with communications. The wreckage itself radiated interference.

In the pale glow of his power ring, matter/anti-matter residue showed black against the paler background of the atmosphere. No biggie. Many faster-than-light drives used minute amounts of matter/anti-matter as a source of propulsion, suspended in an electromagnetic field to prevent it from coming in contact with the rest of the ship. GL launched a blip, searching for another presence. Nothing came back, nor did he expect it to. In the sea of space, the solar system occupied no more volume than a drop of water in the ocean. What were the chances of hitting a specific drop of water, if you fired into the sea? Looking up, GL saw the tiny satellite Pandora winking at him. A lover's moon. The cyclonic storms in Saturn's upper atmosphere were nothing compared to the squall kicked up in his heart.

Jenny-Lynn.

What did a guy have to do to get his girl to say yes? And what was up with the bug killer? There could be only one possible conclusion: She was trying to make him jealous. But that made no sense! It wasn't as if he neglected her. He showered her with affection, told her three times a day he loved her, and had asked her to marry him six times.

A piece of metal debris caught the distant glow of the Sun and gleamed like a diamond. Well, *duh!* That was it! He needed a ring. She was mad at him because he'd put the cart before the horse. You don't ask a girl to marry you without a ring! Especially not a girl like Jen who read *Cosmopolitan* and *Vanity Fair*! Read them? She was on the covers! How could he have been so stupid?

He was in a position to make it up to her. He was in a position to give her the most spectacular engagement ring a man ever gave a woman. No Harry Winston or Tiffany would do. Not for the most magnificent woman in the solar system. A wink of green far below suggested emeralds. The emerald was her stone. But Jenny-Lynn was an old-fashioned girl. The engagement ring had to be a diamond.

The JLA Watchtower sprouted like a portobello mushroom from the Moon's Kepler Crater. The tower rose two hundred feet into the sky, permitting a view over the crater's rim. Not that there was much to see. At a hundred thousand miles, GL blipped to let them know he was coming. The response was almost instantaneous.

"Greetings, Gate. Plas here," emanated from a microdot on GL's uniform.

"Yo, Eel. What's up?"

"Nothin', cuz. Quiet as a confessional around here. 'Course down there they're shooting each other and blowing things up. You coming in?"

GL landed lightly on the tower's entrance/exit platform. "I'm here."

GL felt the lock vibrate through the soles of his feet. A moment later, the outer hatch slid soundlessly open. He walked down a flight of steps into a cylindrical chamber, six feet in diameter. The outer lock slid shut and air filled the chamber with a snakelike hiss. Seconds later, an oval door slid open and GL stepped into the carpeted hall.

Eel O'Brien, aka Plastic Man, stood smiling before him, wearing a pair of jeans, a Giants sweatshirt, a Jets baseball cap and Ray-Bans.

"What brings you to the joint, cuz?"

"Cosmic snipe hunt, Eel. You get a chance to analyze that debris I sent?"

"What am I, a scientist? I sent it to S.T.A.R. Laboratories. They promised results in forty-eight hours. Why? What is it?"

"Remains of a ship I found on Saturn. Nothing special." Kyle examined a small pellet floating at face level. "What is this, a cat turd?"

Eel's mouth formed a suspension bridge. "That damned cat!"

"You the only one here?"

"Except for Minnie the amazing space cat. Come on. Let's go to the lounge."

GL followed the rail-thin O'Brien down a spiral staircase, eerily lit by a series of portholes. The only sound came from the gentle susurrus of the ventilation system. The complex smelled of ozone and sage ever since Wonder Woman had revamped the air cleaners. The staircase opened onto a broad, carpeted lounge with conversation pits. The outer wall was curved, gleaming consoles arcing under windows offering a panoramic view of the heavens and the Earth above. It was warm in the lounge, at least seventy-five. O'Brien kept the temperature up to forestall the psychological effects of being alone. Oscar Peterson played softly over the sound system.

O'Brien sat, reached under the console and grabbed two beers. He held one out. "Beer?"

"What time is it?"

"It's after five in Manhattan."

"Well, all righty then." GL took the beer, twisted the cap off, tossed it in the hopper, and took a drag. It went down well. He looked at the bottle. Fat Tire, from Boulder, Colorado. "Nice."

"Meow!" cried Minnie the space cat. She approached upside down, gripping the carpeted headliner. Her tail hung straight down like a velvet call rope.

"Use the litter box, you dumb cat!" Eel said. "What can I do you for, Kyle?"

"I need to get in touch with Superman."

O'Brien did an elaborate double-take. "Is it that bad?"

"No, it's nothing like that. I need to ask a favor."

"Well the big guy doesn't like to be disturbed for anything less than a threat to life itself. You're going to have to do better than that. I send out a signal to Superman, and he's in the middle of a fight or something, he's likely to be peeved. *Capische?*"

"Come on. Olsen used to call him every time he stubbed his toe."

"They had a special relationship. You got a special relationship?"

"We're all JLA members, Eel."

"True. What do you want him for?"

"None of your business."

O'Brien shrugged his linebacker shoulders. "Be that way. I'll call him, but it's your responsibility."

"No prob, dude."

Kyle watched while O'Brien sat at the console, gathering his courage. Kyle couldn't blame him. He figured O'Brien was apprehensive due to his criminal background. It was one thing for the ex-armed robber to trade *bons mot* with young Kyle, another to tug on Superman's cape.

A moment later, a deep, resonant voice filled the room. "This is Superman. What can I do for you, Plastic Man?"

"Green Lantern's here. Wants to talk to you." O'Brien pushed his chair back and looked at Kyle.

"Superman, it's Kyle Rayner. If you're not busy, I'd like to have a word with you."

"Hello, Kyle. I'm cataloguing a few things at the Fortress. I'll be here for the next hour if you want to drop in."

"Thanks, man. I'll be there shortly."

O'Brien turned off the transceiver. "You want him to figure out your taxes."

Kyle smiled. "Not even Superman could figure out *my* taxes."

A fax machine against the inner wall clicked to life and pushed out a page. Eel retrieved it from the basket. "Here's the preliminary S.T.A.R. report on that junk you found. Traces of iron, molybdenum, plutonium, cesium, and matter/anti-matter residue. Hmmm. Matter/anti-matter residue, how'd that get in here? Wouldn't a matter/anti-matter collision disintegrate Saturn?"

"Apparently there's a whole anti-matter universe out there and they've been trying to infiltrate our universe for eons. Especially the Qwardians."

Eel removed his cap and scratched his head. "I've heard of those guys. Bad news, huh?"

"The worst. Technologically advanced fanatics. Fortunately, they never did figure out a way to invade our universe."

"Is that what you found? An invasion ship?"

"I think so. Looks like it hit Saturn's atmosphere too quickly and broke up, assuming it didn't completely disintegrate upon contact with posimatter."

"Why wouldn't it? Doesn't every matter/anti-matter meeting result in an explosion?

"The Qwardians have been experimenting with electromagnetic fields to hold anti-matter intact while in the posimatter universe. Judging from the remains I found, it almost works. Or it almost worked however long ago that ship came through." Kyle took the S.T.A.R. read-out from Eel. "Carbon dating estimates that the debris is over forty million years old. That's a long time. I wonder why we never noticed it before."

"Saturn is like the Sargasso Sea. You can't see down to the surface. It keeps churning things up that landed long ago. Hey, it took 'em sixty years to find some of those WW II bombers that crashed in the jungle."

Kyle nodded. "Makes sense. Thanks for the beer, Plas. My treat next time."

"Stick around. I'm going to screen *Stormy Weather*. You ever see *Stormy Weather*?"

"Sorry, man. Next time."

Most of the world believed Superman's Fortress of Solitude was located on the polar ice cap. Superman encouraged this belief. The Fortress was actually located in Antarctica, halfway up a sheer rock face, and resembled a black soccer ball approximately one hundred feet in diameter. Anyone wishing to enter had to get a thousand feet up the side of a cliff in hundred and fifty mile per hour winds and twelve degrees celsius wind-chill factor. Talk about stormy weather. They would need Superman's strength to open the door.

Fortunately, Superman was expecting him. As GL approached the black hemisphere protruding from the cliff, a portal opened. Several feet inside, a mild forcefield shut out inclement weather, like a Las Vegas casino entrance. Ten feet past the forcefield the keyhole opened onto a metal balcony with a stair reaching to the main floor, a gallery that made the Batcave look like a closet. The Fortress was a tesseract, a device spanning several dimensions with vastly more space on the inside than it looked like it could hold from the outside.

GL set down his backpack and stared into vastness. The ceiling was fifty feet overhead. The lights were low, but a series of small spots shone on the capsule that had brought Kal-El to Earth. A little further on was the slightly larger than life statue of Jor-El and Lara holding the planet Kypton, recreated by the fortress robots following Dominus' devastation. There was the key to the original fortress: It was sixteen feet long and weighed over three tons. There sat Kal-El himself, halfway across the vast, smooth stone floor, at a desk looking at something under a banker's lamp. Myriad rugs and carpets from all over the universe criss-crossed the floor like railroad tracks. There wasn't a speck of dust. *How does he do that?*

As GL descended to the warm, smooth stone, Superman stood and strode forward, smiling broadly. "Welcome, Kyle Rayner. I don't get many visitors out here."

"I can see why." They shook hands.

Superman turned and led the way toward the interior. Beyond him, the cavern stretched into infinity. "Would you like some hot cocoa? I was just going to whip up a batch."

"That'd be great, man." Superman always made Kyle feel like a little kid, tongue-tied and stupid. Man. He'd just called Superman *man.* What was next? Dude?

"I was cataloguing some of these artifacts I've acquired over the years, trying to at least sort them by dimension, if not civilization. Since I have unlimited space, my fellow JLA members have been dropping off items they've collected over the years. 'Just give it a scan, Superman. Surely with your encyclopedic knowledge and perfect memory you can tell us what they are.' Surely. You know, I now have approximately forty-three million alien objects that need to be catalogued."

"I had no idea."

"I've been thinking of programming the robots, but you just can't rely on robotic judgment. What looks like a dinner plate to a robot may be a sacred icon to an alien race. I found something just the other day. J'onn J'onzz thought it might be some kind of food processor. It was actually a weapon capable of destroying a solar system."

Superman put his hand on the smooth stone wall and it melted into an arched doorway leading into a kitchen the size of the Waldorf's. Eight ovens built into the wall. Sixty-four hot plates. A walk-in freezer. Was he expecting a convention? Superman went to a cupboard and removed a bottle of Ovaltine. He took a quart of milk out of a refrigerator. Where did he get fresh milk up here? Did someone deliver?

Superman mixed the milk and Ovaltine in a glass bottle and warmed it with his heat vision while slowly rotating the bottle. He shook the bottle vigorously and poured the liquid into two ceramic mugs decorated with Japanese brush painting. "Should be one hundred and four degrees."

Kyle tasted the cocoa. It was delicious and spread warmth throughout his body. Superman glugged his down. "Ahh—llama milk. What can I do for you, Kyle?"

Now that he was here, his request seemed petty and selfish. Like asking God to crack your walnuts. But he was here and he had to go through with it. "You know Jenny-Lynn, my girl Jen?"

"Of course. Lovely girl. Her old man and I go way back."

"I'm going to ask her to marry me."

"Congratulations! This calls for a toast. Let me mix more cocoa." Superman got the Ovaltine and llama milk. "How can I help you?"

"Well, you know, I want to give her an engagement ring . . ."

"Of course."

"A diamond."

"That's usually what they want."

"I was hoping you'd, uh, make one for me."

Superman looked up, eyes twinkling. "That's a new one. I don't cut 'em, you know. I just make them. It won't look very pretty."

"I can cut it."

"Did you bring carbon?"

Kyle hefted the backpack. "Picked this up in the asteroid belt. Nearly pure carbon."

Superman took the bag, unzipped it, and removed a black rock the size of his head. "Not taking any chances, are you?"

Kyle grinned. "You're the best, man. Thanks. Thanks a lot."

Superman hefted the rock several times like a softball. "Wait here." He walked into darkness.

By the time Kyle was through cutting it, the diamond weighed five karats.

CHAPTER
18

LaScalia in Greenwich Village was the type of upscale beanery Eddie usually avoided. He preferred fast food joints, but you didn't take a girl like Jenny-Lynn to Mickey D's. He'd been in the LaScalia kitchen chasing down their three cockroaches, and had been impressed with the aromas. He was standing outside in his best Dockers, shirt and sport jacket when Jenny-Lynn walked up, stopping traffic in her little black dress. Guys were trailing after her claiming to be photographers, talent scouts, and directors.

Eddie broke into a grin that completely encircled his head. "Hi!" he said, waving his left hand. He kept his right hand behind his back.

"Hi yourself," she said, taking his hand. "Shall we?"

Eddie had made a reservation. His first. They sat at a linen-covered table on a slight riser toward the front where they could see out onto Bleecker Street. "You look stunning," Eddie said after they were seated.

"Thank you. You look pretty spiffy yourself. What's with the glove?"

Eddie held up his right hand, fitted into a black leather glove. There was a bulge on his ring finger that might have been a ring. "What, this? I got some kind of rash from using a new insecticide. Don't worry—it's under control. The doctor gave me some medication. It's light sensitive so he asked me to wear this glove. No Michael Jackson jokes, please."

A crease appeared between Jenny's eyebrows. "Hazardous! First the rat and now this."

Their waiter was a young man with a hairline mustache, three earrings, and a buzz cut. "Would you like to see the wine list?"

Eddie looked at Jen. "By all means," she said. She studied the red-leather bound volume while the waiter filled their water glasses.

"Do you like merlots?" she asked.

Eddie shrugged. "I'm mostly a beer man, but if they bring it, I will drink it."

When the waiter returned Jenny-Lynn ordered a French merlot.

The waiter nodded his head judiciously. "Good choice." When the wine came, the waiter poured a half-inch into a glass and handed it to Jenny. The wine was the color of Eddie's hand beneath the ring.

Jen smiled. The waiter poured. "Can I tell you about our specials?"

"Please," Eddie said.

"We have an excellent grilled red snapper with fennel and lemon served on a bed of arugala and pine nuts, twenty-two fifty. We also have a roasted pork loin served with a cherry anchovy reduction sauce on a bed of buckwheat noodles with a blackberry glaze, twenty-four fifty. Shall I come back in a few minutes?"

"That would be fine." When the waiter left, Eddie raised his glass. "To the most beautiful woman in Manhattan. 'All beauty comes from beautiful blood and a beautiful brain.' That's from Walt Whitman, you know," he added with a bit of a blush.

Jenny-Lynn smiled. "Thank you, kind sir." They clinked. There was a hush while the world seemed to slip away, the only light emanating from Jen's green eyes. A man could dive into those eyes and never come up.

"Kyle won't be angry?"

Jen made a face. "He doesn't own me."

"I'm sorry. Should we not talk about him?"

"Let's not and say we did."

Eddie refilled their glasses. "Okay. I hope that ban doesn't extend to your father. My grandfather used to watch him on the six o'clock news. How does he stay so young?"

Jen shrugged and smiled. "Good genes, I guess. Green genes."

"I heard your dad loves to sing show tunes."

Jen goggled. "Where did you hear that?"

Eddie couldn't tell her the truth, which was that the information had flowed into his brain courtesy of the ring and the disappearing alien. The ring forbade it. Eddie was being transformed. It was his and the ring's secret. Transformed into what he didn't know. But something important, not just for him, for everyone. He felt himself becoming another person with all the parts of the old Eddie attached. Whatever was happening, it imbued him with confidence. And confidence was very attractive.

"Raised in the Midwest, young Alan Scott made his way to New York City when he began college," Eddie recited. "After several adventures in Metropolis, he moved to Gotham City in early 1940, taking a job with WXYZ, a radio station. He began as a news reporter and soon became a star in his own right, with many reports about the new hero, Green Lantern."

Jen stared, a wrinkle of concern crossing her lovely brow like horizontal interference.

Eddie shrugged. "It's no mystery. I downloaded that information from the Scott Telecommunications web page."

"Nobody knows my dad likes to sing show tunes. That's not on the web site."

Eddie leaned forward conspiratorially. "He didn't exactly keep it a secret. Walter Winchell mentions it in a column in 1946. Your old man belted the complete score to *Carousel* at a party at Damon Runyon's house on Long Island. Teddy Wilson provided piano accompaniment."

"That's one of his favorites. So what are you doing reading Walter Winchell?"

"I like old things. My granddad, Eddie the First, left me his collection of jazz lps. Benny Goodman, Duke Ellington, Sidney Bechet. He was a Green Lantern buff and kept a scrapbook, clipped every mention of the green guys. Your father was usually first with the news, so there's a lot about him in there."

"He did get around."

"How's he doing these days?"

"He's happy as a pig in . . . well, you know the expression. He heads his own media empire. Has the ear of presidents and viceroys. They hate him in Hollywood, but love him in Gotham."

The waiter returned. Eddie ordered the medallions of beef ("a steak by any other name") and Jenny ordered the snapper.

"Very good," the waiter said in an admiring voice, as if she'd just completed a tri-axial spin.

"So how'd you get in the extermination business, Eddie?"

Eddie smiled. "You don't want to hear about that. It's not very interesting." His eyes narrowed and drifted past Jade toward the door. "Oh . . . darn."

"What's wrong?" Jade said, already turning.

In the entrance foyer, wearing his best suit and carrying a dozen roses, was Kyle.

19

S uperman helped Kyle set the ring in a band made from gold Kyle had harvested in the asteroid belt. It had taken a long time to scrape together enough gold for a ring. Superman suggested they leave the detail work to the artisans of Kandor, but that would have taken too much time. Kyle simply copied an ancient Egyptian setting Superman had in his collection as a model. The ring was elegant and beautiful.

Arriving home, Kyle entered his building from the roof and descended to the coop he shared with Jen. He deliberately avoided any route that might take him by a newspaper stand or electronic billboard. He did not want to be distracted by his responsibilities. For this reason alone he tried to stay away from Times Square.

Although he could have used the ring to wash, he showered and shaved the old-fashioned way, splashed himself with Paco Rabanne and put on the Tommy Hilfiger suit Jen had helped him pick out. He stopped at Village Floral and picked up a dozen roses. The young woman behind the counter cast an admiring eye on him.

"I envy the young lady."

"Thank you."

Outside, he stood on Sixth Avenue and launched a blip to locate Jen. Her DNA was programmed into the ring. An instant later, a sounding directed him to Bleecker Street. It was a fine fresh May evening and Kyle felt like walking, averting his eyes every time he passed a newsstand. In the distance he could hear sirens racing to fires, shootings, accidents. Doing what they were paid to do. Every time he heard a siren he cringed a little, knowing he could be on the scene in an instant, wipe out a blaze with a gesture. He always heard sirens.

"Shut . . . up . . ." he said through gritted teeth. His shoulders involuntarily tensed. "Get off my back," he muttered, trying to recall some of the relaxation techniques he'd learned from some of the older JLA members. "A New York City sidewalk is no place to meditate."

Nobody gave him a second glance. People talking to themselves on the streets of New York were not novelties. He passed a pet store. He stopped, turned, went back. In the window, a pair of black-and-white puppies tumbled and played. He went in the store, pungent with animal smells, and watched the puppies. In a few minutes, he had forgotten about the emergency vehicles racing pell-mell through the city and was able to resume his walk. Dogs were powerful medicine.

Jenny-Lynn thrummed at him like a homing beacon, her presence a warm green glow. The light led him to Bleecker Street, a carnival in early evening, an elegant freak show. Skinny Goth heroin addicts rubbed shoulders with supermodels, Nigerian watch vendors, delivery boys, bike couriers, tourists, and harried everyday Joes making their way home after putting in eight. Kyle would have enjoyed it if he weren't terrified of distractions. He did not want to see any beggars, knowing how easy it would be for him to help them. Scan their bodies for cancer. Fill their pockets with silver. Hear their terrible stories. He was walking through a minefield.

A half-block down the other side of the street, he located the restaurant in which Jenny-Lynn was eating and breathed a sigh of relief. LaScalia was a four-star joint, which meant the likelihood of him encountering tragedy inside was greatly diminished. He'd turned off his JLA transceiver and felt guilty about it.

He stopped directly across the street from the restaurant and watched a white stretch limo disgorge a young swell with two gorgeous babes, one on each arm. Kyle's armpits felt damp. Oh, come on! He'd just showered and doused himself with Pit Stop! He was hyperventilating, and it wasn't the sirens. He felt weak in the knees, put a hand out to steady himself against an iron rail.

What was the deal? He'd proposed to her a half dozen times in the past. The deal was, those weren't really *proposals*, which is why she didn't take them seriously. He'd whisper things like, "Why don't we get married?" in the heat of passion. Women wanted romance. Women wanted ceremony. The difference was he was now going to propose to her in public in one of the city's trendiest restaurants. Page Six stuff, just what Alan hated. Hopefully, he would approve of this item. Ideally, it would go unreported, but Kyle couldn't count on that. The city was hungry for gossip, and super heroes were news.

Glancing around to make sure the street was free of paparazzi, Kyle crossed Bleecker, enduring curses in Farsi from taxi drivers and eloquent Italian hand gestures from deliverymen. He realized he looked somewhat conspicuous carrying a dozen red roses. It never occurred to him in a million years that she might be with someone. Jenny often dined alone when Kyle was elsewhere.

Immediately inside the entrance he encountered a knot of nervous theater-goers trying to get in a meal before the curtain went up. He waited patiently while the maitre' d found them a table in the back before returning to Kyle with a supercilious smile. "Sir?"

"I'm looking for someone."

The maitre' d smiled and turned his attention to the next pair in line. "Of course."

Kyle stepped by the mahogany desk and looked around, swinging automatically to the table on the raised deck in front near the windows where his lady love radiated an emerald glow. Seated across from her, the figure at first seemed indistinct, as if viewed through a gauze filter. Then he snapped into brutal focus, every detail etched on Kyle's mind. *The exterminator.* Rocheford.

Their eyes locked. Kyle saw and felt raw hatred. The exterminator felt it too; it was almost an electric current between them. Alternating. The exterminator's brow furrowed, his pupils shrank to pinholes and his lips pulled back in an involuntary grimace. Jenny turned to see what he was staring at.

Sound seeped out of the picture. Only the three of them existed. The rest of the world fell into soft focus. Jenny's mouth went round; she said something: *Ohmigod!* Kyle could read her lips. She started to get up. The exterminator put a hand out and urged her to sit back down.

Kyle had seen enough. Tossing the roses to the floor, he turned on his heel and fled the restaurant. The bitch! Sneaking out behind his back with the exterminator! Some sweaty guy who knocked on the door to get rid of the roaches! Everyone had seen him. Everyone knew who he was. His humiliation was complete. With a snarl of fury he changed right there on the Sidewalk, shucking the Tommy Hilfiger and appearing in costume. A six-year-old boy backed into his mother in terror.

Green Lantern went up and came down in a narrow parabola that deposited him on the roof of his building. Hurt and confused, he stormed down the stairs into his unit, slamming the door so hard it bounced back into the apartment and he had to go back and latch it as Mrs. Milman peeked out of her unit across the hall and quickly shut the door.

He looked longingly at the liquor cabinet. Kyle hadn't been drunk since his junior year in college. The beer he'd had with Spire Raines had been his first in six months. He knew there was a bottle of Chivas in there, a gift from Alan from last year. He was about to reach for it when the door opened forcibly inward. Jenny-Lynn stormed inside clutching the discarded roses, went into the kitchen without acknowledging him, put them in a cut glass decanter and added water. Only then did she turn toward him, hands on hips, mouth a grim line.

"What did you think you were doing?"

Kyle matched her fury. "What do you think? What were you doing with that exterminator?"

"He asked me out. I didn't know where you were or how long you'd be gone so I accepted. I just met the guy, he's a nice guy, there's nothing going on between us. You're not my keeper!"

"Nothing going on? You two seemed pretty cozy to me! Candlelight, fancy wine, sure looked like a date to me!" Kyle imagined pulping the exterminator's head between giant green thumb and forefinger. Pop it like a grape. There was something basically dishonest about the guy. Coming on like this blue-collar grunt, then acting like a well-heeled clubber. That was just *wrong*. There was something off about him. He looked a little too much like Matt Damon. Not the Matt Damon of *Good Will Hunting*—the Matt Damon of *The Talented Mr. Ripley*.

"Kyle," she said with brittle control, "I've told you before that if we're going to have a relationship you're going to have to give me plenty of space. Tonight you interrupt a dinner with a new friend by acting like a jealous lover."

"I *am* a jealous lover!"

"Yesterday, you went to Gotham to discuss my future with my father, as if I were a Moslem bride. Don't ask him. Ask me."

"How do you know that?"

"Kyle, do you think I don't know anybody at the network?"

"I went to ask your father's permission to marry you!"

"That's supposed to make it okay?" she glared. "To me, it seems like you're sneaking around behind my back."

Kyle's mouth fell like a gallows trap. "Me? Sneaking around behind your back? I wasn't the one out on a secret date!"

"There was nothing secret about it!"

"You want to know why I was bringing you a dozen roses?"

She softened a little. "Because you felt bad about crowding me?"

Kyle's shoulders slumped. "No. I wanted to give you this." He reached into his pocket, grabbed the ring, and held it out in his palm. He thought he was going to go down on his knees to do this, but he didn't feel like it at the moment.

Jade looked at the ring, unmoved. She rolled her eyes and said, "Talk about bad timing." She went into the bedroom and slammed the door.

By the time Kyle got the door open, she was gone.

CHAPTER

20

J enny soared above the city, a green goddess briefly glimpsed. She felt like shouting—not just at Kyle, but at all men. Her father with his pipe and his suit and his morals straight out of the fifties. Roger Dupuis at the agency telling her she needed to watch her weight. Her agent John Elwood urging her to try out for some asinine action movie. All *he* wanted was his fifteen percent. And that jerk at the skin rag who kept waving seven figure checks at her to get her to pose nude.

Jade had few girlfriends with whom she could talk. Wonder Woman, but how often was Wonder Woman around? When was the last time Jade and Wonder Woman went out for drinks? Jade couldn't endure the company of the other agency models, constantly running on about their boyfriends and diets and what they were going to wear.

The purple evening gradually shaded into black as she crossed through the exosphere into space, protected by a faint green energy shield. She still wore her little black cocktail dress. She was so angry with men, and one in particular, she performed the equivalent of stepping into a river and swimming downstream. She deliberately jumped to the other side of the earth, burying her trail for any who might attempt to follow. She could teleport to places with which she was familiar, and she had made herself familiar with a number of places people didn't normally go.

She reappeared on an atoll in French Polynesia south of Hao, a place she'd been to several times before. She savored the quiet and isolation. The island was so small it did not have a name. She could count the trees on both hands. Jade liked the place because of the solitude. Guaranteed. She'd created a beach hut, drawing sand and coral up from the ground, causing walls to rise, placing the timbers just so. She searched the shoals for wrecks, using recycled steel and sunken lumber so as not to deplete the tiny island's resources.

Even in paradise trash washed up on the beach. Jenny spent an hour walking around the island, dissipating plastic bottles and bags in a series of green flashes. Finally, when no trace of man remained save for the hut, she collapsed in a green chaise lounge. It had been early evening in Greenwich Village. Here it was late morning. Using the power of the Starheart, she placed a green, pie-pan sized disc over the surf and drew up water, automatically purifying and depositing the water in a wooden barrel she'd retrieved from a sunken Portugese Man of War.

She turned her attention to the island itself. When she'd first arrived it had sustained only scrub grass. She'd planted all the trees herself. Under her guidance they'd grown in three weeks from knee-high to twenty feet. She could easily have caused a luxuriant lawn to sprout all over the island but without her constant attendance it would die. The island received sporadic fresh water from intermittent squalls. She'd planted so many things the island now resembled her. It was green.

She'd discovered the island a year ago in the middle of a stupid argument. Kyle wanted her to go with him while he looked for people to save, and when she wouldn't, they got in a screaming match. Not that she was against saving people. She was not, however, a committed super hero like her father and boyfriend. Jen was perfectly happy leading a normal life, if a supermodel's life could be called normal.

Kyle could be exasperating, with his moon eyes and hang-dog expression. She loved him, intended to spend the rest of her life with him, but she was waiting for him to settle down. He was so damned hyper. Always in her face about this or that. She didn't position the car correctly in the underground garage. He was a neat freak and she tended toward scatter. He wanted to save the world while she wanted to watch *American Idol*.

The main problem, she decided, was that they were living in too small a space. It was ridiculous, really. With their resources, they could buy a place in the country. In Montana, if necessary. They could commute. It was her own insistence on living in New York that kept them there. She loved the excitement, being in the center of the universe. Anyplace else was a step downhill.

"Maybe I should move *here*," she mused, looking around her own little island. A bit like a jungle at dusk, the air fragrant with blossoms. If only Kyle were a little more like Eddie.

Whoa. Where had that come from? She realized it had been there all along, since the dapper zapper had showed at her door. There was something unlikely about the poetry spouting exterminator, and likeable. Was it possible she was not destined to be with Kyle and bear green babies? One way to find out—and she owed him dinner, anyway.

It was a simple matter to locate Eddie. Having been exposed to his unique aura, she had only to look for it. Eddie's aura pulsed strongly from Queens. By the time Jade returned to Manhattan, it was eighty-thirty. She owed Eddie dinner. She went to one of downtown's more chic French restaurants and had them make up two orders of coq au vin, artichoke salad, some upstate white cheddar, crackers, and a bottle of merlot. She could easily have levitated everything but she wanted to feel like a woman on a date, not a freak. She hailed a taxi.

The driver, wearing a Sikh turban, said, "Where to lady?" in a blend of New York and Far East accents. She gave him the address.

A small voice in her head said, *What are you playing at, girl? You got a good man on the line. Why throw it all away for the promise of a thrill?*

"I am not being unfaithful," she muttered. "I just want to have dinner with the guy!"

"'Scuse please?" the driver said over his shoulder.

"Nothing. Just talking to myself."

The driver wheeled daringly into the Midtown tunnel. "How 'bout them Rangers, hah? Are they not incredible?"

"You follow hockey? I find that hard to believe."

"Why not? Is this not the land of the free where you can be all that you can be? Am I making comments because you happen to have green skin? No! In New York, everything is everything, and I am

131

proud to be a part. Nine years I have been here, with my wife, my two sons, and my daughter. My sons play varsity basketball for Sojourner Truth High. My daughter studies to be microbiologist at Columbia!"

"Okay!" Jen agreed laughing. "Okay! How 'bout those Rangers?"

"Well they are going to have a very good year with this rookie Beasley they have signed from Calgary."

They emerged from the tunnel and headed north on 31st Street while the driver expounded on Glenn Sather's skills as a tactician and moral leader. From the corner of her eye, Jenny thought she saw a streak like a falling star in the east, but when she focused, it was gone. A moment later she felt a frisson of unease, ghost spiders on her spine. But she shook it off due to the fact she'd let her concentration slip and she was only wearing the little black dress. She brought her body temperature up with a thought.

"You comfortable back there? You want heat?" the driver asked.

"I'm fine."

Following Eddie's aura, she directed the driver to her destination in Queens. She was surprised when the taxi pulled up in front of a grand estate at 743 York Court, a three story white wedding cake of a house with green shutters. It appeared to be unoccupied, save for a dim light in the front window. Then she noticed the gatehouse, halfway back, with Eddie's exterminator truck parked in the driveway.

"You want me to wait?" the driver asked.

"I'm fine, thanks." Jenny got out of the car. She gave the man a ten-dollar tip and headed up the driveway. The driver stared as her packages followed, floating serenely in her wake.

CHAPTER

21

E ddie sat before his forty-two inch flat screen plasma television, eyes unfocused, mouth slightly open, tendril of drool leaking down his chin, oblivious to Britney Spears' frantic gyrations and thunderous accompaniment. Barkley rested his snout on his master's knee and looked up with a worried expression.

Eddie felt the change coming over him. He had felt it for several days, ever since the alien had activated the ring. It was not as if he were one thing becoming another. He was becoming what he had been meant to be since the moment the monster had appeared and took his grandfather. The change was evolutionary. The ring was meant for him. Eddie the First had been meant to find it and bring it back so that ultimately it could go to its rightful owner—Eddie the Third.

Purpose? He wasn't sure, but it went beyond him. When he closed his eyes he saw the cosmos under siege. The so-called "super heroes," led by Green Lantern. He saw a people and culture older than time, wise and noble, trapped on a dying planet. They needed his help.

Eddie was important, but only a cog in a grand scheme. The human race was at a crossroads. One path led to the stars and exaltation. The other to extinction. They could either welcome the wise and noble race, or they could go down screaming. When Eddie was seven, his parents had died in an automobile accident. A knight of the road driving cross-country in his Peterbilt, up three days on bennies, had crossed the center line and creamed his folks' Buick Park Avenue like an empty soda can beneath a horse's hoof.

Eddie had been visiting Grandpa Rocheford at the time. He remembered the somber-faced highway patrolman coming to the door, speaking softly, asking if he could talk to Eddie the First alone. Later, Grandpa Rocheford sat with his arm around little Eddie and explained God had a reason for everything, and the loss of Eddie's parents was not without meaning.

For a long time little Eddie had thought there was something wrong with him. He wasn't all that broken up at his parents' death. He eventually accepted that it was part of some master plan in which he figured prominently. Nothing else made sense. A just God wouldn't wipe out a kid's parents for no reason because some dumb-ass trucker was hustling to beat his schedule.

He'd grown up a loner in a loner household. He and Eddie the First gave each other plenty of room. Grandpa Eddie became his father and mother, a stern but loving presence who made certain little Eddie got three squares a day, went to school, respected his elders, and did his homework.

Although Eddie's parents had been Episcopalian, he and his grandfather never went to church. Each December, Grandpa Eddie would pull out the all-aluminum Sears Christmas tree and set it up in the living room with the same collection of tinsel and little colored lights. But late at night, when he was in bed alone, Eddie could remember listening to Baptist preachers deliver fire and brimstone on his short-wave radio, the same radio that had belonged to his grandfather. Something about those sermons, warning of dire consequences if humanity did not mend its ways, lit a fire in Eddie's soul. Something in him vibrated sympathetically with those preachers calling down apocalypse on unbelievers. Eddie wanted to believe, if only for the thrill of anticipation it gave him.

But the place in his heart reserved for faith remained distressingly void. Until a couple days ago. For the first time in a long time, Eddie felt direction. Something big was going to happen and he was part of it. Was it possible the world was waiting for him? With a wave of his hand he turned off the television. Barkley whined, stepped back, sat and looked worried. Barkley left the room and returned a moment later with his tuggle rope, which he thrust repeatedly at Eddie.

Eddie tried to ignore him, but when the dog persisted, Eddie grabbed the rope and hurled it from the room. "Beat it!"

Barkley retreated, whining. Eddie peeled off his shirt and raked his hands across his chest and arm. What was happening to him? The influx of knowledge had become a steady, irritating trickle, then a river of itch flowing from his left hand. Eddie went into the bathroom and switched on the light. His lean, tanned body was an ugly purple from the ring hand to halfway across his chest. He looked like Eclipso. He would not have stopped the flow of knowledge even if he had hurt rather than itched. He was learning so many things! Astrophysics. Philosophy. The arts. Forbidden knowledge—things no human being had ever known. The role of electromagnetic fields in holding anti-matter in suspension. He was beginning to see connections where none had previously existed.

Invariably, these involved transition.

He'd better put something on. Jade was heading toward his door with dinner in tow. He could "see" her behind him with a kind of purple-hued omnivision. He'd been aware of her since she'd crossed into Queens, just as he was aware of a wolverine dropping pups in British Columbia, a volcano percolating in Costa Rica, and an old woman sneezing in Tibet.

Barkley eyed him from across the room, muzzle between his paws. That muzzle was usually on Eddie's knee. Eddie patted his knee. "Come here, Barkley." The dog buried its head in its paws and whimpered.

"What's the problem?" he asked conversationally. He could see clear through the animal, see for the first time what a shallow organism it was. Slavish and obedient to whomever fed it. Pretending to love Eddie in return. Transparent. Humans were the same.

The doorbell rang.

Eddie rose effortlessly, went into his bedroom, selected a clean white and blue sports shirt, pulled it on. His hand still glowed a radioactive purple. He put on a white cotton work glove. The doorbell rang again.

"Hold on!" he sang. A moment later he opened the door. The woman who stood before him didn't just smile—she glowed. Even in his state of becoming, Eddie was not immune to her incredible vitality, the ray of approval she directed at him with laser force. Behind her, floating gently in the air like jellyfish, a series of dishes surrounded by a barely visible green nimbus.

"Din-din, Eddie," she said, throwing her arms around his neck and pulling his mouth to hers. Electrons danced. It was like the energy transfer the alien had laid on him, only stronger. Much stronger. As he held her in his arms, Eddie could see all the way back to her birth, and beyond that. He could see a long line of Green Lanterns stretching back into eternity. Hungry for knowledge, he pressed her to him, absorbing her very DNA. At the last instant, she struggled to push him away.

At that last instant, an unearthly glow erupted behind her, accompanied by the smell of ozone. Eddie knew that smell. That smell had haunted him for twenty years. He thrust her back and away, straight into the arms of the giant who had killed his grandfather.

The giant grabbed Jen by the shoulder, eliciting sparks and a harsh crackling noise. His hand covered half her torso like a serape.

"Kyle," she whispered.

CHAPTER

22

Kyle stood in the harsh glare of the bathroom examining the Little Pink Pregnancy Test. Why did all personal hygiene products sold to women come in pink boxes? He was ripping off the cellophane when he realized the box had not been opened. Why was it there? Nobody bought a pregnancy test just to have one around. It was not a common household item. Like the Honda Rune, you had to want one.

Perhaps Jen herself was afraid to know. But that was unlike her. She was fearless. If she were in a family way, she'd want to know. But wouldn't she know simply by scanning herself? How could a woman with her self-knowledge not know? She was not without powers. Unlikely scenarios unreeled in his head. The kit was for a friend. What friend? Wonder Woman? The kit was for the future. If so, why didn't she say "yes" already? The diamond ring burned a hole in his pocket.

He was trying to put his finger on the odd sensation he felt when it came to him: disappointment. He was disappointed she hadn't applied the test and run to him with the news. If there were news. Fact was, he could prevent conception just by thinking about it, but then his mind would be messing with her body. They'd never discussed it, but he assumed she could do the same and had left the responsibility to her. If she wanted to get pregnant, all she had to do was think about it. With him, of course.

Maybe they needed a break from each other. Maybe they needed counseling. Kyle didn't now what they needed, but he knew things

137

were not going as planned. The love of his life was moody as Portland weather. Half the time she acted as if she wished she were alone. He worshiped the ground she walked on. Why couldn't she just love him back simply, directly? Why all the horripulations, the moods, the attitude? Why the secrets?

Was she pregnant or not?

KYLE!

He winced as her cry reverberated in his skull. That's how whipped he was—he felt so guilty pawing through her things that he heard her screaming at him in his head. Quantum mechanics were easier than women. Saving the universe was easier.

What in the world did she want?

The phone rang. Kyle plucked the nearest, in the bedroom. Caller ID fingered Alan Scott in Gotham. "Yes, sir," Kyle answered.

"What the hell's going on?"

"Excuse me, sir?"

"Didn't you hear Jenny-Lynn's mental cry?"

"Holy cow," Kyle said softly.

"What's that?"

"I hear it now, sir. I'll find her. Don't worry."

"You'd better get your butt in gear, son!"

The rest was lost as Kyle dropped the telephone, morphed in mid-air, and phased through the window. Experience had taught him that the best way to locate someone was to take a high position and launch a blip. The ring was attuned to Jen's DNA. Within a second of launching the blip, he had a ping from Queens, charted and dove.

He'd mistaken Jade's cry for help for a guilty conscious. *Way to go, Ace.* Five years on the job, he still couldn't tell his ass from a hole in the ground. He still didn't know what was important.

Except this. Jen was important. What was she doing in Queens?

Jenny-Lynn froze in the giant's grip, her mouth open in a silent scream. Even her hair froze—an art nouveau swirl. She looked like a doll in the monster's hand. It was the same giant who'd killed Eddie the First. Eddie didn't know how he knew, but he knew. It was a combination of things—the way it looked, its ozone smell, that same jittery manner, the electricity that swarmed over its skin instead of sweat, the mean little eyes. Eddie also knew the thing was called a Destroyer. The monster smashed its way out of his house, holding Jenny. Eddie followed.

The giant took a step back, almost as if it were afraid of him. But that was crazy. What did the thing have to fear from him? It was twice his height. It must have weighed six hundred pounds. Eddie gazed fearlessly into those slot eyes, dark save for a miniscule gleam in the center. Eddie's skin felt hot. Not like a fever, more like a hot-plate. His shirt began to smoke and curl, but strangely, he felt no pain, no burning sensation. He felt as if nothing could hurt him.

He was furious.

The giant had interrupted the greatest moment of his life. The giant held the girl of his dreams in its shovel grip. For some reason, the horned giant seemed to fear him. Eddie pointed at it.

"Let her go."

Its stoic expression didn't change as it hesitated, taking another step back. It *was* afraid of him! Why? What could he do to it? Eddie looked down at his hand in wonder, the yellow ring pulsing through the glove with a light of its own. There had been a reason the purple alien had crossed space and time to bring him this gift.

Here was the reason: To stop the creature and rescue Jade. Eddie felt the power within him. It was a new sensation, like the first time you put it all together in whatever sport you loved—karate, baseball, basketball—when strength and reflexes met skill and coordination, and you knew they couldn't lay a hand on you. That's what it felt like, but also something else: An electric spring, a charge, a source within himself strong enough to topple buildings. It hadn't been there before.

Eddie felt it in his toes and his gut and as he made a fist he felt it in his hand. His ring hand. The ring strobed yellow, a pure sort of yellow like you see in the pistil of a flower. The giant was retreating now, turning with Jade. Eddie knew what to do.

"Stop," he barely whispered, extending his hand toward the giant.

A green battering ram slammed into Eddie, knocking him off his feet, driving him ten feet back against the house, where he slammed into the porch with a shudder that caused the shingles to flap. For an instant he was breathless. Life, power and anger flooded back into him. What had hit him?

"Where is she?" demanded Green Lantern, fury in his teeth, fists, and neck tendons. He stood three feet from Eddie practically smoking with anger, a hair's breadth from striking again.

"I don't know," Eddie said, almost conversationally. "I was about to rescue her from the giant when you butted in."

"What?" Green Lantern said, suddenly unsure of himself.

It all came together. The deep electric well Eddie felt boiled up and over. The concentrated bolt of fury he'd meant for the giant went to Green Lantern instead. It had been meant for Green Lantern all along. The battering ram leaped from his clenched fist, striking Green Lantern hard and hurling him out of sight.

Yes! Eddie exulted, every muscle straining in joy. The transformation was complete. He glanced in the front door window and saw his reflection. His face was purple. There wasn't a square inch that wasn't purple, except for his hair and his eyes. The life force crackled within, a thing alive, begging for release. At last he understood his purpose: To oppose the Green Lantern, whose selfishness and megalomania threatened all life.

Eddie became aware of incessant barking. Barkley had backed under a lawn chair, his tail between his legs, alternately showing his fangs and yapping furiously. Eddie regarded the mutt. Barkley had joined the other side. Too bad. With a casual flick, he imploded the dog. A bloody ball of fur and guts hovered inches above the ground, then fell with a wet thud.

Somewhere deep inside, Eddie felt a twinge of regret. It passed. Fate filled him like a gas. He was one of the Chosen, one of the men of mystery, and had been ever since the giant murdered his grandfather. Even before that. Fate had decreed Eddie the First bring the ring home to him. The alien had chosen him. He was a ring-bearer and a ring-caster.

Lights had gone on in the house and across the street. Someone leaned out their window and yelled, "Hey, I just called the cops!"

Eddie looked around, bewildered. What had they seen that caused them to call the cops? His front yard looked as if a giant ice cream spoon had dipped down and scooped up a couple tons. Part of the rear of the main house had imploded from the force of his blast. He could "see" a faint trail of glowing green particles tracing Green Lantern's flight from where he'd knocked GL out of the borough.

Green Lantern. The dude would be back in a minute. Better if Eddie took the fight out of his neighborhood. He spread his arms and soared into the air.

CHAPTER

23

K yle was more surprised than hurt. There hadn't been a new paranormal in years. Eddie came out of left field. The exterminator! A guy you wouldn't give a second glance on the street. How had it happened? But Kyle had no time for leisurely study. Eddie's blast had knocked him four miles through the air. Only his ring had saved him from blunt force trauma and serious injury when he came down in a junkyard. And that had been the kid's first blast. Who knew what he could do once he'd had a little practice.

But where had that power come from? Kyle got out of the junkpile, hovered a half mile in the air and scanned. Whatever the source of Eddie's power, it wasn't the Starheart or any derivative. It smacked of the same trace elements Kyle had discovered circling Saturn. The remains of an alien ship. It was not an isolated incident, it was connected with the new paranormal. Kyle was looking at a giant jigsaw puzzle with most of the pieces missing. He needed help but had no time. He clocked the yellow streak coming for him at four hundred miles per hour. The yellow streak was Eddie. Kyle used his ring to grab a reinforced concrete bridge abutment, whipping it into place like a catcher's mitt.

Eddie struck the barrier like a safe hitting the pavement. The steel-reinforced concrete shattered, raining debris. Green Lantern realized his mistake in time to scoop up most of the falling debris, but the delay cost him. In the two seconds it took him to clean up after himself, Eddie seized a three-hundred-foot broadcast tower and used it for batting practice. Kyle was the ball. His ring again protected him,

143

reacting automatically, but the blow sent him reeling across Queens to Flushing Meadow.

He'd always been good at thinking on his feet. It didn't take a Superman to realize the transformed Eddie was not on the side of the angels. Kyle resolved to pin him down in the meadow's relatively open space, with minimal damage to citizens and infrastructure. He rose from the ground and hovered at five hundred feet, waiting for his enemy.

And waiting.

Eddie hovered at the same altitude over the East River, reduced to a softly glowing nimbus, barely noticeable among the tethered drones, helicopters and airplanes criss-crossing Manhattan. Using his powers to cast his voice, he spoke softly in Kyle's ear.

"Dude, sorry about that. I mistook you for the giant."

Quivering with tightly bound anger, Kyle spoke through clenched teeth. "What giant?"

"The giant who seized your girlfriend."

A WABC News helicopter circled two miles out. Kyle and Eddie heard their transmission. "This is Alva Reedy in the WABC News chopper over Flushing Meadow. A bizarre situation is developing with Green Lantern and an unknown opponent in some kind of stand-off, a half-mile in the air. Mere moments ago, they clashed over Queens, creating a spectacular nighttime display and disrupting tele-communications in the tri-state area. Uh-oh. We just received warning from Ellis Air Force Base to clear this area. Apparently, the Defense Department is as concerned about this confrontation as we are. This is Alva Reedy . . . "The transmission broke up in a storm of interference. Only Kyle could detect a hair-thin tendril of energy emanating from his opponent to the helicopter.

"This place is going to be swarming with F-16s in one minute," Kyle said. "Where's Jenny?"

"I don't know. The giant took her. May I suggest we combine our efforts in tracking her down?"

Kyle nodded tersely, held out his ring and launched a blip. Giant? What giant? In a second, he had his answer. The ring picked up the bright yellow contrail identical in structure, though much stronger, to the trace elements he'd noticed in the Saturn wreck. Eddie apparently did not know how to use his ring to trace *residual* radiation.

Eddie immediately duplicated Kyle's trick with a yellow blip. *Shut my mouth*, Kyle thought. He's a quick learner. The trail arced over the Manhattan skyline and came down on the other side. Kyle followed, Eddie right behind him.

"Describe the giant," Kyle said.

Eddie closed the distance between them so that they were flying side by side. Kyle refused to look at Eddie. The dude was poaching on his girl. He had to let it lie for now, but they'd come back to it. "Over seven feet, built like an oak sea chest, boots, chain mail, bullet helm with wings protruding. Sort of Viking-like."

The description rang a chime deep within the ring's memory. An image appeared. It was fleeting, evanescent. Kyle shoved it aside in the rush to get after Jenny. The thought of her in the grips of some creep drove him crazy. He inserted himself into the radiation trail and rode it like an electron down a platinum wire. It dead-ended in a cliff halfway up the Jersey Palisades. Kyle had a nanosecond to realize this was a gate before he passed through the cliff like long-wave radiation through water.

Eddie had the same time to arrive at the same conclusion, but his ring had not finished downloading all the data. He didn't know that it was a gate. A lifetime of experience taught him that to hit the cliff at high velocity would result in instant death.

Kyle passed through a meat grinder. He felt himself break down molecule by molecule in an enormous rush, world's biggest domino fall, down to a single point. He felt himself rebuilt molecule by molecule in a jumble of pain, pleasure, ennui, sensations he couldn't identify. He felt as if he had been turned inside out. The first thing he saw was his hand before his face. Beyond lay chaos. This was no recognizable world, this was no world at all. It was a space between universes, insulation, filler, gap, sumphole. A place the universe forgot. He was like a sock caught in a washing machine. Round and round in a rush of noise and fury from which there was no escape. Every sense receiving on every frequency. Total cosmic overload.

Green Lantern fell to his knees. That meant there was gravity. Its focus kept shifting: up, down, sideways. His stomach oscillated like an egg in a blender. His gorge rose. The savior of billions heaved his guts out, bile burning his throat. His eyes teared. He couldn't see the ground hidden beneath a swirling foglike miasma. He felt rather than heard the thud of approaching footfalls, something massive.

He looked up like a dog to its master. Pale colors emerged: yellow for the boots and helmet. Glittery silver for the cuirass. The ancient image of the Destroyer emerged from the mists clutching a jagged bolt of fury.

CHAPTER

24

T he man hovering two hundred feet in the air over the Hudson went unnoticed in the dark. Barges and pleasure boats passed underneath, oblivious to his presence. The spot where Green Lantern had disappeared was a rock escarpment jutting over the swift-flowing waters. Atop the bluff was nothing but a hurricane fence festooned with blown trash, a rocky field, and the edge of a lumber-yard.

Eddie cautiously extended a plasma tendril toward the cliff face. He could feel its resistance to his touch, but with minimal effort he was able to force the tendril through—like having a forty-yard-long finger. He intuitively understood the nature of the yellow plasma as an extension of himself subject to his will. He also understood that the spot where Green Lantern had disappeared was a gate. Not an end but a beginning. On the other side of the gate lay the answers to so many of his questions. The source of the ring; why he was chosen; his ultimate purpose.

Come, the gate whispered. We're waiting for you, Eddie. It's your destiny.

Still, he hesitated. He'd lived most of his life as an ordinary man, and ordinary men didn't overcome a lifetime of experience instantly. It would take an act of faith to follow Green Lantern through the rock. He willed himself closer until he was floating an arm's length from the bluff. This time he used his hand. He pushed right through the granite face into a space beyond. Warm breezes caressed his fingers. He could smell through them. A tropical paradise awaited him on the other side of the rock. It was a familiar feeling. It felt like home.

Come on, the gate whispered. *What are you waiting for?*

No. A trick! Searing heat grazed his fingers and he withdrew them sharply, looking to see if they were burned. He willed a soft yellow glow from the fingers. They were all right. Some kind of electromagnetic barrier designed to keep out unwanted organisms, but not him. There was no way he could discern what was on the other side without passing through.

The gate called to him with Jenny's voice. The demon had her—the thing that killed his grandfather. The thing he'd taken an oath to kill. Well, it was put up or shut up time, buddy. If this wasn't a defining moment, there weren't any. His entire life, since that day he'd found the ring and lost his grandfather, had prepared him for this. Eddie jumped through the gate feet first. It might have been undignified, but he'd grown up around shallow water.

He landed in a spring meadow, redolent with the scent of flowers, familiar but unidentifiable. He'd landed in a park on the outskirts of an impossibly clean and futuristic city, like something you'd see on the frontispiece of a nineteen-fifties science fiction novel. Smooth plastic towers ended in sleek, appliancelike grills. Soaring gull-wing roofs enclosed vast public spaces, visible through shifting transparent barriers. Shiny craft traveled invisible but well-defined corridors, banking and reforming in new configurations with balletic grace.

A half-mile away, a pair of kids in blue jumpsuits tumbled in and around a bright, puffy-looking jungle gym under the watchful eye of a woman. To Eddie's astonishment, he found that by concentrating, he could see their faces in detail. Like his vision had suddenly become ten times as sharp. The woman, the kids were purple. The same color as his skin. He'd made the right choice. He'd come home.

"Eddie," said a familiar voice.

Eddie already knew who it was before he turned. It just seemed like the most natural thing in the world. It was Grandpa as Eddie remembered him, still relatively young, a trim hundred and fifty pounds, dressed in crisp olive fatigues wearing his Distinguished Service Cross. And the ring: Gramps had his ring on. Eddie looked down. He had his own ring on. It had fused with his flesh. So obviously Gramps wasn't wearing that ring.

There was another explanation.

"Hello, Gramps," Eddie said, as if it were the most natural thing in the world.

Eddie the First beamed.

"Is this heaven?" Eddie asked. What the hell, maybe the monster *had* creamed him. Maybe he really didn't have a future.

"No, Eddie. You're very much alive. This is where you belong. This is Qward."

Qward. Strange, yet familiar—like a word that had been hovering on the tip of his tongue forever.

"What are you doing here?"

"I'm here to help you. I'm a manifestation of the inner you created to guide you through your new home."

"You're not real?"

Eddie the First shook his head with an Andy Griffith grin. " 'Fraid not. But I couldn't be prouder if I were. The ring." He reached out and touched Eddie's ring. Eddie felt a smooth electric jolt. "It channels your memories, combines them with the central data bank, and voila. Here I am."

They began walking slowly toward the street. All the time in the world. Eddie noticed gull-like birds with feathers a bright cerulean blue, and crimson beaks. They would frequently disappear against the sky, leaving only their beaks visible like random arrowheads. The street bore little traffic, an occasional yellow capsule-like vehicle gliding by on invisible wheels. The wind hummed in the trees. The ground was a uniform violet-colored moss, highlighted by pink blossoms.

"So this is Qward."

"This is Qward, son."

"You know where the Destroyer is? The one that killed you? I've got a score to settle with that big bastard."

The phantom Eddie put his hand on Eddie's shoulder. "Let's not go running off half-cocked, son. You've got a lot to learn about this place. Those Destroyers, as you call 'em, are a vital part of the Qward defense posture. They're called Weaponers."

149

" 'Scuse me, Gramps, but why do I give a hoot about the Qward defense posture?"

" 'Cause you *are* Qward, son. Look in a mirror lately? The change wouldn't have taken place if you didn't want it. I resisted, and look what happened to me."

Eddie stopped and wrinkled his nose. This made no sense whatsoever. If Eddie the First was so gung-ho on Qward, why had he refused the ring?

"'Cause I'd had enough fighting. Why do you think I opted to be a medic in the first place? I didn't want to have to carry a rifle and put some other poor bastard down. Some of us have got the killer instinct, and some ain't. You got it. I never did."

They came to the street. There was no sidewalk, but a well-worn path in the moss showed evidence of foot traffic. "Gramps, that thing has got Jenny. I've got to get her back. You know who Jenny is?"

"Yup. She's the green goddess. Only reason he grabbed her was to get you to cross over. Can't grab you. You took the ring. You would have blown him to smithereens. But they know you want the girl. Smart."

"If this is where I belong, why didn't they just ask?"

"The Qwardians never do things half-assed. They like at least two back-up systems for every plan. Back in the day, you'd see some gentlemen wearing both belt and suspenders. I guess they're like that. Guess they figured this was the best way."

"Gramps, there's another guy who crossed over. Kyle Rayner."

Eddie the First squinted and the corners of his mouth turned down. "They don't want him. He wasn't invited."

"Jenny's his girl. What did you think he was going to do?"

Eddie the First scratched his jaw and followed one of the red beaks. "Kinda' comes under *your* job description, getting rid of that guy."

Eddie rubbed his hands together in anticipation. He'd dreamed of punching Kyle Rayner since the first moment he'd met him. "Point me at him."

"See, that's what I mean about running off half-cocked. You don't even know where you are. I'd like to show you the city, introduce you to the big guy."

The big guy. Of course. There was always a big guy. At Terminator

Too, it was Eugene Kleiser, son of Earl Kleiser, founder and bug squasher supreme. Eddie had learned a lot from Eugene.

"Take me to the big guy."

Out of nowhere, one of the smooth, capsulelike vehicles veered silently to the curb and lifted a gull-wing in greeting. Inside, soft umber cushions beckoned. Eddie noticed that Gramps didn't make a dent when he sat. The interior walls were seamlessly transparent to provide a view of their surroundings. The driverless vehicle smoothly blended back in with the flow and joined a thicker column of vehicles arcing toward the center of the city. They passed an enormous, multi-level parking garage that appeared jammed with military vehicles. Other military vehicles, obvious from their uniform gray color and markings, sifted in and out of traffic. It looked like a city on a war footing.

Traffic joined a vast circle around an immense thumb-shaped government building. At least Eddie assumed it was a government building. It had the planned-by-committee look. Millions of symmetrical windows for worker drones. The vehicle swept through an opening big enough to swallow an ocean liner. An immense plaque on the wall read PARLIAMENT OF QWARD. Eddie realized he could read the strange alphabet.

"Ay-uh," Eddie the First said. "That's your data dump kickin' in."

" 'Scuse me?"

"Now that you're home, the ring has access to the central data dump—it's bringing you up to speed on Qward history, and so forth. Like, for example, the fact that Qward predates civilization on Earth by three hundred million years. During that time, the Qwardians have often found themselves in conflict with the so-called Guardians, who seek to extend their rule by force. In an unprecedented display of arrogance the Guardians took it upon themselves to divvy the universe up into 3600 districts. As if *they* had created it. As if it were *theirs*. Central planning has never worked. It doesn't work on a tiny scale, it doesn't work on a grand scale. Yet the Guardians refuse to concede their mistake, even after three billion years. It is *their tyranny* that prevents humanity, among other species, from reaching its full potential. Like you."

"Like the Commies."

"That's right. This Kyle Rayner, he's one of their top enforcers. And I hate to be the one to break it to you, this Jenny dame carries a Guardian membership card. She's known as Jade."

"Come on, Gramps. It's not like she's some ideologue. She goes along to get along. She could care less about imposing order on Earth! She's a crime fighter. A part-time crime fighter. Everybody's doing it. I thought I'd do a little myself, I ever get back."

"You'll get back all right. You're the chosen one, son, and don't you forget it. It may be you can work things out with Jade so she comes over. But you got bigger fish than muggings and bank robberies. We're talking future of humanity here."

Eddie gazed through the vehicle's transparent wall at the massive bureaucratic façade sliding past, tiny figures occasionally visible through myriad windows. The light behind the windows was yellow. They passed by an enormous monument, some kind of spacecraft angling upward like a leaping sailfish. It looked like something Stalin would have commissioned.

"What's that?" "The *Sid* Monument."

"What's the *Sid*?"

"The probe ship they lost on Saturn."

A chime went off deep in Eddie's soul. He'd always known about the *Sid*, the way goslings know to seek their ancestral mating area.

"Do I have to give a speech?"

"It's a formality, really. Strictly rear-echelon stuff, but Sinestro, he's the real deal. If we'd had him on Iwo. . . . Unfortunately his participation was viciously resisted by the Green Lantern of sector 2814 and thousands of good men had to die. Okay, whelp. You ready for this?"

The automated vehicle pulled over at a vast circular curb similar to the passenger arrival area at an airport, only more orderly. There were several hundred people going about their business in the shaded, open-air garden, most of them wearing similar brightly colored jumpsuits. The men were of a kind: smiling, pink-cheeked, with handsome, intelligent foreheads, bald on top, thick white hair curling around the backs of their heads. The women were cherubic and seemed ageless. There were others, humans who didn't conform to the mold, and aliens. Everyone seemed to have a mission. There were no idlers, no street musicians, no aimless teens. Eddie watched as an elephant-sized creature slithered across the platform twenty yards away, followed by a cheerful janitor in a blue jumpsuit wiping up a trail. Tall, palmlike trees stood in rows like silent sentinels along the street.

A huge figure exited the building, standing head and shoulders above the throng. Eddie boiled with rage. He felt his grandfather's hand on his arm. "Steady, son. Remember what I said. *Besides*—the Weaponers all look alike. That's probably not the one you seek."

"The one who killed you—is he still alive?"

"I expect so. They're pretty much indestructible."

Eddie stared with loathing as the giant strode across the public space and entered a large automated vehicle. Intellectually he knew that what Eddie the First had told him was the truth, and he had no reason to doubt it. His hatred of the Weaponer was irrational. It had only been doing its job. Tell that to a nine-year-old kid cowering in the attic. Some images never leave or lose their power to unnerve. That's how Eddie felt about the Weaponer. Only when the hatch wing closed did Eddie relax and allow Eddie the First to steer him toward the main entrance, a huge arch that could easily have accommodated an armored panzer division, dwarfing the line of trees that grew around the base.

There was something about the massive, orderly public space that made Eddie uneasy. He couldn't put his finger on it. Unless, of course, it was being a human on an alien planet. That could make you uneasy. Several of the smiling cherubs nodded at them as they strode across the vast plaza toward the steps. One side of the plaza was dominated by an heroic, Giacometti-like sculpture, twenty feet tall, similar to the alien Eddie had met at the lake.

Eddie the First nodded at the statue. "That's him. That's the big guy."

Although no one stopped them, Eddie got the impression they were being scrutinized as they strode down the great hall that was at least sixty feet high; the arched ceiling was decorated with a series of striking geometric patterns, punctuated periodically by balconies, some of which were large enough to launch flying cars. Light filtered in through a series of enormous lenses. The light was yellow. Happy light. Men and women criss-crossed the great hall in midair, defying gravity as they smiled at one another.

No bums, no panhandlers, no one parading in front of Starbucks with a grudge and a sign. The streets were spotless. Eddie couldn't see a trash receptacle anywhere. Did they not generate trash? The lack of conversation was also eerie. Plenty of smiling and waving, hardly any words. For such a large public space in the middle of the day it was unnaturally quiet.

Eddie the First snapped his fingers. "Let's levitate." He rose a foot in the air, taking a slight forward tilt like the figurehead of a ship. Eddie felt a gallop of excitement as he willed himself to follow. Effortlessly they glided down the hall, plenty of room on both sides for like-minded individuals. Eddie realized that he had come to a world filled with geniuses. A world filled with demi-gods, or at least a superior sort of being, above the gross violence that had characterized most of humanity. That was another thing. No cops. They didn't need any. No wonder there were no trash cans. These people existed in perfect harmony with their environment. He saw wisdom in their sameness.

Differences among people gave rise to grievances. The poor hated the rich. The thin hated the fat. The Mods hated the Rockers. Here, no differences. No one rose above the mob in a graceless display of ego. It was a socialist paradise. But what did they do for a living?

"Gramps, what do they eat? Where are the supermarkets, the cafes, the restaurants? Are there farms?"

"No farms. Thanks to those green bastards every bit of food has to be imported, or raised underground. They've perfected a form of fungus with taste and texture not unlike tofu. It's their primary source of protein but they don't make a big thing of eating like humans do. In fact, you'll find the Qwardian approach to bodily functions entirely different than what you're used to."

"What about sex?"

"They don't have sex. They reproduce by parthenogenesis."

"You're joking."

"Nope."

"Doesn't sound like much fun."

"You're not here to have fun."

The floated into a side corridor twenty feet above the floor. The corridor had rounded edges and was decorated with softly glowing geometric patterns, some of which doubled as doors and windows. Everywhere the light was yellow.

They turned down another corridor. Eddie took one look at the figure guarding the door opposite and felt his neck muscles tighten, his hands close in fists. He was without fear, filled with a terrible power. Again, he felt his grandfather's hand on his arm.

"Easy, son. It's his job to guard the head man. He's not the one you seek."

"They all look alike," Eddie said through gritted teeth.

"That's what they say about us."

Eddie fixed his eyes straight ahead and did not look the Weaponer in the eyes. For his part, the Weaponer might as well have been a statue. Eddie the First said, "We're expected." The creature gave no sign, but the door opened. They floated in. The chamber was immense, easily one hundred feet across and oval-shaped. Eddie thought of the Oval Office. No. It was like the signet on his yellow ring. He looked at his hand. The ring was glowing, sending a warm, happy pulse through his body. The domed ceiling was a dazzling mosaic in every shade of yellow, from deep gold to burnished copper, to the pale yellow streaks of Arctic summer. The tiled floor mirrored the ceiling's design. Exactly in the center was an oval desk that seemed to rise of a piece with the floor, made of the same exquisitely worked rock and tile. Behind the desk sat an imposing figure in a leather-like chair.

He was purple. Las Vegas Naugahyde purple.

"Is this the new sleeper agent?" the head man said.

25

K yle was in hell. Suspended in a viscous purple gel, he was a
castle under siege. Pathogens stormed his system. Jolts of
electricity fried his nerves. Generators mounted outside the
tank broadcast high-frequency sounds designed to drive him mad.
Only the ring protected him—automatically—from certain death. Cut
off as it was by the power-sapping gel on all sides, the ring would
eventually run out of power, his immune system would break down,
the electricity would break in and he would either suffocate or die of
a massive stroke. He was naked. The ring didn't have enough power
to generate the costume.

The Qwardians had chilled the gel to make it as uncomfortable as
possible. He figured the reason they hadn't simply frozen him was
they were extracting the power from his ring at a fixed rate. Two
diminutive Qwardians, so like the Guardians, had come by with their
clipboards and their palm discs, never once looking him in the eye.
Just the facts, ma'am. They studied the read out, did their calculations
and left.

Struggling against the overwhelming resistance of the gel, Kyle
felt the parameters of his cell. It was a transparent cylinder two yards
in diameter by four yards high. Kyle saw similar cylinders nearby.
Some appeared to be occupied. When he tried to move he realized he
was tethered in place by a series of monofilaments, below and above.
There was enough leeway for him to twitch but not enough for him
to make contact with the cylinder's wall. Cautiously, he tested the
limits of his freedom. Motion caused him excruciating pain in his

joints. Arthritis as a weapon. It jolted out of his knees and elbows, meeting in his chest. Could arthritis kill? You bet.

Through his misery he sensed that the Qwardians had left the chamber. He wasn't a very good show. Slowly, millimeter by millimeter, he strained against the filaments to bring some part of his body in contact with the cylinder. The pain was excruciating. He could almost touch the wall with his left foot but countless filaments pulled him back like rubber bands. He thrashed in frustration, reeling in nausea, afraid of vomiting and drowning in his own vomit. He could breath through a bit they'd put in his mouth connected to a clear plastic tube running up to the top of the cylinder. It supplied just enough oxygen to keep him on the edge of suffocation. They wanted him to suffer. He tried yanking the tube free with his jaws but was unable to.

His thrashing stirred up the viscous purple fluid, sending bubbles drifting lazily upward. It was like hanging in STP oil additive. He practiced the yoga breathing and relaxation techniques Green Arrow had taught him. He brought his pulse and breathing under control, but he was weaker now. Every effort drained the ring. When the ring gave out, so would his immune system. Pathogens would rush in like a tidal wave would overwhelm him. His cellular structure would decay. The soft tissue would slip off and fall to the bottom, leaving his skeleton hanging in the tube.

After a few minutes—it only felt like years—he tried gyrating up and down like a puppet held by someone with cerebral palsy. The filaments began to stretch. Emboldened, Kyle spun. In slow motion, he flapped his arms through the viscous fluid and jumped up and down, ignoring the spiked pain burrowing through his limbs. His skull felt like an oil drum filled with ball bearings. But the monofilaments stretched and his left foot touched the cylinder wall.

He couldn't keep it there. The combined tension of the remaining filaments drew him back to a central position. Now he knew the filaments could be stretched. He waited for his nausea to subside before trying again. To an observer, he must have looked like some bizarre over-developed fetus jerking spastically in a glass womb. Extending himself to the limits of his bonds, he found he could just touch the wall of the cylinder with one foot. Now if he could maintain contact long enough to launch a blip, however feeble . . .

Yes! The desperately weak sphere ballooned outward, invisible to all but Green Lantern eyes, a hint of emerald that became fainter as it grew. Kyle snapped back into place, exhausted. He had no time to rest. If Jenny were in the vicinity, the answer would come back instantly. Again the awful dance. Again his foot made contact with the cylinder wall. Almost immediately the ping registered in his head, a pure celestial chime. It was Jenny. No more than several miles away. She would know he was alive . . . if the blip had been strong enough. He was afraid it had been so weak she hadn't even felt it.

Please God, he prayed. *Let Jen be all right. Bring her to me.*

He sobbed involuntarily. He hadn't prayed since becoming a Lantern. What did it mean? That he recognized a power greater than the Guardians? Greater than Ion? Greater than Parallax? Greater than the Spectre? Greater than Superman? And if that were so, then the Guardians were mistaken about the nature of the universe. There *was* a natural order. Which meant the Green Lanterns were superfluous, if well-intentioned. He certainly wasn't doing himself or anyone else any good in his present circumstances.

There are no atheists in foxholes.

Kyle's parents had been good, church-going Episcopalians. They had dutifully trucked young Kyle to church every Sunday where the Message of Deliverance cruised over his radar. One thing the minister had said stuck with him, though. It never hurt to pray. Kyle shut his eyes against the cruel glare and prayed.

Dear God, deliver me from my enemies. Return Jenny to me safe and sound. Smite these poxy little bureaucrats. Please!

He opened his eyes. A series of dark shapes surrounded the cylinder. Qwardians. A group of dignitaries getting the grand tour. They parted like wheat before the Weaponer who strode directly to the tube, glared at Kyle, and made an adjustment. Instantly more filaments jacked out of hidden chambers to attach themselves to Kyle's extremities. By the time they were through he was unable even to wriggle a finger.

CHAPTER
26

T he creature stood, leaned over his desk and extended his hand. He was eight feet tall. Eddie gingerly gripped the shovel-sized hand, was surprised at the giant's gentle grip. A firm but not overpowering salesman's handshake. The hand felt less dense than it looked, like a cleverly painted piece of Styrofoam. Warm memories flooded Eddie's purple arm. He'd seen this creature in the ring's ancestral memory. Despite the creature's disturbing appearance, Eddie found him reassuring. Like Eddie the First.

"Sinestro," the creature said. He relaxed back into his throne and indicating a chair that resembled a tulip, made of soft, foamy material. "Have a seat, Mr. Rocheford."

Eddie sat. Whoever these people were, they'd gone to an immense amount of trouble to meet him. Eddie felt lucky. He felt good. He felt like the hottest rookie in the major leagues, and a free agent to boot. He made himself comfortable. The chair conformed to his body perfectly, and when he shifted, the chair shifted with him.

"What's up, Mr. Sinestro?"

"We need you, Mr. Rocheford, and we're prepared to make it worth your while. As you've already observed, we have already made it worth your while, for it is due to us that you possess extraordinary powers. Powers to rival Green Lantern's."

Eddie looked around. They were alone. Eddie the First had disappeared.

"Where's Gramps?"

Sinestro made a shooing motion. "A mere construct to facilitate your assimilation. Why? Do you want us to bring him back?"

"No. Who's us?"

"The Qwardians of the Qalaxy. In a minute you'll meet our Council of Elders, those who determine qalactic policy."

"Whaddaya need me for?"

Sinestro grinned. His teeth were surprisingly small and even. He looked like a Pixar creation. "Our world is dying as a direct result of our ability to tame nature. We have tamed nature so that it does not utter a peep. There are no wild places left on our planet. Every square inch of surface has been improved. The seas have been improved to the point of sterility. The earth has been sucked dry of every nutrient. No wild things roam wildernesses. No wilderness exists. We seek green earth. Will you help us?"

Eddie grimaced, wriggling like a bored child. "Let me get this straight. You don't want any old planet. You want Earth, correct?"

Sinestro displayed his perfect teeth like a series of ceramic semi-conductors. "Officially, I'm not permitted to comment. The Elders will explain."

"You want me to betray my own kind by turning Earth over to you."

"No, that is incorrect. The Qwardians represent the highest form of moral order. By imposing our rule on Earth, we will save it. I don't have to tell you that Earth is suffering from many of the same pathologies that have made it necessary for us to seek a new home."

"Well dude, excuse me if I'm dense, but what makes you think you'll do any better on Earth? You already trashed one planet."

Sinestro steepled his fingers like a spider doing push-ups on a mirror. "Events leading to the abandonment of the home planet were set in motion over a billion years ago. The oldest present Council Member is only two million four hundred and sixty-three thousand years old, Earth time. We like to think we've learned from our mistakes. The Qwardians are all about wisdom."

"What would you do differently?"

"Everything. Really, this is more the Council's purview."

"What about the people? The human beings who live there? What rights will they retain?"

Sinestro's pitch-dark brows arched into his smooth forehead. "The same rights they now have. We do not intend to interfere with Earth society."

"How many Qwardians are there?"

"Four hundred million. Less than the population of several of your largest political entities."

"Wow. That's a lot of Qwardians. Where were you planning to settle? I got to tell you, real estate prices in Manhattan are ridiculous."

"That need not be your concern. Suffice it to say, we plan to integrate with Earth society as smoothly as possible. We do not intend to upset your delicate economy."

Eddie scratched his head. "You sound like a typical politician. Four hundred million Qwardians without upsetting the economy? Come on, Sinestro! What are you guys going to do for food? Raise your own?"

"I told you, we plan to integrate with your economy as smoothly as possible. I've been to Earth, as you know."

"Dude, was that you in the spaceship at Lake Agnes? You almost took my head off."

Sinestro's tiny smile resembled on octopus's beak. "A manifestation calibrated to your DNA. We've been waiting a long time for you."

"How'd you find me? How do you even know about me, man?"

"Your grandfather came to our attention during one of your regional conflicts. He would have been perfect, but he refused to serve. He was a pacifist, you know."

"Not with me he wasn't."

"Your father lacked the necessary genetic structure. These gifts often skip a generation. We knew you had arrived by a signal received by a listening station on Saturn, the sixth planet in your system."

"What signal?"

Sinestro formed the Sydney Opera House with his fingers. "Green Lantern, your mortal enemy."

Anger foamed in Eddie's mouth. "I'd like to kill that son of a bitch."

"We're counting on it. But first, you asked how we planned to integrate into Earth society. I've seen your markets. Qwardians will convert their native currency to that of whichever country in which they reside. Those who choose America will convert to dollars. Those who choose Europe will convert to Euros. Those who choose Saudi Arabia will convert to dinars."

"Horse puckey. Who's going to choose to live in Saudi Arabia, or even Brussels, when they can live in the good ol' U.S. of A? Nobody. That's who. You're all coming to America, aren't you?"

Sinestro's eyebrows performed a complex *pas de deux*. "No. You place too much value on your native culture. Moreover, the Qwardians have the ability to terraform arid land, turn it into a garden. We could transform the whole of this continent." Sinestro pointed to a map of Africa hanging in the air.

"Then why don't you terraform this planet?"

"As I explained, the ground lacks the necessary nutrients. We perfected our terraforming technique after we had depleted the land."

"Don't you guys ever learn?"

A ripple of annoyance quivered Sinestro's smooth brow. "It is of course possible that the Council erred in choosing you as our representative. Should you wish it, we will erase all memories of this incident and return you to your former station unharmed."

Eddie blanched. Wait a minute. He didn't want to talk himself out of the best gig he'd ever had. He at least owed it to himself—and the people of Earth—to hear what the Council had to say. After all, these guys had been around a long time. Give them credit. They had to know a few things.

"Okay, okay, don't get your panties in a bundle. I just want to be sure I'm doing the right thing here. It's a big decision. I mean, I'm not just representing myself, you know. I got six billion human beings to worry about."

"I understand. That is why we are most anxious for you to meet our Council and hear their wisdom. Will you accompany me?"

Eddie stood, grinning. "Let's do it."

Sinestro stood. A yellow disc appeared on the floor next to Eddie. "For your convenience."

Eddie stepped on the disc, which gripped the bottoms of his soles like Velcro and rose two feet in the air so that he and Sinestro were at eye level. Sinestro strode smoothly toward the wall, the disc keeping pace. Eddie leaned forward slightly to maintain his equilibrium. It was better than a Segway. As they reached the wall, an arch formed.

They moved through and the arch closed behind them. The corridor stretched a half-mile to a more grandiose arch sealed with a rippling sheet of energy. Floor-to-ceiling windows on both sides of the corridor looked out on the perfect parklike city. Military vehicles floated past in formation. Eddie caught a glimpse of himself reflected in a window. His skin had turned a uniform purple. He was the same color as his host.

No one was in a hurry. No one honked their horn. There were no trash receptacles because there was no trash. There were no pets fouling the sidewalk. The sky was cloudless and blue.

They want to trade this for Manhattan? Eddie thought.

They passed through the arch and were engulfed in thunderous applause. Several hundred Qwardians, all wearing robes of office in the same hue as Sinestro's skin, stood to honor him. Heady stuff for a young man who had achieved little of significance in his life on Earth. Sinestro gestured for Eddie to take the podium that stood in the center of the vast saucer-shaped chamber. It was like the Senate, or a theater in the round, with tiers of concentric seats rising to the rim.

One man strode forward, arms outstretched, sleeves like the wings of some strange bird. As he approached, the little man rose slightly in the air so that he was at Eddie's eye-level without the aid of a disc. Eddie submitted to the man's embrace, stepped back and regarded their leader. He was similar to every other man in the room. High, bald forehead, fringe of luxurious white hair surrounding the back of the head, clear, widely set intelligent gray eyes. Small of stature.

"Welcome, Eddie Rocheford the Third. I am Marshak, Prime Minister of the Qwardian Council. We have searched far and wide to find you, Eddie Rocheford the Third."

"Please call me Eddie."

"Very well, Eddie. I speak for the entire Council when I say I hope you will accept the mantle that has been prepared for you and become our herald in the posimatter universe."

"Marshak." Eddie raised his voice and addressed the entire council, surprisingly comfortable with himself. "Gentlemen of the Council! I appreciate your faith in me, but before I accept this position I have a few questions. Number one: Why me?"

"We have searched long and hard for a champion," Marshak said. "Each time we sent forth a herald, a Green Lantern would murder him. The Green Lanterns are the sworn enemy of progress. They are the enemies of life!"

At this declaration the entire Council, several hundred, began stamping their feet in unison and making a whooping sound. Eddie found himself caught up in the emotion. He'd experienced the Green Lantern's treachery first hand. Green Lantern, and all the so-called super heroes, treated the people of Earth like mushrooms. Kept in the dark and fed a steady diet of manure. What chance did the man in the street have to learn the truth? On the one hand, you had this race of superior beings, ensconced in their fortresses, their caverns, their satellites, their halls of power issuing fiats "for the good of humanity." On the other were those lonely prophets who dared point out that many of the so-called super heroes weren't even human. So how could their desires coincide with humanity's? It was all a big con job. Superman, J'onn J'onz, Hawkman, these were only a few of the openly alien super heroes feeding off Earth's largesse. Who knew how many others were of unknown origin?

"We have sent countless heralds, expeditions, scout ships into your universe over the millennia. All have either been destroyed by the Green Lanterns, or broke up on contact with positive matter."

"What do you mean, positive matter?"

"We Qwardians exist in an anti-matter universe, relative to Earth. Of course we here at home regard our own universe as the positive model, and yours as negative. It's relative to your position. Particles that carry a positive charge in your universe carry a negative charge in ours. When matter meets anti-matter, there is always an explosion. However, due to your unique cellular structure and DNA, you are able to reconstruct yourself on either side of the gate in whatever charge that universe carries. Because of your unique gift, you have provided us with a template so that others may follow.

"We have learned to transmit humans and material into your universe by deconstructing them and reconstructing them on the other side in positive template matter. We have been able to insert various expeditions into your universe over the years. But until you came along, these were all doomed to failure. Some of them are quite famous. In 1908, large portions of Siberia were devastated by what was assumed to be a meteorite. In fact, it was a Qwardian scout ship exploding in contact with posimatter. It failed to reconstruct properly.

"Before that, we sent through two thousand eight hundred and twelve probes dating back to two million B.C on the posimatter Earth. In so doing, we encountered a planet in your home solar system that is uninhabited. You call it Saturn. Because of the unique electromagnetic charges in its atmosphere, it is possible to insert negative matter protected by an electromagnetic field from coming into contact with positive matter. This is of course not a permanent solution."

"*Sid,*" someone whispered. Others took up the chant.

"*Sid. Sid. Sid.*"

Eddie peered at Marshak in disbelief. He had not been a brilliant science student but he understood from the ring's data dump that Saturn was a gas giant. "Dude, that planet is totally uninhabitable. Why would you want Saturn? Sinestro said you wanted Earth."

Marshak darkened. "No, no, no! We do not want Earth!" His flashing eyes sought out Sinestro who gazed skyward as if none of this concerned him. Was there a power struggle going on? Who *was* Sinestro? Eddie knew from the ring the last Sinestro had been consigned to a jade coffin and had never escaped. Jade, because his captors believed its spectral vibrations would act as insurance against his resurrection.

"Sinestro is in error. The Council has specifically stipulated that we do *not* intend to inhabit any planet already hosting an advanced civilization. The reason we have chosen Saturn is because its unique electromagnetic field and gas structure are ideally suited to the creation of a matter/anti-matter conversion gate."

"Which means, what?"

"We can live there without setting off a chain reaction that would destroy the universe. Our craft and people will reconstruct positively."

"There is a problem," Sinestro rumbled. "The Green Lanterns oppose us."

"Yes," Marshak said. "The Green Lanterns exist for two reasons: To enslave the human race, and to prevent the Qwardians from offering their stewardship to the posimatter universe."

At the mention of Green Lantern, Eddie once again experienced a visceral rush of hatred. He knew the Green Lanterns were evil. He had always known. "One of them tricked me through the gate hoping to destroy me."

"We know the one of whom you speak," Marshak said. "We have him."

"You have him?"

"Yes."

"What about the girl, Jenny-Lynn?"

"We have her, too."

There was a pause. Eddie did not dare speak.

"She is for you," Marshak said softly. "She is waiting for you, contingent upon the assignment."

"I accept the assignment."

CHAPTER

27

J enny dreamed in green. A verdant, rolling, hilly country with majestic mountains looming, stern patriarchs rising from a distant haze like the prows of enormous ships. She stood in a high country meadow—she could tell from the air—surrounded by a clover field. Their blossoms were purple and yellow. Young, three-pronged goats soared through the field like flying fish. A chill wind filled the air, turning the gently swaying field into an uncharted sea pulling itself into spasms. Towering cumulonimbus gathered overhead like old world prophets. They put their heads together. With a rumble, they set their fury free.

Jenny woke up. All was still and sweetly scented. There was no field, no mountains in the distance and certainly no clouds. She lay on a soft bed between yellow silk sheets. At least it felt like silk. Through an open gallery she could see neatly trimmed trees—were they palms? It was like the place in Cabo that Kyle had taken her. Beyond the palms loomed smooth spires.

A hand caressed her cheek. Without thinking she reached up and took it. No one touched her like that but Kyle. She rubbed her cheek against it and kissed the fingers. They were the color of port wine. Instinctively she jerked back. Suddenly, she noticed the scent that she had thought of as honeysuckle. It wasn't. It was something sweet and strange, tinged with a lick of rot. The colors that had seemed so gay and natural now seemed slightly off. The cool smooth fabric against her skin—it wasn't silk. She could tell by the weave. And the man sitting on the edge of the bed clad in a blue and black jumpsuit was definitely not Kyle.

It was Eddie. Eddie the Exterminator. Only now he was something else. The purple stain had claimed him entirely. His forehead was beginning to elongate, like an eggplant. He gazed at her with an expression of mild amusement.

She realized she was naked. Her last memory was of going to visit Eddie in his little house in Queens. Then, nada. She had been dressed then. Now she was not. She automatically put a hand to her breast, drawing the sheets up higher.

"What am I doing in this bed butt-naked, Eddie Roach?"

He really did have a charming smile, so much more sophisticated than the rest of his face. "Hi. You don't remember the Weaponer?"

She tried to hide her consternation behind an expression of mild interest. This was just too weird. She'd been hit on by everybody from Skeet Ulrich to Donald Trump, and she was getting the same vibes from Purple Eddie. "What's a Weaponer?"

"Eight foot Nordic giant, kinda. Remember coming to my house last night?

"Yes. We had a dinner date."

"Just as you appeared, Green Lantern and a Weaponer landed in my yard trying to kill each other. The *residual* energy knocked out Con Ed all the way to Providence. I was able to save you from being crushed, but the Weaponer grabbed you. He and Green Lantern took off. I followed. They led me through a trans-dimensional gate. We are no longer in the known universe. This is the Qwardian universe. And it's anti-matter. The reason you don't explode, I was able to reverse your molecular structure." He held up his hand. "With the ring."

Jen didn't blink. She gulped. "Wow."

Eddie grinned self-consciously. "Yeah, I know. It's, like, everything you've ever been taught is wrong. Don't worry. I'll explain."

"Explain what I'm doing under these covers naked."

"Oh that. The clash between the Weaponer and the Green Lantern tore off your clothes. Don't worry. Nobody tried to take advantage of you."

Jen was not worried. She had complete knowledge of her own body and would have known if anyone had tried anything. She wondered at Eddie's expression of smug virtue. He really had come quite a ways from the hayseed charm of the exterminator who'd knocked on their door a mere three days ago. How? What had happened to her was a piece of a bigger picture. Weaponers, the Qwardians, this transformed bug killer. Something big was going on. She'd felt it days ago but foolishly disregarded her woman's intuition. *My problem*, she mused, is *too much data. I need one of those rings like Kyle or Eddie has to filter it down.*

"Why am I here, Eddie?"

"I told you. The Weaponer brought you through."

"Where's Kyle?"

The blood rose so suddenly to his face Jade was afraid his head would explode. "Forget that treacherous piece of dirt! He was fixing to sell out the human race, and the Qwardians!"

"Oh, Eddie!" she laughed. "That's just silly."

She realized her mistake as soon as the words were out of her mouth. He stood up, backed away from the bed as if it were contaminated. His purple face turned ugly, like a drama mask, the eyes cold. "You think too much of yourself. You might have showed a little gratitude. I saved your life, you know. Green Lantern was going to kill you."

This last lie was so outrageous she could only gape.

Eddie pointed toward an armoire decorated with a psychedelic explosion. "You'll find a variety of garments in your size. Please get dressed. We're returning to Earth shortly."

"Wait a minute." Too late. Without a backward glance Eddie left the room, the door irising shut behind him. Wow, indeed. She sat there clutching the sheet to her neck, head swimming. Talk about a strange date. She remembered nothing past the sudden glow that had enveloped her outside of Eddie's place. If what Eddie said were true, and that was a big if, Kyle was somewhere on this side of the gate.

What gate? God, she hated these inter-dimensional excursions! She never was good at quantum mechanics and time theory. But she was sufficiently in tune with the Starheart to recognize an alien universe. No, she wasn't nauseous, unable to extract oxygen, or puffing out like a jellyfish in reaction to local toxins. Her body could handle all of that, automatically. Her link to the Starheart enabled her to convert when traveling from positive to negative. Kyle clearly could do the same. What Eddie had told her wasn't true. Maybe *he* believed it, but she had made the switch on her own.

With a rush of guilt, she recalled hers and Kyle's last stupid argument when he'd thrust a ring at her like a morning muffin. It had been quite a ring. With a quiet jolt of belated recognition, she pictured the humongous diamond in its twenty-four karat setting. Yeah, quite a ring.

Nor had it come as a surprise. She'd been expecting something like this for months, ever since Kyle got on his marriage mount. The way he'd begged and badgered was more akin to some Victorian heroine than a member of the Justice League. The woman was supposed to do the badgering.

Jenny-Lynn loved Kyle and intended to spend the rest of her life with him. So she thought most of the time. But her nature ran counter to convention. She was no more capable of adapting societal norms than of painting the ceiling of the Sistine Chapel. She had that wild streak.

"All the good super heroes do," she said to herself. Whenever Kyle went into his marriage shtick, she invariably envisioned Ed Bundy-like scenes of domestic duplicity, ennui, and desperation. She couldn't picture herself wheeling a baby tram in the park. Two A.M. feedings. Mini-vans and car pools. And yet . . .

"Come on, girl," she growled. "Don't be a lotus eater." There was something about the place that was more than tranquil—it was anesthetizing. She had to get out of there before she fell back on the sheets and slept.

Where was Kyle? She knew he'd followed her through the gate. She could feel him somewhere nearby, but her senses were damped, as if she were trying to peer through a dense fog. Something they'd fed her? Something in the air? Or was it the place itself, its gravity and electromagnetic fields that prevented her from functioning at full capacity? No time for a shower. With an audible ping she cleansed herself. A faint green outline showed on the sheet. She got up, went to the large, hive-shaped armoire Eddie had indicated, and found it stocked floor to ceiling with soft, cottonlike garments in various styles and patterns. She quickly found what she needed, dressing in a loose-fitting cottonlike Kelly green shirt and baggy pants, more at home in a martial arts studio than a harem.

She quickly passed through the arch leading outside. She was on a patio in a garden. The garden was perfect. Shiny bushes burst from reddish soil like yellow bubble gum. Tiny violet blossoms lined the perfect bluegrass lawn, yielding only to a pathway of crushed pink coral. In a corner of the garden was a bronze monument to a space-ship. There were no birds or insects as far as Jade could see, but the scent was delicious. She placed her hands on the balustrade and inhaled. She shut her eyes, letting the scent take her back to half-remembered idylls, places she'd dreamt or visited long ago. Something blotted out the light.

She opened her eyes. The flesh-toned thing she saw was nine feet tall with a Viking's helmet. What did Kyle call them, a Weaponer? She shuddered with involuntary revulsion, took a step back from the balustrade. Not that she was afraid of it. She'd faced worse, but she had no idea what, if any, of her powers survived in this place and was not about to do anything rash. Her disintegration and reconstruc-tion as negative matter had already put an enormous strain on her system. Her body was struggling to catch up. Since she was biologi-cally linked to the Starheart, she had a limited capacity to restore herself.

The thing didn't even look at her. Just planted itself with its arms folded and stared through her at the building. Its meaning was obvi-ous. She was not permitted to leave.

"Oh yeah," she muttered. "We'll see about that." Unconsciously, she put her hand to her flat stomach. She'd felt a spasm. How long had it been since she'd eaten? She went back into the bedroom, willed the bedclothes to straighten out. They fluttered, but she was unable to control them. It was as if she had a little power, but not enough to shake a tree. She'd lost projectile dexterity. She lofted herself in the air, hovered six inches above the thick, jute-like carpet, fell lightly on the balls of her feet. When she tried to soar around the high-ceiling room she smashed into the wall. Some kind of energy damper at play.

Calmly, she sat cross-legged in the middle of the room. Yoga pos-ture. She searched herself top to bottom for an implant or injection.

Nada. She even searched her hair, teeth, toe and fingernails. She was still master of her own domain. Her body remained untouched. Whatever was affecting her performance lay in the environment.

A jolt disturbed her equilibrium. A little mental shove. *Kyle.* He was alive, and he needed her. Hope bloomed. Her eyes opened wide and green. She had to get out of there! Kyle was in trouble. She could feel his suffering in the split second the ping made contact. It had not been the kind of firm exploratory he would have launched unfettered. They were holding him down somehow. He was in pain, under enormous stress.

Without moving, or giving any outward sign, she launched her own blip. It returned a second later from a north-easterly direction. At least the damned place had magnetic poles. Without a glance toward the garden, she rose and strode to the door. Locked, of course. Did Eddie the Exterminator intend to keep her prisoner? And how in the name of Oa had he ascended to the level of—what? What was he now?

He was the new Sinestro. The Qwardians had turned Sinestro into a program to be fed into a single frame: their hero. Hal Jordan had long ago theorized that the original Sinestro had been converted into a program.

She couldn't worry about that. She had to save Kyle. In order to do that, she had to get past the Weaponer. *Hope there's only one of them*, she thought. She knew it would be useless to try and overpower, or do an end-run around the giant. With a jolt, she realized where she'd seen it before. On Earth, seconds after arriving at Eddie's house.

She'd seen what it could do on Earth. She looked around the room for a heavy object, something to throw. Her eyes fell on three smooth round stones artfully arranged at the base of a strange hearth. The smallest was the size of a chicken's egg. The largest the size of a softball. She picked them up, stuffed the smallest into one of her baggy pockets, held the others in each hand. She looked out. The Weaponer stood as before, but as she walked out onto the patio, consciously cleansing her mind of coherent thought, it glanced at her.

It was too well trained. It knew. But she was into the motion now and there was no holding back. Striding forward with her right leg she brought the softball-sized stone to shoulder level and whanged it guy-style with her left hand at the Weaponer's chest. She followed its progress, shifting the baseball-sized stone to her left hand. The first stone struck the giant dead center and momentarily staggered it. The second stone struck its metal nose cone with a sound like a gong, snapping the helmet straight back and off, leaving wires quavering like seaweed. The creature's slotlike eyes slammed shut. It began to lurch, stepping first one way then another like a robot dancer.

'*Yes!*" she crowed. "The hat! I knew it was the stupid hat!"

She soared ten feet in the air and fell on her butt in the soft grass. "Damn!" she exclaimed. There was something in the air that prevented her from flying. It wasn't just in the room, it was everywhere. She was in an alien environment. Despite her reconstruction as negative matter, she would still be susceptible to air-born pathogens, perhaps more susceptible since she'd had no opportunity to build up immunities. The Weaponer continued to lurch about, its movements becoming more frantic, an inchoate bellowing issuing from its throat.

Jen got to her feet and ran. She was barefoot. The unusually robust grass was stiff and crinkly but it didn't hurt. She sprinted through the garden to a low wall topped with an electric crackle. She looked over the wall and gasped. The city spread before her like an enormous hieroglyph. Smogless, trashless, gleaming benignly in the yellow sun, candylike vehicles flowing through its antiseptic arteries. Large patches were devoted to military vehicles and mustering. Clouds of dust hovered over armored troop carriers lined up to board enormous warships. Squads of military vehicles converged on these massive staging areas.

The city stretched to the horizon, punctuated by teased and tamed green domes that bore the air of ancient matriarchs with nothing to do but sit and gossip. She saw pedestrians. No one hurried. Everyone looked the same. If she attempted to flee she would stand out . . . nothing new there.

She couldn't simply wait for Eddie to return. She had to find Kyle. Using one hand, she bounded over the wall and scrambled awkwardly down a steep escarpment covered with shiny yellow pointed leaves. She landed on the sidewalk adjacent to the perfect street. A man came her way. He wore a caramel-colored jumpsuit, like a construction worker, but his bald pate and fringe of white hair marked him as one of the ruling elite. He smiled at her as he approached. She smiled at him.

With a prickle of apprehension, she passed him going the other way. Either they were too polite to notice, or they were accustomed to outré visitors. Jenny looked around. She needed to launch another blip to locate Kyle. Higher was better. The villa she'd just left was on a hill with countless other private homes, each shaded by bushy, yellow-leaved trees that resembled oak. There were also palmlike trees in various shades of aquamarine. It was astounding, a cartoon universe, but she couldn't take time to sight-see. She began walking up the hill. The Sidewalk was three feet wide, surfaced with some kind of smooth glossy pebble. The ground felt cool and clean to the bottoms of her feet.

As she passed smooth stucco walls guarding hidden estates, she noticed there were no gates, only elaborate markings painted on the walls hinted at access. The occasional crimson-beaked bird was the only wildlife. No nannies walking trams. Where were the children? Were there any children? With the exception of Eddie, everyone she'd seen had looked old. She walked on, consciously emulating the Qwardians' businesslike little steps. When in Rome. *Ha!* she thought. She had about as much chance blending in as Boy George at a Z.Z. Topp concert. She had no abilities beyond the blip and the ping. And she hadn't had that on Earth. Something in the atmosphere granted her that gift.

She passed a few more nicely dressed pedestrians, all of whom acknowledged her with a nod and a smile. God, they were polite. A color-blind society. Or maybe everyone was in on the joke. *Listen, there's a big green girl coming toward you. Act natural. We'll get her 'round the bend.*

There appeared to be a park ahead at the crest of the hill. The lawn was the color of ornamental copper, blushing bronze at the tips. Aquamarine fronds swayed in the gentle breeze. There was a hint of ozone in the air. From the rounded crest of the park Jenny could see down into the endless city, the march of towers past the horizon. The hill itself was covered with walled villas. And there was a child.

No more than three feet high, the chubby purple boy tumbled on the lawn under the watchful eye of a mature woman. He looked like a Teletubby. No telling their age. Jenny stared in fascination. This was the first child she'd seen. She instantly knew what had been missing—the sound of kids, laughing, shouting, crying. The city seemed dead without them. The matron regarded Jenny suspiciously. The woman smiled, but it was cold and menacing: Come near this kid and you're dead meat.

Jenny smiled reassuringly.

The lack of activity was eerie, child notwithstanding. Jenny half-expected to hear sirens and see a SWAT squad descend at any second. Not that she'd broken any law, but she was an exotic beast loose in a controlled environment. They could no more tolerate her walking around freely than Hot Springs, Idaho could permit a grizzly bear to walk down Main Street.

Well, here she was on top of a hill. Maybe the tallest hill in town. That was another thing she noticed, the sameness of the landscape. No better place to launch a blip. The telepathic bubble went forth. The woman down the hill slapped her neck as if she'd been stung. Instantaneously, the ping returned from a series of long, low buildings on the horizon, in one of the less genteel, more industrial sections of the impossibly clean city. She fixed it in her memory. It was on the edge of one of the vast military complexes. Why did they need such an enormous military presence? Were they expecting an invasion?

She may have lost her powers, but she still retained an uncanny sense of direction, her own inbuilt magnet.

What now? Hail a cab? She needed information. There was no one to give it. Except the matron. Putting on her best Julia Roberts smile, Jenny rose to her feet and approached the woman who sat on a wood bench not far from her charge, ready to pounce. Jenny prayed her JSA translator was working. She unconsciously touched the implant behind her right ear.

"Hello!" she sang. "Isn't it a lovely day?"

The woman stared at her as if she were a bug. Jenny experienced the sinking sensation that the translator was not working. Probably fried its circuits passing through the gate.

"It is not a bad day, but tomorrow will be better," the woman finally replied in a mellifluous sing-song. She didn't crack a smile.

"I'm sorry to bother you, but I'm a visitor to your fair planet."

"I would not have guessed," the woman replied without blinking.

"How do I get around the city? Is there some form of public transportation?"

"If you wish to return to Central stroll down the hill and signal for a purple cab."

"A purple cab."

"Yes."

"How do I do that?"

The woman bounced to her feet, threw out one arm in what looked like a Hitler salute and barked a multi-phonic chord that gave Jenny a headache. She smiled briefly and sat. "Thus."

Jade smiled back. "I don't think I can do that. What if I just hold my hand out like this?" Jade offered the standard New Yorker's finger.

The woman nodded. "They will recognize your intent."

"Thanks," Jen said. "That's a cute kid you've got there."

"I have always thought he resembled a breadfruit," the woman replied, returning to her charge.

I didn't know they had breadfruit here, Jenny thought as she strolled down the hill. She could see all the way to the main thoroughfare, approximately a half-mile distant. Curiously there were no pedestrians whatsoever. Halfway between her and the main thoroughfare, a large figure appeared rounding the corner and striding toward her in seven-league boots.

28

O h, no," she gasped. The Weaponer. Or another one. They appeared to be identical, and this one was wearing its hat. There was a disturbance in the air behind her. She turned. A second Weaponer, identical to the first right down to the yellow speedos and the nose-cone helmet. She noticed in passing they had no nipples. Their smooth muscular chests looked like plastic.

She stopped between them. It was pointless to run. Where could she go that they couldn't follow? At the same time she sensed that they were reluctant to harm her. She realized that this almost certainly had something to do with Eddie. And that gave her an advantage. "Where you guys get your clothes? Erik the Red's?"

The Weaponer coming up the hill toward her, which she thought of as Uphill Erik, to differentiate him from Downhill Erik, raised his right hand and pointed a bratwurst-sized finger at her. "You must return with us." His voice was surprisingly mellifluous.

"O-kay," she said, waiting for Downhill Erik to reach her. She was hemmed in, the two giants a few yards apart and still closing. Then she took a step toward Uphill Erik, using his extended thigh as a springboard to gain altitude, and became a human pinball. She landed on Downhill Erik's chest, kicked off and whacked Uphill Erik smack in the helmet. She let her foot fall to his collarbone, stood on it and lashed out behind her with a back kick.

Bingo. She took off Downhill Erik's helmet with a sound like adhesive tape ripped off a package. The two Eriks started to smoke and stagger like bad robots. Downhill's helmet rolled down hill. Uphill's rolled against a fence.

Jenny landed on the balls of her feet, scooped Uphill's helmet and ran toward the street. After a second, she looked behind her. The Weaponers were on their hands and knees on the sidewalk as though looking for contact lenses. She couldn't see the second helmet. With any luck it had rolled down a sewer grate.

The helmet was heavy. She looked inside. The domed interior was designed to plug into several leads extending from the Weaponers' skulls. It was packed with micro-circuitry and tiny glowing points. She had a wild urge to put it on. Oh yeah. Talk about your document dump!

Not my style, she thought, reaching the street. But she wasn't about to ditch it—it might come in handy. Leather straps retracted into the sides. She pulled them out, fastened them to make a handle and carried the helmet like a purse. She was on the main road now, purple capsules zipping past a foot above the smooth rose-colored pavement. Before stepping to the curb she looked up and down the broad thoroughfare. The few pedestrians were scattered far and wide.

She stepped off the curb and held up a hand in the universal gesture. Within a minute, a lozenge-shaped vehicle had zipped soundlessly to the curb, lifting a gull wing door in greeting. Toting the helmet, she got in. The car rocked once like a rowboat before righting itself. The gullwing closed, leaving no seam. She could see out in all directions through a single continuous wraparound window. She was the only occupant. There were no badges, licenses, or vehicle ID's. There was no telephone number to call for complaints.

"Where to?" rang in her head.

"I don't know the address," she replied. "But I can picture it in my mind."

With the sound of a cork leaving a bottle, a circular rubber device popped from the ceiling on a shiny metal stalk. "Place the bowl against your forehead and picture your destination," the vehicle said.

She did so. Instantly, the industrial complex she'd glimpsed from the top of the hill occupied the front of the windscreen. "That is the Green Lantern Detention Center. It is off limits to off-worlders."

"Does that include Green Lanterns?"

"No."

"Are you going to take me or do I have to find another cab?"

Soundlessly, seemingly without inertia, the cab pulled away from the curb and joined the flow of traffic. "No need to take offense," it said. "I am required by law to state these facts."

"Do you get many off-worlders here?"

"Quite a few. But they mostly confine themselves to the city center."

"How 'bout them Rangers?"

"Excuse me?"

"Never mind."

The taxi fell silent. She looked around for a badge number and a picture. Nada. Maybe they didn't have taxi crime here. No maybe about it. They didn't have crime here at all. Unless it was government sanctioned.

A moment later the cab pulled to the gleaming curb outside a series of low stucco buildings. The gullwing door opened. Jenny sat there. "Whom do I pay?"

"The service is provided by the Qwardians, qomrade. Have a nice day."

"Yeah. You too." She got out of the cab and looked around. Both sides of the broad thoroughfare were filled with low, light industry type buildings, many topped with fantastic arrays of antennae: Alexander Calder meets Atlanta Cutlery. The smooth stucco fronts were painted in brilliant tribal patterns, crimson, gold, aquamarine, black—every color in the rainbow except green. A few pedestrians in gunmetal jumpsuits ambled with unhurried pace from building to building. Each hundred yards or so was a little park replete with swaying fronds in which citizens sat and chewed the fat. Way down the street, the unmistakable profile of a Weaponer headed her way.

She faced the building she'd seen. Here at last was a patch of green. The dread Green Lantern logo in a black circle with a line through it, the intergalactic symbol of the banned. An elaborate circular pattern that reminded her of a Tibetan mandela dominated the façade. She placed the flat of her palm against the wall. Nada. She suddenly remembered she was still toting the damned helmet! How could she have forgotten? It weighed close to ten pounds.

"This could kill my modeling career," she said, placing the gleaming helmet on her head. It was heavy and tingled, and she had to hold absolutely still so it wouldn't fall off. But at least it wasn't squirting her full of evil alien enzymes. She felt like she was trying out for *Der Ring des Nibelungen*. She cleared her throat operatically and sang a few arias. "I'm going to kiww the, kiww the wabbit," she sang in Elmer Fudd's voice. She placed the flat of her palm against the wall and an opening immediately spiraled outward. She stepped into a white-tiled corridor with a clear view of the street, as if the outside edifice weren't stucco but glass.

A Weaponer looked at her from his desk just inside the entrance. He looked through her. He raised a hand in greeting and went back to reading. Jenny craned her neck. The thing he was reading was tri-angular and sparkled like Hong Kong at night. Maybe he wasn't reading.

Jenny pulled the little straps down and fastened the helmet around her head. The thing weighed a ton. Carnival time. Apparently the helmet gave her some kind of immunity. The Weaponers seemed unable to distinguish their elbows from holes in the ground.

"Whatever," she said, launching another blip. The ping returned instantly, guiding her through a series of security gates toward the center of the structure. Midway through a darkened gallery she stopped, frozen in horror. Behind a transparent plate hung the skeletal remains of a Green Lantern, its green uniform clinging in tatters. At least it wasn't human. Jenny shuddered. This building was dedicated to the torment and death of Green Lanterns. *Kyle*! she blipped. There was no answer. She might already be too late.

No! she raged against herself. She mustn't think like that! In that instant she realized how much she loved him, how much she needed him, and what a fool she'd been playing up to Eddie.

What a fool! What a silly, empty-headed little-girl thing to do. Because she was bored and annoyed.

The door at the end of the corridor opened and one of the little red men entered. He stopped when he saw her. "You are in the wrong building," he said with a trace of panic.

Jenny was already in motion. His eyes widened in terror as she lofted herself in the air, turned sideways, and smacked his head into the door with a flying sidekick. He bounced back like a high rebound and hit the floor on his face.

"Sorry about that," she said, landing lightly on her feet. She didn't have much time. She knelt, felt for a pulse. Yes, the little sadist was still breathing. Without a backward glance she pushed through the door he'd come through and found herself in a chamber of horror.

The circular room was lined with transparent cylinders, like the columns of a temple. The columns were filled with a viscous, translucent, roseate fluid. Suspended in the fluid were four shapes. Not all the cylinders were occupied. She sensed movement, a desperate, spastic twitching motion. The viscous fluid momentarily cleared and Kyle stared at her with desperate, pleading eyes.

Controlling her panic, she swept the cylinder for controls. They were utterly alien. She dared not touch anything for fear it would only increase his agony. That he was in pain was obvious. He tried to stretch, twitching like some hideous perversion of life.

"Don't move!" she cried, going to the cylinder and placing her hands on it. "Don't move, my love. I'll get you out of here, just don't panic."

Something warm and sinuous snaked around her waist, yanking her back. She looked down. She had been seized by some kind of magenta energy beam. She twisted and beheld the grinning, beet-faced Eddie, now wearing a skintight costume. Black and blue. Where had she seen it before?

Instead of resisting Eddie's power beam she went with it, kicking off from the floor, hurling in midair, reaching out to rake his eyes with her fingers. He held her inches away. "I should have known you were too perverted to appreciate what I was offering."

She hung there like a kitten, trying to reach his eyes. Her efforts seemed to amuse him. "You're not going to save your boyfriend. He's going to hang there until he dies. Then we're going to finish deprogramming his ring and use that data to find and destroy any other Green Lanterns still living in this galaxy."

She gasped. Her father was the *only* other Green Lantern in the galaxy, and although Eddie couldn't know that, Sinestro would. She couldn't allow that to happen, but what could she do? She felt helpless in Eddie's mental grasp. His power had increased exponentially. Hers had dwindled.

He grinned at her. "Nice hat. You look ridiculous."

The hat. It weighed a ton. She grabbed the strap beneath her chin and pulled it loose. Twisting in Eddie's grasp she swung the helm like a mace and let go straight at Kyle's cylinder. It struck the cylinder with the tapered point.

The cylinder cracked and began to spew fluid. Klaxons sounded with skull-imploding force. Suddenly Jenny was out of the building, helpless in Eddie's grip as they soared straight up. A half dozen Weaponers converged on the building.

It was up to Kyle now.

CHAPTER
29

He saw her through a haze of pain and nausea like a green oasis. They hadn't anticipated that much green entering the chamber. She beckoned to him like the Sun itself. And then, when she let fly with the helmet, he wanted to kiss her. He would kiss her. But first he had to get out of the prison in which they'd placed him.

The exterminator, who Kyle now recognized as a Sinestro-in-training, took off at the first sign of trouble, choosing to let the Weaponers control the rogue Green Lantern. It was the smart move. Kyle would have stayed and taken care of business himself. Maybe this Eddie, this Junior Sinestro, was something of a coward. Kyle would dearly love to find out.

First, he had to free himself. He was nearly exhausted, his reserves of energy all but depleted. The ring was useless. He'd used the last of its energy to launch the final ping. But the cylinder had been breached. The way it spewed fluid across the room, he knew it was under extreme pressure. Summoning whatever reserves of energy he had left, little more than adrenaline and desperation, he twisted one more time, lashing out with his feet, bracing his upper body against the roof.

As the first Weaponer entered the room the cylinder exploded, dumping Kyle on the slick ceramic floor. The rush of purple gel caught the Weaponer by surprise, depositing the giant on its tailbone with a jarring thud. Kyle tried desperately to get to his feet but he was weak as a newborn kitten. The Weaponer sat and smiled. *Where you going, buddy?*

Kyle felt a jolt, a frisson of power tingling his ring finger. He looked down to where his hand was spread palm-down on the floor. He was feeling something *through* the floor, a source of energy. Of course! All these Green Lanterns, they had to siphon the energy off to somewhere. There had to be a central battery in the prison.

Kyle lay face down on the floor with his arms spread. *Give it to me*, he willed, seeking whatever residual energy was escaping. He spread his body as flat as possible, trying to expose as much of himself as he could to the trickle of raw energy. Its flow was like a gigantic static shock, nearly lifting him off the floor. The Weaponer's eyes narrowed to buttonholes as it scrambled to its feet, reaching for a bolt.

Too late! Like a boxer getting his second wind, Kyle felt energized. His extremities tingled as if blood were rushing back to them after they'd fallen asleep. He leaped in the air and lashed out with a roundhouse kick, snapping the Weaponer's helmet off its head.

Ouch! It felt like he'd kicked an oak, but it worked. As soon as Jen had appeared with a helmet in her hands he'd intuited that the Weaponers could be disarmed. Why hadn't he seen it before? The helmets served no obvious functional purpose—they had to be tech.

Kyle dove through the floor like smoke through a fissure, finding himself in a sealed chamber not unlike the reactor core on a submarine. Only in the center of the core, instead of a nuclear fuel and rods, was a Green Lantern power battery! A very old design—older even than the one Alan Scott had used. Somehow, the Qwardians had harnessed one lantern as a slave unit in which to store the life energy they'd stolen. It was residual Green Lantern energy that now sustained Qward. He instantly intuited their purpose in gaining access to the posimatter universe. They wanted, Earth, yes. But they also craved the few remaining lanterns—perhaps even the main power battery on Oa—as a source of energy!

Who knew how long the lantern had been used for its sinister purpose? How much energy could it possibly hold? It was, after all, a battery. There were limits to what a battery could store. Batteries didn't create energy, they merely held it. Moreover, they were in the Qwardian universe. No telling what that might do.

Kyle could sense energy swirling all around him. This laboratory was now the focus of whatever passed for law enforcement on Qward—Weaponers were converging from all points. He could "see" them as if he were perched above the building looking down. The lantern containment chamber was a large ovoid cylinder, translucent and amber. But Kyle could feel the green inside reaching out to him. He extended his ring.

The containment capsule pulsed dull yellow once, a heavy blink. A dot of green burst from a whisper to a scream as the stored energy of eons rushed forth in a single zap. Emerald light arced into Kyle's ring. Green St. Elmo's fire embraced him. It dove through his skin like rain into parched earth. In a nanosecond he was fully charged, the torment of the previous hours a dim memory to be brought forth at a later date for examination.

I live! he raged. *I breath! I will see our son grow to manhood!*

He paused, panting, and willed the ring to reconstitute his costume. It grew from his neck down in a single seamless burst.

The steady pounding on the chamber's thick metal door could not be ignored. He was standing inside a massive drum. The Weaponers systematically assaulted the door with a bludgeon. He pictured them swinging one of their own, head-first. Kyle guessed that his escape and the subsequent energy surge had shut down power in the neighborhood, if not the city. If not the planet. They must be having a Green Alert out there. It was funny. On Earth they'd call it a Red Alert. Condition Red, the highest state of readiness and alarm. But like Australia or the Bizarro World, the Qwardians chose green as the color most indicative of tension and danger.

WHOOM. WHOOM. WHOOM. The metal door began to buckle. It was hexagonal, ten feet in diameter, and made of some metal Kyle couldn't recognize by touch or scan. But when he put his hand against it it felt familiar. It was made of the same material as the wrecked probe circling Saturn.

Anti-matter.

Why didn't it explode on touch? How could he survive in an anti-matter universe? There could only be one explanation. His ring had reacted to the qualities of the gate, instantly breaking him down into molecular components and reconstructing him on the other side. In reverse. Jen's connection to the Starheart must have caused the same reaction.

WHOOM. WHOOM. WHOOM. The middle of the massive gate peaked. Brilliant yellow light licked through a tear like a snake's tongue. The Weaponers were using energy bolts. Each subsequent bolt caused the rift to widen. They'd be inside in seconds.

Kyle left the way he'd entered, through the ceiling, projecting himself through the circuitry that had gathered energy from the dying Green Lanterns. He emerged in the lab, coalescing in the middle of the floor. Two Weaponers and two Qwardians looked at him with distaste. The Weaponers simultaneously loosed their bolts. The bolts collided where Kyle had been, exploding and setting off a chain reaction that began to spread through the building.

Kyle watched from two miles up. It was terrible and beautiful, like the lava flow at Mauna Kea. Only this had nothing to do with nature. The Qwardians had long since buried nature. Flame erupted through the prison's perfectly smooth facades, spreading under the thorough-fares, causing the streets to heave and buckle. It spread outward like ripples in a pond, an ever-expanding circle of fireworks.

Ululating klaxons sounded from every point of the compass. Emergency vehicles began to converge. Invisible beams stabbed at him. For all their seeming middle-class indifference, the Qwardians were not without serious self-defense. A series of dart-shaped ceramic craft rose from platforms circling the city and headed his way. Kyle did not stick around to wait for them. He booked toward space, launching a ping in his wake.

Where was Jen?

One vector bounced back strong, its trace ending in what appeared to be a residential unit. Kyle committed the location to memory before turning his attention to the fighters closing in on him. He could detect no one on board. They were using drones as if he were some kind of bug. His heart filled with rage for Eddie the Exterminator. Yellow particle beams converged where he'd been a split-second earlier, creating a miniature sun over the city. One of the commanding spires began to melt.

Green Lantern was gone. He conceived a plan the moment the arrowhead-shaped vehicles rose from their ports and with exquisite timing permitted them to fire to create a diversion. Using refracted light as a cloaking device, he sank to street level and zeroed in on Jen's trace vector.

It appeared to be a plush residential neighborhood with opulent villas surrounded by seven-foot walls covered with striking patterns. There were no doors or gates. The walls themselves moved to permit entry. The place where she had stayed would have been obvious to any Green Lantern. A faint green glow hovered over the property. Kyle leaped effortlessly over the wall to find a Weaponer on hands and knees in the garden, wires dangling from its denuded scalp. It rummaged through the bushes as if searching for keys. The thing didn't even look up as Kyle passed it on his way into the house.

Cold fury seized him when he came to the bedroom. The big round bed spread with pale green sheets and what looked like rose petals, her scent everywhere. And *his*—that scum, the exterminator, the new Sinestro. Kyle had glimpsed Eddie's new coloration in the lab. Of course. That's what this was all about. Grooming a new Sinestro to open up Earth for invasion. He should have realized it the instant Eddie had manifested his own power ring.

What did Jenny have to do with this? And where was she? *Calm yourself man*, he heard Hal Jordan say. You know she loves you. She risked her life to save you! The danger now wasn't that Jen would fall in love with Eddie.

As if. The danger now was that Eddie would hate Jen and try to destroy her.

With the clarity of super-vision, Kyle realized he'd been a perfect jerk, demanding she answer his proposal. And her carrying his child! She had been wrestling with questions of cosmic responsibility, weighing her needs and desires as a biological entity against her duties. Most people didn't choose to become parents. But she had chosen to become a super hero. Where did their kid fit into the big picture?

With a jolt of pure satori, Kyle realized the kid was paramount. Whatever happened, the kid came first. They were, after all, creatures of nature and the first obligation of biology was perpetuation of the species.

The image of the fresh-scrubbed Spire Raines popped into his head. Holy Moly and Shazam. Spire Raines was possibly his great-to-the-nth power grandson!

Spire Raines might even be his and Jen's son.

Klaxons sounded as Weaponers converged on the villa.

They had found him.

30

K yle glanced out the window. The Weaponer continued to comb the shrubs for his hat. Kyle dragged his gaze inside and forced himself to scan the room for a clue. His broadband view reflected countless glittering microscopic elements dancing in the yellow sun. They cast the same hue as the debris he'd discovered on Saturn.

Well, duh. He should have guessed that the probe had come from the Qwardian universe! Traces of anti-matter everywhere. Now his girl was mixed up in their sick plan, thanks to Eddie, the new Sinestro.

A Weaponer appeared in the doorway, raised his hand and loosed a bolt. Without thinking, Kyle held up one hand, a glowing green nimbus forming a shield that scattered the bolt. Shards of energy pierced the walls. He flicked the Weaponer from the room with an immense green finger.

"That's right, pinhead," he exulted. "You didn't expect this. I've got the juice you've been draining from all the Lanterns you murdered."

He felt more powerful than when he'd been Ion. As Ion, he'd operated on a macro-scale without the satisfaction of hands-on labor. Now he had a unique opportunity to deliver a message to the Qwardians. For one fleeting second he toyed with the idea of nuking the planet. He could do it. End the Qwardian threat once and for all. Elegance and simplicity. He could insert his power into the core and blow it up like a bubble, bursting the planet apart. He felt that strong. Subconsciously, he began to power up.

That's not the way, Hal Jordan whispered. Startled, Kyle looked around. Was Jordan here? No. It was his conscience. Or the Green Lantern charter, which expressly forbid species extermination. It was one of the thousands of moral restraints that civilized people adopt.

The curving wall melted at one-hundred-and-twenty-degree intervals, revealing three Weaponers. They fired their bolts. Laughing, Kyle spun straight up through the ceiling, boring a hole as round as an augur, ignoring the pinprick irritation of the bolts.

"I am *juiced!*" he exulted, flying over the city, backtracking the exterminator's radiation trail. From an altitude of several thousand feet he spotted a large open area crawling with activity. He was over it instantaneously. One hundred thousand Weaponers were lining up in formation. Five hundred gleaming shark-shaped ships waited to receive them. Each Weaponer carried a pack the size of a washing machine. These Weaponers were clothed in protective gear, like a SWAT squad.

They were preparing for invasion.

Kyle was once again seized by an overwhelming urge to let loose—rain fire on the whole field. Fry them where they stand. It would only be a symbolic victory. The Weaponers weren't people. They were weapons designed to look like people and the Qwardians could punch them out quicker than doughnuts. It would only harden their resolve.

For millennia, one thing and one thing alone had prevented the Qwardians from invading Earth. The barrier. It would do no good to destroy the Qwardians on this side of the barrier. For Earth to live, the barrier must stand. He flicked back to the vector he'd been following.

It led to an immense government complex built around a vast, intricately decorated dome, the center of government. Government was in session. Kyle could sense the myriad bodies in concentric circles through the walls. Government was *always* in session. The Qwardians were nothing *but* government backed by an iron fist.

Kyle knew what they wanted. Same thing they always wanted: Death to Green Lanterns and more space for themselves. Having thoroughly screwed up their native environment, they were looking for new digs. The exterminator was their Pathfinder, their Sacajawea, their Wild Bill Cody. Eddie, the new Sinestro.

Arrogant creeps. They were in for a surprise. Executing a perfect seven hundred and twenty-degree coaxial twist, he dove for their Parliament. He fell through its skylight and coalesced on the podium next to a dapper little dude who was talking monetary policy. The sudden appearance of their most hated enemy in the very heart of their empire elicited a collective gasp that almost sucked all the air out of the chamber.

The speaker fell back, ashen-faced.

In your face, Qwardians. Grinning fiercely, Green Lantern gripped the polished wood balustrade surrounding the dais. "You know who I am. You brought me here to kill me. I shouldn't even be alive. You had me where you wanted me. But you blew it. Now I stand at the center of your world, impervious and unassailable. Imagine what will befall you on the other side, where other Green Lanterns are waiting along with super heroes you can never hope to defeat. You'll never take our universe. Stay home!"

Thumping his right fist to his chest, he spiraled upward into the sky, into the range of five crimson dart-shaped drones. He was too fast for them; he was twenty miles away when they collided. Crimson darts converged from all over the city. All over the planet. They launched weapons—broad channel rays designed to upset his molecular structure, particle beams to pierce his organs, poison gas to seize his nervous sytem.

None of it mattered. He had absorbed too much power from the Qwardians' captive battery. Maintaining a random orbit to avoid missiles, Kyle blipped the city looking for Jen. Gone. Off planet. Sinestro had her. He blipped for Sinestro. He, too, was gone.

There could be only one Sinestro, the ring told him. The program now inhabited Eddie.

Kyle had to find the transfer gate and return to his home universe.

The ping came back instantly from the only logical place, the lab where he'd been held in the Green Lantern prison, now teeming with the Qwardian equivalent of forensic specialists and cops. These came in two packages: wizened little guys with gray skin and Weaponers. Emergency vehicles surrounded the now devastated building, forming a beetle-like carapace in the air. Black smoke rose in fat skunk tails to the ochre sky. Green Lantern flowed among the cars like a smoke snake.

The lab was a burnt-out hulk. It reminded him of the abandoned warehouse on the other side of the gate, the one through which he'd visited the Zip-a-tone planet and met Spire Raines. He used the refracted light trick to render himself invisible but he must have triggered something on one of the sensors. Within seconds of landing on the lower level, a Weaponer looked up from a hand-held device and pointed directly at him. A Qwardian cop followed the Weaponer's finger, put on a pair of round goggles with a gnurled adjustment next to each lens.

"You. Green Lantern," he said in a snippy little voice. "I see you."

"Gold star for the midget. Where's the gate back to Earth? I'm checking out."

Several other Qwardians noticed and leaned over the makeshift barriers from the upper levels to watch. The Weaponer remained where he was. He could fire a bolt at any instant from any part of his anatomy.

"What makes you think we'll just let you walk out of here?"

"What makes you think you can hold me? Look what I did last time. I suggest we call a temporary truce. I can do a lot more damage here if you want. All I'm asking is for you to politely show me the way out. I'm tired and I want to go home."

The Qwardians froze. They seemed to be having a mental summit. The only part of them that moved was their foreheads. The Weaponer snorted in disgust and chewed on his mustache. The first Qwardian to have seen him pointed to a pattern on the curving wall behind Kyle that had survived the fire. When Kyle turned, the pattern irised open revealing a corridor that ended in a large, dark chamber from which an eerie glow spilled.

"The staging area lies at the end of the corridor. The gate to Earth is clearly marked."

Kyle saluted and ducked through the opening. It closed immediately, leaving him in the darkened corridor lit by a series of tiny floor lamps like miniature landing lights. The corridor ended in a large ovoid chamber that reminded Kyle of a train station. Twelve rhomboid apertures were set in the wall around the perimeter a few feety above the floor. Above each glowing opening appeared a symbol. The symbol for Earth was green and blue and showed the North American continent. It could have been taken by NASA. Another symbol was clearly Saturn.

An instant before he dove through the gate, he willed the eleven other gates to collapse. His last glimpse of Qward was of chaos and explosions.

CHAPTER

31

Jenny-Lynn remembered nothing of the journey from Earth to Qward, but the journey back was a nightmare. She felt as if she'd been stretched, twisted, torn apart and put back together with parts that didn't quite fit. A python coiled around her waist, holding her fast in Sinestro's grip.

Eddie *was* Sinestro now. The transformation was complete. He was eight feet tall. His skin had turned pulp purple, the color of a high school newspaper called *The Crimson Tide*. There was a sinister cast to his features. What had seemed charming and boyish had turned devious and truculent. Jenny caught him looking at her sideways, the way one looks at a mess on the floor.

They had emerged from a wormhole in the vastness between Sol and Alpha Centauri. Jen got the impression that Eddie had miscalculated and was unhappy with himself. He had not intended to emerge so far from home. She didn't speak as he dove toward Earth trailing Jade like a U-haul. Their passage through space may have taken hours. It may have taken days. There was no way to tell. Time ceased to have meaning out here, without the passage of the Sun. The spectacular view seldom changed.

"Eddie," she said, knowing her words reached him through the energy conduit that linked them. There was no response. When she tried again he shook her once, like you'd shake a naughty puppy. It made her nauseous. She shut up and enjoyed the view, protected by Sinestro's energy. If that failed, her own system would kick in but she'd be stranded a million miles from nowhere with no way of getting home. She was at Sinestro's mercy. A bad place to be.

Tentative telepathic forays ran into a brick wall. Eddie Rocheford may not have been the sharpest knife in the drawer, but the Sinestro ring came with a lot of software. The Qwardians had found a way to preserve the original Sinestro's personality. For all intents and purposes this was the same Sinestro her father had fought. And Hal Jordan, Green Arrow, and Black Canary. In fact, Sinestro might be nothing more than a sophisticated program whose mission never changed: Kill the Green Lanterns. Take over Earth.

They stopped, relative to the Sun. Sinestro had taken a fixed orbital position over Saturn. The enormous gas giant spread beneath them like God's own aggie. In the game of cosmic marbles, only Jupiter was bigger. She craned her head, observing the moons Titan, Rhea, and Janus. Sinestro floated like a dead man, staring down into the swirling atmospheric horror. He extended his ring and cast a pale cone downward. His fingers were longer, more attenuated than Eddie's, like a human spider.

He was looking for something. Jenny became aware they were moving, criss-crossing the planet. At this rate, she thought, we should be done in twenty-five million years. The creature seemed preoccupied.

"Psst!" she said. No response. "Sinestro," she said. Nothing.

"Eddie."

He was totally absorbed in his task.

Now or never, she thought. While his attention is elsewhere. She might not get another change. She spoke the name Sinestro must not hear.

"Kyle," she blipped, spanning the known universe. Telepathy was a powerful tool but the human mind was only so strong. Like a tiny battery, it pumped its message into the universe praying for a response, like a note in a bottle. As the message expanded and fled its source it became exponentially weaker with each passing mile.

Jenny's message disappeared like a pebble in the Atlantic.

Abruptly, she had trouble breathing. The massive coils enclosed her neck. Sinestro did not even favor her with a glance. His entire demeanor was focused on the search.

"Please," Jenny gasped. The coils released her. She pulled in a hawser of breath, rubbed her throat with her hands. She willed her throat back to normal. Slowly, like a heavy blink, her body responded.

Dreamlike, her captor seemed to coalesce before her, grinning. She could still see a hint of the charming young man who'd come to kill roaches. "Eddie," she gasped.

"Eddie doesn't live here anymore. Do you see the debris? Do you see it?" He grabbed her tightly by the back of her head, forcing her to look down. A cone of yellow light extended from his ring, illuminating a trail of glittering space flotsam that went on for hundreds of miles.

"Two hundred million years ago a group of peaceful explorers tried to enter your solar system. They were the kindest, gentlest people the universe has ever known, and they were viciously attacked. By your father."

Jen's head whipped up, eyes fierce. "That's a lie! My father has never killed anyone! Oh Eddie, what have they done to you?"

"You love your father. I respect that. But the truth is the Green Lantern Corps is a criminal organization formed by the so-called Guardians to prevent the Qwardians from surviving."

"No one is trying to prevent the Qwardians from surviving! Why don't they find a world in their own damned universe?"

The blow came so swiftly she didn't see it. Only a hot, stinging sensation on her cheek and the ghost of a report in the thin shell of air that encased them. Her response was automatic. She kicked the bastard right between the legs.

Imbued as he was with the power of Sinestro, he was still vulnerable to an attack, particularly coming from within his own forcefield. Sinestro's eyes bulged like ping-pong balls. He floated back, doubled over, breathing shallowly through his gun barrel mouth.

Jen waited, breathless. She didn't regret striking him. It had happened so quickly she hadn't had time to grow fearful.

If he's going to kill me, I'm ready.

Sinestro gingerly straightened and regarded her with a wry smile. "Good one," he said. "It's a shame you're in love with that freak. He's a killer too, you know. All the Green Lanterns are killers."

She looked toward Arcturus, gleaming red in the sky. "Why are you showing me this space junk?"

"I want you to understand."

"Why? What do you care? Do you think we're going to be boy-friend/girlfriend? You're not even human anymore."

His rictus smile frightened her. "I want you to understand the per-fidy of the Green Lantern Corps. It and it alone is responsible for the bulk of human suffering over the millennia."

"How is that possible? My father was the first Green Lantern on Earth. He didn't appear until 1940. How can you blame the bulk of human suffering on the Green Lanterns?"

Sinestro's eyes bulged like hard-boiled eggs. "The bulk of human suffering has occurred since 1940, has it not? Had the Japanese won the war . . ."

Jenny-Lynn barked in disbelief. "Eddie, what are you talking about? Hasn't it occurred to you that the Qwardians have fed you a line of bull? I mean, you're a human being. You're not Qwardian. They've got you betraying your own planet."

Sinestro bristled. "There is a higher responsibility, you know."

"I can't imagine what it is."

"The ideal of cosmic justice."

"Oh, Eddie." She laughed.

Enraged, Sinestro seized her in a crimson coil and dragged her like a reluctant cur down into the toxic atmosphere. Debris lay in clumps. Monstrous buzzing filled the thick, foggy atmosphere. He shoved her face to within six inches of an object that at first she couldn't identify, something burnt and twisted. With a sickening jolt she realized it was a Qwardian corpse, eye sockets staring sightlessly back at her.

"You see?" Sinestro hissed. "You see what your father did?"

Amid the din of Saturn's shrieking winds, the blip was all but lost. So faint she almost missed it, but not quite. Hope swelled like a nova. She looked quickly at Sinestro to see if he'd heard it, too. But he was too involved in his anger and hadn't heard it.

Green Lantern had just reentered Earth's atmosphere.

CHAPTER

32

G reen Lantern came out on the fifth floor of the abandoned Gotham warehouse. Was it the same gate he'd used on the Jersey Palisades? Did that mean the gates were mobile? And if so, did they have predetermined fixed positions? Or were the Qwardians able to access a number of gates on Earth? Perhaps the outlet gate was strictly a matter of chance, or involved some automatic selection process.

Green Lantern stared at the free-floating rhomboid, a bubble of white noise in the otherwise dark and silent building. As he watched, it dwindled to nothing and blinked out. He used his ring to illuminate the closet where the Shamrocks had holed up. Nothing. It was just an abandoned closet devoid of meaningful radiation.

Hoping against hope, he rocketed out of the building, shot like an arrow toward Manhattan. *Please let Jen be home when I arrive*, he prayed. In his fear, he didn't notice an Aer Lingus skybus until the JLA satellite informed him that fighters were scrambling to intercept him. He had to take ten minutes to explain to the Air Force and Homeland Security, holding steady while the fighters buzzed him.

He felt like a speeder who'd just got a warning as he resumed flight at reduced speed and lower altitude. He could have ignored the Air Force and Homeland Security. But that would have violated the understanding. He could hear Jen's cat wailing from two floors below when he landed on the roof. Kyle took the steps three at a time, let himself into the apartment. Mauser meowed accusingly.

Kyle knew instantly that the apartment was empty. He checked all the rooms anyway. He refilled the cat's water and food and was about to contact the JLA when the phone rang.

"Where the devil's my daughter, Rayner?" Alan Scott boomed from Gotham.

Kyle instantly felt like a feckless child caught in a misdemeanor. He had lost the man's daughter. Except he hadn't. Sinestro had. "Sir, I'm working on it. She must be trapped in the Qwardian universe."

"What?"

"Sir, the Qwardians seem to have found a champion here on Earth to become the new Sinestro. This guy they chose, we knew him. He was the exterminator for our co-op."

"What are you telling me, son? The Qwardians have taken some laborer and turned him into the new Sinestro?"

"Exactly."

He could hear Scott grinding his teeth over the phone. "Sir, please stay where you are. There's nothing you can do that I and the rest of the Justice League can't."

"Have they been informed?"

"I was about to when you phoned."

"All right. I'm in my office. I want you to get in touch with the Justice League and call me right back. Will you do that?"

"Yes, sir."

Kyle used the desktop to contact the JLA satellite. Eel O'Brien peered back at him. "What's shakin', Jim?"

"You still solo?"

"Until my wayward sheep come home. What's up?"

Kyle explained the situation. He'd searched for Jenny but couldn't find her.

"Not so fast, Jim," O'Brien said. "I have a reading here indicates she might be on Saturn, although it's hard to tell—some kind of negative energy is blocking her signal."

Kyle's pulse quickened. Hope leaped to his throat. "Are you getting two readings?" he asked softly.

"Only one that's human. I got another reading here but it's an energy sink. Could be a wormhole. I don't see how she could maintain that close to a wormhole, but we just had the system checked out. If what you say is true . . ."

"We're looking at a possible Qwardian invasion," Kyle finished for him.

O'Brien's eyebrows went spastic. "Perhaps I'd better put out an alert."

"I don't want you pulling members off jobs on my say-so. I can still stop it by shutting down Sinestro. He's the key that allows them to convert to positive matter."

"You and what army, boyo?"

"Don't sell me short."

"I'm jerkin' your gherkin, Jim. Wasn't Sinestro discombobulated?"

"Yeah—he *was* dead. Hal Jordan killed him when he went crazy, before he became Parallax and the Spectre. But the Qwardians have created a new one. Apparently there can only be one at a time. They've been working on generating a human candidate for decades. They seem to have found their man. Guy used to be Eddie Rocheford."

O'Brien shrugged. "Doesn't ring a bell."

"He's a nobody," Kyle snarled with unexpected vehemence. "That sample I sent you, that stuff is all over the Qwardian universe. Looks like they tried to turn Saturn at some point."

"Turn?"

"Generate enough anti-matter through a gate to start a chain reaction."

O'Brien did an elaborate flop and double-take that took him out of the picture for a second. "Isn't that dangerous?"

Kyle nodded. "Yeah. It would screw up everything's electromagnetic field. And possible upset the orbits of the entire solar system, in which case Earth would readjust at a level not conducive to life. At least not *our* lives. *And* inadvertently detonate our stockpile of nuclear weapons. Now they have a new plan that doesn't involve blowing up the universe. They want to take over. If they succeed in opening a gate on Saturn, it's going to be Doomsday Times Nine down here on Earth."

O'Brien cringed with each revelation until he'd stretched himself so far back Kyle was afraid he would snap and hit the monitor. "They're idiots," he said.

"They're trying to create an electromagnetic shell that would encase the whole planet. They'll pop out on Saturn and be instantly transported to Earth."

"Why not open a gate on Earth?"

"Something about electromagnetic fields. They've been trying to establish a base on Saturn for eons. Once they get established they'll use it as a staging area to invade Earth, never mind the consequences. Their hatred has blinded them to science. It's been growing unchecked for years on their creepy Stepford planet. Far as they're concerned, the Green Lantern Corps are the Anti-Christ, Count Dracula, and the Nazis all rolled into one. And they don't like you very much, either."

"Man, I'd help, but I'm no good at this space stuff."

A faint green ping impinged on Kyle's consciousness. Relief flooded his blood.

"Fuggedaboudit. I'm just glad you're at the wheel there, man. You've been a tremendous help. List, gotta go. Gotta blip from Jen."

"Where?"

"Saturn."

"Keep the transceiver on. I'm getting some anomalous readings from all over North America."

Kyle was over Liberty Island. "What kind of readings?"

"Beam broadcasts. I'm tracing one of them right now to an abandoned factory in Gotham."

"Holy Crow, Eel. That's one of their gates. The other readings must be other gates! Are you mapping them?"

"Of course. But why are they activating now?"

"Maybe you should alert the other members."

33

G reen Arrow crouched in the limb of a mahogany tree in the southern Yucatan, motionless, clutching a digital camera. Since "taking it easy," he'd become fascinated with wild-life photography. Maybe it was all that time spent with a bow and arrow in the wilderness. He'd eaten everything he'd killed, but lately the desire to prove himself a natural-born killer had diminished. Maybe it was having his kid around. Maybe it was dying and being brought back to life. He wished he could bring back all the creatures he'd slain, enough to stock a game preserve in Kenya.

Oh well. Life goes on. He'd learned to forgive himself with his son Connor's help. The important thing was that he wasn't through growing as a man. He could admit past errors and change for the better.

Green Arrow was waiting to photograph a jaguar. He'd been camped out in the forest for three days eating grubs and tubers so that his sweat and waste would smell of the jungle. Signs of the jaguar were everywhere: spoor, prints, a half-eaten iguana. It was pure joy to be out of touch—no ringing cell phones, no honking horns. No one to save but himself. He'd left behind every communications device except his JLA implant, which had been deactivated years ago.

A shadow flickered through the green, a dark evanescence. Green Arrow drew the camera to his eye. The pool was little more than a shallow hole in the rock where water poured off the forest canopy. As Green Arrow held his breath, a paw protruded from the green. Silently the jaguar padded forward, slightly hunched, low to the ground. GA framed the animal as it dipped its pink tongue, and gently depressed the button.

The bong went off in his head so loud he thought he'd been hit with a rock: "JLA TO ALL CURRENT AND FORMER MEMBERS. EARTH IS UNDER ATTACK."

Green Arrow dropped the camera, stunned. It fell twenty feet to the ground and hit with an expensive report. The jag looked up, stared at him a second, then faded into the forest. It took Green Arrow a minute to realize what had happened—they'd switched the transceiver back on from the other end. GA tapped his skull.

"Who is this? Why are you shouting?"

"Green Arrow! It's Plastic Man. Sinestro's on Saturn trying to open a gate to the Qwardian universe. Gates are opening up all over Earth and converging on Saturn. Looks like a full-scale invasion is under way."

"Sinestro? He's dead."

"He's back."

"Damn it! Why don't they stay dead when we kill them? Are you alone?"

"Yes."

"No—he's not," said a voice from behind O'Brien.

Eel just about jumped out of his skin. He turned around and saw the hulking figure of a derelict . . .

"Hal Jordan here," said the man. Eel looked at him more closely and thought, *How the mighty have fallen.*

"Uh, yeah . . ." said Eel. "The Spectre just showed up. Out of nowhere—but I guess that's in character."

"Put him on."

"I'm here, Ollie."

"Hal. What do you want from me?"

"O'Brien put out a general alert and no one answered. Unfortunately, no one will answer, because Sinestro is jamming everyone's frequency on the emergency signal. Fortunately, he couldn't jam your's because it was inactive. O'Brien turned it back on after the jamming burst went out."

How the heck does he know that? Eel thought. *Oh, right—he's the Spectre.*

Green Arrow sat at the edge of the pool with his knees drawn up. "You mean you can't get in touch with anyone—Superman, Batman, Wonder Woman, J'onn J'onz?"

"We will, eventually," Jordan said before Eel could speak. "But right now, you are the only one we can contact."

Green Arrow thought Jordan sounded more alive than he had in years. Since becoming the Spectre he seemed to have lost his personality. "I don't know what I can do to help. I'm in the southern Yucatan. Left a Jeep up the road a couple miles."

"Ollie, you're among a handful of JLA members who have actually fought Sinestro. Maybe if we put our heads together . . ."

"You're too kind, old buddy. All I did was hold your coat. You and Black Canary did the rest."

"Where is Black Canary?"

"Back in Star City—probably baking lemon bars. Wait a minute. You're not thinking of asking her to go out there?"

"It worked before."

"How do we know this is even the same Sinestro? Has anyone checked the coffin?"

"We can't find the coffin."

"What?"

"I tried searching for it. It's gone."

Great, Green Arrow thought. Maybe Sinestro got out somehow. But how would that account for his awesome power? Power to open a gate between universes had to come from somewhere else—the Qwardians. "Do you think it's the same guy?"

"No. Eel says Kyle told him they made a new Sinestro out of some human kid."

"What makes you think Black Canary can use the same trick on him? In space?"

"I can place her there."

"Hal, why don't you just off the guy? You did it before."

There was a pause. "I can't do that."

"Why not?"

"There are certain restrictions. Moral restrictions."

"You're back to no killing again? Oh, man! "

"It's not that simple. But if we can get Black Canary up there we might not have to kill him."

"Okay. Let's see what we can do." Green Arrow picked up his things and headed back to his Jeep.

"Do you really think that you and GA and Canary can take this new Sinestro, Hal? Hal . . .?"

But Eel O'Brien found that he was talking to himself. The Spectre had vanished as mysteriously and quietly as he had appeared.

CHAPTER

34

W hile Jenny-Lynn watched frozen in stasis, Sinestro recreated the ancient Qwardian scout ship molecule by molecule. The vehicle taking shape under her gaze resembled a great silver shark with parts missing. It was unbelievable. Not in a million years would she have thought he could have made something from a cloud of interplanetary dust. But there it was, held in place with a tenuous yellow membrane. Sinestro sat opposite Jenny—eyes shut, legs crossed, hands on knees, mentally directing the reconstitution. It was like watching an explosion in reverse.

Whenever Sinestro came across mortal remains, he installed them in gleaming yellow caskets he conjured from his ring. Unlike Earth caskets, these were lozenge-shaped with no flat surfaces, meant for disposal in space. The caskets began to pile up. Without ever opening his eyes, he indicted Jenny and her kind. She could feel his insinuations nibbling at the edge of her consciousness. *Your fault. You and the Green Lanterns.*

"Lies," she fired back, as if the word would knock him down. He kept his eyes shut, concentrating. The probe continued to coalesce. The reconstruction looked like a ghost ship; a haunted vessel; dinosaur bones. It took enormous concentration to put it back together. Jenny guessed they'd been sitting there for at least twenty-four hours while Sinestro worked his reconstruction. Where the parts were unavailable, he intuited their shape from their surroundings. The ultimate jigsaw puzzle.

Due to the fragment of Starheart that lived within her, Jen wouldn't need food or water for days. From time to time she dozed. She had vivid dreams of her and Kyle arguing; her and Kyle loving; her and Kyle with a baby. At random intervals she would sweep the heavens with her thoughts, looking for him. It was like shining a flashlight into the night sky, hoping to illuminate a particular moth. No answering ping returned. She could feel Sinestro's nimbus robbing her of strength, dampening her senses, keeping her dull. At least she wasn't barefoot and pregnant. Whatever Eddie had become, he seemed to have lost interest in her as a woman. Thank God for small favors. There could be only one purpose for which he was keeping her around.

Bait.

Think I'm just a worm on a hook? she thought. *Think again.*

There was plantlife even here. It clung to the pores of her lungs and her body hair, microscopic fungal pores endemic throughout New York. These were normally harmless unless you were allergic. Jenny could control them to a certain extent. Purple skin or not, Sinestro was based on a human being, a sweet kid named Eddie. She hated to hurt him but she didn't have any choice. It was no longer just her life that was at stake. Nor that of her family. It was the entire human race.

She attacked. She directed fungal pores through the yellow isthmus connecting her to Sinestro. Under her direction they danced along the yellow beam and gathered before Sinestro's nostrils. Within moments, he had inhaled millions of them. Jen went to work massaging their molecular structure, using the rich nutrients of Sinestro's human/alien blood. They became fruitful and multiplied. Under her guidance they turned green. She turned his body into a fungal machine.

His eyes popped open like sprung blinds. The boiled-egg eyes flashed, slash mouth twisted in anger. Green spots stippled his cheeks; the spots spread. He gasped, clawed at his face. Jen redoubled her efforts, encouraging the fungus to grow, feed off his alien blood, take over his body. *Kill him!* She had seldom known such rage and hatred. She nourished it like an infant. Sinestro twisted and writhed. Strange growths appeared on his once smooth skin, sea cucumbers, green warts spouting tufts of moss.

With a wild gyration, Sinestro staggered backward, separating contact with Jenny-Lynn. She was free, on her own, kept alive only by her natural Starheart energy pack. Already she could feel cosmic rays bombarding her. Her power reserves were miniscule. It would only be a matter of minutes before her personal forcefield degraded, letting out the air. She didn't care. She'd rather die than aid this monster in his assault on humanity.

She turned toward the Sun and tried to soar. She fell back toward the center of the planet instead. She had no power, nothing like a real Green Lantern. She had once, but not anymore. All she could do now was make plants grow. Faster and faster she fell, hurtling through ice fields—frozen clouds that collapsed with a vast tinkling sound, showering her with needle-sharp pricks. Falling through chandeliers. She turned her gaze upward. No crimson foe followed. No yellow rays appeared. With luck, she'd killed him.

Kyle, I love you! she thought as she hurtled to her death. The atmosphere itself attacked her forcefield with toxic chemicals and anti-matter debris. It became thicker, the friction of her descent causing her to heat up. In a matter of minutes, all her moisture would boil away. *What a way to die,* she mused. Heat and dehydration on Saturn. Her tongue began to swell and she gasped involuntarily as her air ran out. She saw green and purple spots. Darkness closed around her.

At the last instant, she was bathed in a green light. An angel appeared beneath her, arms spread. Caught her light as a feather, like a pop fly to center field. They were rising, ascending to the heavens, accelerating away from the gravity well of Saturn, and she could breath. A glowing green nimbus surrounded her and straight ahead was her angel.

Still weak, she reached up and touched his cheek. "Kyle. I knew you'd come."

He dipped down and kissed her, then whipped his head up, eyes probing the heavens like locomotive beams. "Sorry I cut it so thin. They tried to turn me into soup on Qward. Where is he?"

"I don't know. He was with the remains of that scout ship, trying to put it back together. What's going on?"

"The Qwardians are trying to use him to take over Earth. They think they can open a gate on Saturn and use a form of anti-matter flashover to flip-flop Earth."

The atmosphere scraped by like steel wool. It became thinner as they rose, more cloudlike. Vistas opened, allowing glimpses of towering cumulus monsters, the occasional gleam of debris, but no sign of Sinestro and his death ship.

"Flip-flop?"

"Matter/anti-matter. That's how we were able to survive when we passed through the gate. If we'd kept our normal molecular structure, we would have exploded. But they don't want to reverse the polarity. They want to invade our system and have that explosion."

Green Lantern burst free of the last vestiges of Saturn's atmosphere just beneath the plane of the rings, which stretched over their heads seemingly to infinity, a ceiling of icy pebbles rushing by overhead as if they were flying upside down. Jen tightened her grip around Kyle's neck and shuddered.

"They're looking at a controlled explosion," Kyle said. "They don't want to shatter the atmosphere or affect the orbit. They've found a way to slow down the reaction so that instead of instantly, it takes about a minute. I can't describe to you what would happen in that minute."

He didn't have to. He couldn't stop his thoughts from permeating her skin. She saw human beings literally turning inside-out. Eyes dribbling down skulls, intestines exposing themselves, a river of blood rushing to the gutters. A charnel house of unimaginable proportions.

"I know," he whispered. "I'm going to drop you off at the JLA tower and get some reinforcements."

Inertia caused Jenny to surge forward, but Kyle held her tight. Between them and the Sun, a giant crimson hand had descended in the universal traffic cop's gesture. Stop. The hand shrank, turned purple, and attached to it was Sinestro. He hovered a mile away slightly crouched, like a jockey. The position the human body assumed in saltwater, with no conscious effort. The posture of a floater. He looked up through yellowish eyes beneath his huge dome.

"Stick around," he said over Kyle's JLA transceiver.

Kyle cued the satellite. Nada. Sinestro was blocking. "Can you contact the JLA?" he whispered to Jen.

"No. He's blocking me."

Kyle looked around for someplace to stash her while he and Sinestro had it out. The JLA tower was a trillion miles away.

"I'm going to have to put you someplace. I need my hands free."

"Where?"

"The probe."

He zinged "up" toward the debris that formed Saturn's rings. Almost instantaneously, he had accessed and entered the airlock on the ancient, reconstituted Qward probe. Unbelievably, Sinestro had restored it to near original condition, making what he needed from the surrounding elements, intuiting what he needed from the design itself. The interior board room had been restored to its original grandeur, huge, form-fitting chairs waiting to encapsulate, massage, sooth, and heat the weary.

Jenny clung to Kyle. "I thought I'd never see you again."

"You know better."

"Why isn't he following us?"

"He's waiting for me." Kyle handed her what looked like a pen. "It's a plasma bomb. You can set a timer by twisting it, although I don't know where you'll go. If Sinestro gets me, don't let him have the ship. It's the key to restoring their gates."

Jade took the tiny object. She knew what it was. It was capable of pulverizing a large moon. If it detonated it would destroy everything within a million miles. Kyle held her tight, kissed her on the mouth. He seemed about to say something but he bit it off and stepped back.

"Hang tight. I love you."

Jenny watched him step into the airlock.

Outside, Sinestro was waiting.

35

Plastic Man scanned the monitors, alarmed at what he saw. Gates had opened on a dozen locations on Earth and were converging via curved beams above the surface of the Moon in seeming defiance of the JLA tower. He fought down a wave of panic. He was the least of all Justice Leaguers. Oh, they pretended he was their equal, included him in all the meetings, gave him plenty of responsibility. But to think he could hold his own against Superman, Wonder Woman, or Batman was wishful thinking.

Eel O'Brien had been a petty thief and second-story man. He'd grown up during the depression and carried its baggage with him into the super hero life, even into the twenty-first century. He'd blundered into a vat of chemicals and came away with amazing powers. He might have become big-time bad, but borrowing a page from a man he greatly admired, the criminal Two Face, Eel O'Brien had decided to become a good guy on the flip of a coin.

"Lord, I'm just a cheap hustler," he said to himself. "This is out of my league."

A low chime began to sound throughout the station, booming hollowly like bells announcing a fire drill. Plastic Man looked at the screens with alarm. There were now at least two dozen tendrils of energy arcing up out of the atmosphere and converging above the Moon. Control board lights went on like Christmas at Rockefeller Center. On the station's surface invisible beacons automatically activated, broadcasting throughout the known universe.

"Warning," a woman's mellifluous voice spoke. "Inter-dimensional gates have been detected at sixteen locations. There is a high probability of an environment-altering event. This is a stage-one alert."

Trying to remember the crash course in physics Wonder Woman had given him, he moved to systems analysis. What were these portals and what did they mean? Why were they converging at the Moon?

"Trace radiation of anti-matter residue at each gate suggests possibility of portal opening between matter/anti-matter universe," the woman's voice explained as if conducting a tour of the garden. "Possible attempt at radiation flashover."

What the hell was flashover? Firestorm had explained it to him once. It was a phenomenon whereby fire could race along a smoke corridor like electricity through a copper wire, igniting fires down the line. In this case, someone was trying to open a massive gate. Planetwide. But where? The surface of the Moon? It made no sense.

"Warning," the woman said. Plastic Man pictured Hedy Lamarr. "Beams converging at the Moon."

Plastic Man stared in horror as the tracers flowed around the Moon, met, glowed, flared, and launched a beam away from the Sun. The target popped up: Saturn.

Plastic Man's face fell to his waist. "Thanks!" he muttered. "Thanks for leaving me in charge for the galaxy-spanning crisis of a lifetime!"

"You're not alone, Eel."

Relief buoyed Plastic Man's face. Hal Jordan had returned.

"Man, am I glad you're back. The whole solar system's gone haywire. Gates are opening up all over Earth, converging at the Moon and shooting on to Saturn. What's going on?"

"The Qwardians believe they have found a perfect match: their champion versus my successor. They act to fulfill their destiny, the destruction of the Green Lantern Corps and occupation of Earth."

Plastic Man flapped like a flag in the wind. "Solid, Jackson! I thought it was something serious. I mean, you're the Spectre, right? You got some juice."

They emerged into the carpeted curving corridor. "My ability to affect the physical world is nugatory."

"Say what?"

"No juice, Eel! My job these days is mostly just watching."

Damn—no help here. O'Brien's frustration got the better of him. He cast a jaundiced eye in Jordan's direction and said, "Say, how come you're dressed like a hobo?" Immediately, he regretted it.

Jordan took no offense. "These days I wear what's comfortable," he said with a shrug. "Show me what you've got on the big screen."

They walked along the corridor to the control center. The outer rim of the wheel looked out on space and a big chunk of Earth. The inner rim was devoted to controls and myriad monitors covering most aspects of the solar system. Several of the screens charted the energy lines that stretched from Earth to Moon to Saturn.

"Isn't there some way you can skirt around Sinestro's jam and make contact with the JLA's heavy hitters?"

Hal Jordan looked grim as he said, "No, Eel. They cannot be contacted in time to help. That leaves you, me, and Kyle."

"Well, GL's right in the middle of a donnybrook with Sinestro. What are you going to do? You going to take us to Saturn?"

"We're not going out there right now. Kyle has the means to stop him—and the need to stop him. And," he added in a whisper, "he will stop him."

"What makes you so sure?"

Jordan's eyes flashed. "Faith."

"Great," Plastic Man muttered.

CHAPTER

36

Jenny-Lynn walked through the interior of the probe, fingers tracing its inner wall, a vinyl-like substance decorated with fantastic tribal whorls. She found it hard to believe that the same uptight buttoned-down Qwardians she'd met had once created art like this. So wild. So primitive. Could it be that with their perfectly ordered lives they secretly pined for wildness? Did they not know that by conquering nature they had only forced it to strike back?

The ultimate question, did the Qwardians lack self-knowledge? All the scientific mastery in the universe was useless without self-knowledge, which came down to an understanding of one's own limits and shortcomings. Those who aren't aware they're screwing up have no incentive to change. Sometimes they knew and still had no incentive. Jenny didn't think that was the case.

There were huge areas of the Earth where people had never heard of psychotherapy and the display of any emotions was considered untoward. Here was a race that had been around for millions of years. Clueless. It forced her to reconsider her definition of intelligence. Perhaps the Qwardians' so-called "intelligence" was a built-in self-destruction factor for the safety of the universe. At what cost? If the Qwardians succeeded in opening an anti-matter gate into the positive universe, they could suffer blow-back, which would destroy the Qwardian universe. They might even trigger the Big Bang in reverse, a massive implosion of the entire universe into a pinprick smaller than a period.

Heavy.

One heavy dot.

It could happen. Jen had read Stephen Hawking and understood the nature of the universe. The explosion of matter and anti-matter could result in a singularity—a black hole—that would suck it all in. Every bit of it. It reminded her of her father's recording of Tom Lehrer's "We'll All Go Together When We Go." Every Hottentot and every Eskimo.

Weak with the idea, she collapsed into one of the form-fitting chairs, which automatically adjusted to her shape. Sinestro had restored the craft to like-new condition. His powers were enormous, able to regenerate all the pieces, put them in the right places, remove any sign of the terrible destruction. The after-image of the hollow skull he'd showed her burned into her retina. There was something in the ship's air, the faintest whiff of death. Not even Sinestro had been able to banish that.

She looked out the portal. All she could see was a storm, thrashing currents of toxic gas. Flashes of yellow and green sometimes illuminated the mountainous folds, like heat lightning from a distance. Her telepathic attempts to contact Kyle were blocked. There was a strange aura to him, as if his powers had been tainted. He reminded her just a little bit of Ion. She wondered what had happened to him in that Qwardian lab before she'd arrived, and shuddered.

Her JLA transceiver had been destroyed during her return from Qward. She scanned the instrumentation in front of her. Although designed millennia ago for an alien race, she immediately intuited most of the basic controls. If she could recalibrate their transceiver for parabeam, she might be able to contact the JLA. Jenny eased herself into the com officer's chair in front of a curving screen geometrically divided into buttons. Her hands felt the screen like Oscar Peterson exploring a piano.

Within thirty seconds she had learned how to broadcast and was shooting off messages like a burning fireworks factory. Many of these would be absorbed in the atmosphere. The craft was deep in the soup. Others would simply fly off in the wrong direction. But surely one would get through.

The message said: "Attention JLA. Jade and Green Lantern on Saturn. SOS!"

Maybe some kindly fishing trawler would forward it. Saturn, she thought. That really pins it down. By now she was working the craft like a pipe organ and they would be able to find her simply by back-tracking the broadcasts.

If anyone heard her. If anyone was coming. Certainly Sinestro and Green Lantern heard her, but they were too busy to do anything about it. She looked out the portal. The armada of gleaming yellow coffins hove into view. She shuddered and blanked out the screen.

The transceiver crackled.

"Yipe!" Jenny shrieked, leaping in her seat.

"This is Hal Jordan," came the world-weary traveler's voice, as if picked up from a great difference by your grandfather's Grundig on shortwave late at night.

"Hal! Thank God. Where are you?"

"I'm at JLA headquarters. Plastic Man and I are the only ones available, I'm afraid. Where are you broadcasting from?"

"I'm on board a reconstituted Qwardian probe ship above Saturn. It was just debris when Sinestro found it. He recreated it perfectly. I don't know where Sinestro and Kyle are. Can you bring help?"

Static overwhelmed the system. "Come on!" Jenny shouted in frustration, kicking the console. The static abruptly cleared up.

" . . .even if we could get out there, I'm afraid. It's too danger-ous—Sinestro would kill you with the speed of thought if he even suspected that reinforcements were on the way. You say he recreated the ship from debris?"

"That's right."

"And this Sinestro is an Earthling whom the Qwardians have turned?"

"I didn't tell you that."

"Is it true?"

"Yes. How did you know that?"

"It's their way. They've done more than lie to him. They've pro-grammed him to believe their drivel. Told you a Green Lantern des-troyed the ship, didn't he?"

"Yes! That's impossible. The ship was here for millennia before my father was born!"

"I know that. You know that. But Sinestro doesn't know that. All right, listen. If he recreated the ship intuitively he may have recreated the ship's log. See if you can find it. Go back to the day it entered our system. Find out what really happened. That may hold him long enough for us to . . ."

The console went dead. Every dial and aperture flared crimson as if it contained a tiny nuclear explosion. Intense heat drove Jenny back. She fell, and when she looked up Sinestro towered above her, the top of his head making an indentation in the padded ceiling. His eyes narrowed to slits.

"I spared your life because you once meant something to my human host. If you call for help or try to escape I'll erase you without a thought."

She glared at him with raw hatred. Where was Kyle? Was he all right? Sinestro's gaze turned upward. He gasped and rippled, mass disappearing until there was nothing left but an afterglow.

The lights, circulation and ventilation system still worked. But when she investigated the communications console, it was toast. The interior had fused into a black, sticky mess.

In the meantime, what had Hal said? The ship's log. What if it were part of the fried com system? There was only one way to find out. She had to search for it. The craft was trout-shaped, about a hundred yards long. The main chamber, incorporating both the bridge and passenger accommodations, filled half the length. Behind were several smallish staterooms and lavatory facilities. The final quarter of the craft was devoted to hardware. It seemed to radiate a sense of alien antiquity. Although Jade was able to stand upright and move about freely, it had clearly been designed for people who were smaller than the current American norm.

Jen felt her way toward the rear of the craft, hands on the soft ecru walls. The plasticene material was warm and gave slightly under pressure. Some of the patterns were obvious, such as the water closets and food facilities. Others were enigmatic. She had no way of knowing where they might have kept the flight recorder or even if they had one. If it had been in the cooked console, she was out of luck. But most airlines kept their flight recorders separate from the control consoles to avoid being destroyed. It was a universal principle.

And even if she found the recorder, what then? What if it proved the ship had simply disintegrated under the extreme pressure? Was Sinestro likely to abandon his mission? Oh, sorry. Well I guess I'll go home now.

Not likely. She had no choice but to continue. The only other option was to admit defeat. She felt a tingling beneath her feet. Kneeling, she touched the soft plastic floor. There was something dense and alive beneath her fingers. She felt the floor for a seam and it sprang up in her hand like a hinged Spongebob Squarepants. Nestled in a velvet bed was a black object shaped like a can of sardines.

The flight recorder. It was incredibly dense. Jenny needed both hands to lift it. Once free of the floor it resisted being turned onto a vertical plane as if had gyroscopes. In her hands it hummed to life and projected a holo-beam that bounced off the wall and shimmered into shape in the middle of the craft. A vast public plaza seen from a height. Hundreds of thousands of citizens wearing gray tunics marching in military precision past a reviewing stand. Jen concentrated on the reviewing stand and it seemed to swim into focus and come closer. She could see the dignitaries' faces clearly. They were Qwardians, all members of the same clan, except for a pair of Weaponers flanking them on either side of the platform.

Hundreds of Weaponers marched in formation. What at first had sounded like a series of random bird chirps transformed into language—a man's voice, mellifluous and deep, like the recordings of Walter Cronkite her dad had insisted she watch.

" . . .Gathered here on the twelfth day of Zha in celebration of our heroic leaders and the brave Qwardians who will undertake this venture on behalf of the Qwardian people. Our need is desperate. If we do not find a new planet within the allotted span, the Qwardians will cease to exist as a race.

"Our birth rate long since fell below the minimum necessary to sustain a vital economy and it is only through the most desperate measures we have been able to stabilize our population. Our children are few and sickly. The Guardians attack us at every turn. The Guardians bid us die on our desiccated corpse of a planet. The Guardians seek to rule the universe. They have created proxies to prevent us from crossing the Great Divide: the Green Lantern Corps. The Green Lantern Corps are the shock troop bully-boys of the

223

Guardians. Never in the history of civilization has their been such a collection of sadists and thugs."

The image changed from the vast military display to a lone Qwardian at a podium in a darkened theater. His words and gestures reminded her of old newsreels of Hitler. She'd seen this tape before. Examining the recorder she found buttons indicating forward or backward. She fast-forwarded through the rest of the march, the speeches, the farewells and the launch. The craft prepared for insertion.

Jen's world went blank.

CHAPTER
37

They faced each other across a plane of debris, separated by less than a mile. Every nerve in Kyle's body twitched in anticipation of blasting the purple alien to hell. He fought that battle with himself and won. He didn't shoot. He waited to see what Sinestro would do, just as it said in the JLA manual. He felt so charged from the Qwardian battery, he didn't think Sinestro could hurt him. He would see.

With the utmost delicacy, he probed the depths for Jen, or that smaller heart that might beat within. Nothing. He couldn't conduct a more thorough search without letting down his guard. He could tell just by looking that this Sinestro, newly minted from an exterminator, was as lethal as any foe he'd ever faced. Thousands of years of martial experience had been retrofitted into Sinestro's elongated brain. The eyes that glared with unblinking hatred were ancient. They faced each other like two gunslingers, each with his hands by his sides. Kyle wondered what Sinestro would do if he were to suddenly conjure up a pair of Colt Dragoons and start blasting.

"Yo, Eddie," Kyle said, spitting the words out like watermelon seeds. They struck Sinestro's forcefield and translated. "This is the biggest sell-out since Benedict Arnold. What did you get? Immortality? Big thoughts?"

Sinestro smiled thinly. Although they were in a vacuum, they could hear each other clearly via telepathy. The force of thought alone was a potent weapon and both were aware of it. Either could kill with a thought.

"How apropos," Sinestro said.

"What do you mean?"

"How fitting that I end your reign of terror on the very site that you and your ilk destroyed a ship filled with innocent pilgrims."

"Whoa, Eddie! Those are awfully big words for a home exterminator. You sure this isn't the chemicals talking?"

A surge of rage tinged Sinestro's bubble orange. Then it receded and he was back in control. That answered one question—a little bit of Eddie still survived. Green Lantern had a chance. If he could somehow reach Eddie, get him to reject the parasite program. . . .

The creature laughed as if reading Kyle's thoughts. Which was unlikely, since their brain patterns were as different as two sentient species' could be and still communicate with one another. The laughter reached Kyle as a hollow cackle tinged with subtle nuance beyond his ken. He experienced the first fissure of doubt. This was no home exterminator pumped up on steroids. Here was the culmination of millions of years of concentrated energy, the personification of the Qwardians' racial imperative. Invested with the power of a planet and whatever dark star they worshiped.

Kyle had pulled a strange energy from the Qwardian battery culled from a thousand Green Lanterns. Memories came with it, as if a part of each fallen hero lived on in the battery. Kyle knew they weren't real. The Green Lanterns were long past dead. But their powerful emotions and ideas lingered on with a life of their own. Alien thoughts squalled through his mind, leading him down one false path after another. All the Green Lanterns had encountered Qwardians in some form or another. Each had a different solution.

Burn him, said the Green Lantern of Sector 14.

Encase him in gold, said another.

Off with his head!

Train a microwave beam on his liver.

He had a family. Find them and kill them.

Destroy his home planet.

Kyle was appalled. These were not Green Lantern thoughts. Sensing his confusion, Sinestro struck. Asteroids the size of cabooses converged on Kyle. He felt his hand twitch like a ghost limb; the forcefield expanded. The rocks slammed together all around him, minutely compressing his envelope. Shattered rock tumbled away in all directions. Two more boulders the size of freight trains smashed together on a perpendicular vector. Again the ring responded. Kyle now stood at the center of his own little expanding universe, consisting mostly of rubble.

Why am I standing here? he thought. He flicked. The next set of asteroids smashed where he'd been standing, so close the shrapnel rattled off his forcefield like hail. Kyle reached out encompassing a hundred cubic miles of rubble, sweeping it over the place where Sinestro had stood.

You want to throw rocks?

Green Lantern swept the skies. Where was the bastard? The blip came back yellow from below. He embraced a sea of debris and channeled it into a raging river, an unending onslaught at a hundred miles per hour at the yellow blip.

"You missed," hissed in his ear. Kyle whirled, had an instant to register the rock wall inches from his face. The ring did its thing. Kyle saw an impression of his own face punched into the smooth rock as it struck. *My death mask*, he thought, falling backward into Saturn's toxic soup. Sinestro followed him down, grinning sardonically, pushing, pushing with his yellow power, pushing Kyle to the center of the planet.

They had a long way to go. Sinestro was forcing him to accelerate faster than the pull of gravity. Kyle had to get out from under. He reached for something solid, trying to gauge Sinestro's strength. He needed an anchor, something big he wouldn't pull out of orbit. Snaking around the ice fields, through clouds close to absolute zero, he found the mid-sized moon Enceladus and dug in with his green hand. Applying all his strength, he wrenched out from under Sinestro's battering ram, watching in awe as it continued to plunge toward the center of the planet like a freight train of stone. It took a long time to pass. Enceladus oscillated. Kyle hoped it wouldn't smash into other moons.

True, nothing lived here and it probably wouldn't matter, but JLA policy was clear. Leave things as you found them. He had no time to ruminate on the ramifications of his action, pulling a moon out of its orbit. Sinestro intuited what had happened and stepped off his pillar, which disappeared into the thickening depths. A golden strand arced out of the depths and attached itself to the wobbling Enceladus. Precious nanoseconds passed while Kyle registered the line tighten and the icy little moon begin to move toward him.

With stunning rapidity, Enceladus grew to encompass the heavens. Sinestro was using it as a tetherball. Kyle acted on pure reflex, diving to the side, barely escaping its gravitational pull as it rushed by. An instant later it disappeared in the primordial fog. It would continue until it joined the core. The greater heat and pressure near the center of Saturn would melt it to nothing. Saturn was short one moon.

Sinestro was tearing apart the solar system.

38

J ordan and O'Brien watched the destruction of Enceladus with grim fascination.

"Think that will affect Saturn's orbit?" O'Brien asked.

Jordan leaned over the screen, one hand on each side, staring like a castaway watching a ship slip over the horizon. "No telling. It's far enough from Earth that no matter what happens it shouldn't affect us. Of course you never know. The sudden absence of one moon could have a destabilizing effect on the other moons and the rings. If Saturn readjusts itself either closer in or farther out, it could affect Earth's orbit. Even a distance as miniscule as a thousand miles either way could have a devastating affect on our weather."

O'Brien regarded the haggard Spectre with a sick expression. "Wish I had a cigarette," he muttered. Jordan pretended not to hear him.

"Don't worry, be happy," Jordan sang softly.

"Huh?"

Jordan turned toward him smiling. "You heard me, Eel. There's nothing we can do about it at this moment, so we might as well relax."

"Nothing we can do? Excuse me? Your successor's out there fighting a solar-system-collapsing event! We've got to do something."

Jordan lowered himself into a chair and turned to face Plastic Man. "You know, Eel, over the years I learned to accept my limitations as a man and as a super hero."

Plastic Man's jaw hit the floor. Literally. "That's funny, coming from you. I always looked up to you like a god. I mean, look at me. I ain't much. Small potatoes. I can impersonate a toaster or an inflatable raft. Big deal. Biggest bust I ever made was the Rosencranz Gang. Art thieves. You, you've saved the universe. You're not giving up on me are you?"

Jordan put his hands behind his head and stretched so that O'Brien could hear his vertebrae cracking. "A little while ago I was praying that I could cash it in."

Eel's eyes bulged like cathode tubes. "You?"

Jordan shrugged, a Gallic gesture suggesting volumes. "I'd seen too much. I felt sorry for myself. I let my personal pain overwhelm my concern for others. I was going to give it the old Justice League try, but a wise coyote pulled me back from the edge."

"A coyote."

"God takes many forms. Do you believe in God, Eel?"

O'Brien felt uncomfortable. Now he was sorry Jordan was there. Of all the super heroes associated with the JLA, Jordan was the most enigmatic. You were never quite certain where you stood with the guy. Batman, he let you know right off whether he liked you or not.

"You're not going to try to talk to me about accepting Jesus Christ into my heart and soul, are ya? I'm Catholic, you know. Or I was."

"You didn't answer the question."

"Aw, who knows. I ain't been to church in a dog's age. What are you sayin'? Yaweh's going to step in before things go completely down the drain?"

The Gallic shrug. Eel stared at the man who had been through so many changes. Just being a test pilot was enough excitement for most men. But Jordan had also been Green Lantern. He'd been Parallax. And now he was the Spectre. Did he even know who he was anymore? Man, the damage he could do if he went bad. Eel shivered. Then he remembered: Hal Jordan *had* gone bad. Now he was good. Perhaps infinitely good.

"You could do it, couldn't you?" O'Brien said in a voice hushed with awe. "You could reach out and set things right. Just like that." O'Brien snapped his fingers. "Why don't you?"

"You're giving me too much credit, Eel. I believe that we're in good hands. You might say I have faith in Kyle. That's what I was asking you. Do you have faith?"

"Faith in what, Hal?"

"A supreme being. A guiding light. Order to the universe."

Eel slithered, clearly uncomfortable. "I don't know. Being raised Catholic . . . well, you know, you either let the Church take over your life or you leave. I left. I got burnt out on religion. Then, when I turned into this I had to rethink everything. I mean, I'm no big noise. But Superman." Eel held out a hand palm up.

"Superman is not God."

"Closest thing to Him I've ever seen."

"Would you pray to Superman?"

"Come on, Hal. What are you getting at?"

Jordan leaned forward, arms on knees. His eyes burned with a holy intensity. "I'm saying that the fate of the universe may very well depend on your faith, Eel. And yours alone."

Plastic Man wobbled like a cheap roof in a hurricane. "What? That's nuts! You can't pin this on me! This has nothing to do with me!"

Jordan held his hands up in a placating manner, reminding Plastic Man of Jesus blessing the crowd. "You misunderstand me. I'm not some all-powerful being making an arbitrary decision. I'm saying you're in a unique position to affect things. For one thing, you're at the wheel. I'm not even an active member now. For another, you're the only one who's getting the big picture. You see the gates opening on Earth. You know Kyle is fighting Sinestro on Saturn. Connect the dots."

"What are you saying, Hal? Spell it out for me. I'm no good at this enigmatic stuff."

Jordan sighed as if Eel just wasn't getting it. Eel felt stupid, and a little bit pissed off. He hated this cosmic crap. If the man had something to say, why didn't he just spit it out?

"Will you pray with me, Eel?"

The board lit up. A familiar face appeared onscreen.

"I'm coming aboard," said Alan Scott.

CHAPTER

39

The Qwardian dreadnaught *Sid* emerged from a wormhole, bringing with it enough matter/anti-matter debris to form the nucleus of what would become Sedna, the solar system's tenth planet. It happened five hundred million years ago. The *Sid* carried thirty Qwardians and two Weaponers, by far the greatest expeditionary force ever sent into the posimatter universe.

Sixteen previous expeditions had failed at a cost of thousands of lives and billions in credits. The first of these expeditions predated the *Sid* by millennia. The Qwardians were a patient race. Having reduced the universe to a binary code, they had no doubts and no humility. The universe in which they lived was sterile. Life existed, witness the Qwardians. But life did not thrive. All life in the Qwardian Universe was in a slow, downward spiral brought about through simple exhaustion, like soil that had been over-farmed.

The Qwardians had brought this upon themselves by killing off any organism that did not fit their plan. Their destruction of "vermin" led to unexpected consequences. The Qwardians could not conceive that their methodology was at fault, so they reasoned the universe itself was dying and set about finding a new one. Many thousands lost their lives before the Qwardians succeeded in transferring a personality to the posimatter universe. That personality encountered the Green Lantern Corps and a feud was born.

Had the Green Lantern Corps not handed the Qwardians their ultimate weapon, they may very well have remained consigned to the anti-matter universe until the last of their breed withered. But the

Corps erred and erred badly. They consigned Sinestro, a renegade Green Lantern, to the anti-matter universe, where he thrived. The Qwardians recognized a good thing when they had it. Sinestro became the key to gaining entry to the posimatter universe. Sinestro would prove the key to permitting antimatter to convert to matter and thus survive the transfer.

How could the Guardians have made such a mistake? His physiology lent itself to transfer through a wormhole. He was somehow able to accomplish the complete inversion of polarities that passage from the matter to the anti-matter universe requires.

The Qwardians recognized what the Guardians could not: the Green Lantern ring formed a symbiosis with Sinestro, resulting in a new personality. A new life form. The Qwardians quickly substituted their own yellow power ring for green. From the anti-matter universe, Sinestro was able to return to the posimatter universe far earlier than he had left it. Certain gates opened on the past: deeper, deeper. It was Sinestro who led the Qwardians to Saturn, with an eye on Earth. He planted the beacon that beckoned them through. He was waiting for them on the other Side. He had traveled back in time five hundred million years to nip humanity in the bud.

As the *Sid* prepared for transmission through the wormhole, they received sporadic updates from Sinestro on the other side of the gate. Sinestro alone was able to communicate between the two universes because of his unique physiology.

It all came down to the big day. The big day was now. Thirty Qwardians in posimatter traction suits lay strapped in their lounges while the two Weaponers ran the ship. Sinestro signaled the ship, which lay in an underground dry dock. The launch would take place beneath the planet's surface. All was ready. Silence within the shark-shaped vehicle was complete. No one prayed. The captain offered no invocation or pep talk. All eyes were on the consoles in front of them counting down the seconds, watching the bars reach equilibrium

"Thirty seconds," the Weaponer rumbled in a low frequency that every Qwardian could feel in his bones. "Twenty seconds." Smooth faces remained calm. A few Qwardians gripped their arm rests but otherwise you might have thought they were waiting for a bus ride to Atlantic City. Did they think about their loved ones, those they left behind? Did the ponder the greatness of the Qwardian civilization? Did they know fear? No one knows. The Qwardians paid little heed to individual histories. To them the group was paramount. It was a rebuke to all Qwardians to stand out from the group.

"Ten seconds." The ship's matter/anti-matter drive began to hum. The hull vibrated in frequency with the gate. Enormous electromagnets focused their beams on a single point, while in the posimatter universe, Sinestro used his power to open up the other end, like the pair of locked doors that connect adjacent hotel suites. Four billion Qwardians watched the final countdown. All activity stopped while the *Sid* set forth. An observer would have seen Qward as a lifeless planet, a monstrous city that seemed abandoned. All Qwardians were indoors, glued to their telecoms.

"Insertion," the captain announced. Surrounded by a shifting matrix of crimson beams, the ship slid forward on rails toward the burst of static that had appeared in the tunnel. The pulsating white dot formed an opening no more than a yard across. The ship slid its needle prow into the opening and like a child first entering the world struggled to widen the gate with its own mass. The gate widened to form a band of dancing white static the encircled the ship like a belt. It slid from the nose to the tail. As it progressed toward the tail, everything behind it disappeared. Finally there was nothing left but the pulsating white dot and soon that, too, disappeared.

The Qwardian Congress of Elders waited in silence.

Within the *Sid* there was a sense of scraping through a tight passage, sudden changes in air pressure and temperature. Every portal and screen showed white storm. Miraculously, the storm blew away, leaving behind the clear blackness of space pierced with a billion pinpricks of light. To the right, a massive white and red atmosphere filled the sky. Saturn.

Sinestro beckoned in space like a crimson beacon. He smiled, proud of his accomplishment, anticipating revenge. "Welcome Qwardians!" he sang, using a ring-generated monofilament to transmit his voice.

"Hail Sinestro," replied the captain. "The field holds." The captain was referring to the powerful electromagnetic field that permitted the negative matter *Sid* to exist in the posimatter universe. The field maintained a wafer-thin envelope around the ship and, theoretically, around each individual Qwardian.

Sinestro beamed with pride. His physics had made the field possible.

The first asteroid, mostly iron, smashed through the ship's forward portal, removing the captain's head. The space rock tumbled about the interior, killing three Qwardians before exiting. The ship's electro-magnetic field, which permitted the Qwardians to exist in our universe, was attracting every chunk of ferrous metal in the neighborhood. Within seconds the ship completely disappeared in a blizzard of meteorites and matter/anti-matter explosions. The bizarre mechanics of the electromagnetic field operating in the posimatter universe caused polarities to go haywire.

Sinestro watched in dismay as the *Sid* was reduced to rubble in a matter of seconds. Then he set about covering up his mistake.

40

J enny-Lynn sat surrounded by ghosts. Carefully, she turned off the recorder. The destruction of the probe and its passengers had been Sinestro's fault. He had used his mistake as a monstrous lie to stoke the fires of hatred. Perhaps by now he even believed it. What would he do if she exposed him? What would the Qwardians do? Stop trying to invade? She doubted it. Their civilization demanded that they try to project themselves into the posimatter universe. It was their only chance of survival.

In order to do that they needed Sinestro. If he realized his life was built on a lie, he might go away.

Ha, she thought. *Dream on.*

There had to be a way to use this knowledge against him.

Eddie. The way was Eddie. Somewhere inside the purple madman, Eddie Rocheford still lived. If only she could reach him. First, she had to find him.

Jenny launched a blip. It hit the inside of the *Sid* and bounced back. Her energy was sealed inside the Qwardian craft. Only by leaving the craft would she be able to communicate telepathically with Eddie or Kyle. The craft itself remained up and running. Cautiously, she made her way to the bridge, a crescent-shaped console facing forward. A wraparound screen showed the view ahead as if it were glass. It was not glass. It was a Qwardian substance that transmitted light images with a millisecond delay for analysis and protection.

Jenny settled herself in the captain's chair. It closed around her, shrinking and fitting her form, sliding forward so the controls were within reach. The controls looked like her grandmother's pin-cushion, an assortment of multi-colored switches and knobs.

"Tracking," she said. "I need tracking."

A pod detached itself from the console and rose on a narrow stalk to face her. "Where is Sinestro?" she said into the pod. The console hummed and crackled. She smelled a faint electric burn. A tendril of vapor escaped a seam and rose toward the ceiling. The ship was essentially five hundred million years old, but if Sinestro was able to recreate it, it should be good as new.

Yeah, right. It only had a billion parts. Even the latest batteries were perishable after a couple years. A nuclear reactor could be coaxed into its centuries. But millennia? She was kidding herself. She hoped she hadn't burned the ship down.

The viewscreen went blank. Slate gray. A black point appeared before her like an anti-matter planet in the distance, grew with startling speed to encompass the screen and turned into a chart. Saturn, the rings, the planets, the ship, the combatants. The ship was shown in bright yellow outline. The combatants were green and purple. They were five thousand miles overhead, in the rings.

"Ship what's your name?" "*Sid*," the ship rumbled in basso profundo.

"*Sid*, take me to Sinestro."

Sid shook itself like a dog. The humming and crackling seemed to extend all the way to the stern. The ship began to vibrate. When Jenny strained forward, the seat held her gently but firmly.

"Please remain seated for the duration of the journey." The voice was both resonant and metallic. With no sense of motion, the ship began to move. She watched the swirling miasma of rocks and gas through the screen. It was like rising through a swamp. Debris slid down the hall with a hideous scratching noise. Sinestro had reconstructed the ship out of posimatter. It was now truly in the universe for the first time, and therefore vulnerable.

"Come on, baby," Jenny urged *Sid*. "You can do it." Just like her old Camaro. It only needed some encouragement. The half-billion-year-old ship swam up through Saturn's murky depths, a tapered yellow cylinder. The hull groaned and sang. A crack appeared in the bulkhead with a sound like a rifle shot.

Jenny laid hands on the control console willing it to hold together. "Come on, *Sid*," she cajoled and prayed. "You can do it! You're a good old ship!"

An asteroid the size of a Volkswagen banged off the hull, momentarily altering the ship's orientation. *Sid* righted itself and continued to climb. The storm of ice particles began to break in spots, permitting some vision. She caught glimpses of the rings gleaming faint sunlight and a massive dark shape that could only be a moon.

The graph before her charted her progress. She was closing the distance quickly. She would be within sight of the combatants within minutes. "Clear the screen. Show the view ahead."

The black chart disappeared, replaced by a wraparound vista of swirling gray and pink columns of frozen ammonia reaching thousands of miles into the atmosphere. Far ahead she saw tiny alternating flashes. Yellow and green. The boys were having at it. She didn't want to distract Kyle at a crucial moment, but she had better let him know she was coming.

"*Sid*, I want to speak with the Green Lantern."

"It is forbidden."

"*Sid*, this is your captain speaking. I'm overriding your programming. Contact the Green Lantern now."

"Impossible. Such action would result in immediate self-destruct."

"Hera help me," Jen muttered. Nor could she communicate with Kyle telepathically while inside the ship. If she wanted to speak with him she'd have to go outside.

Outside.

Could she risk it?

She had no choice. She'd felt Sinestro's power on Qward. It was greater than Kyle's. Hal Jordan hadn't been able to put Sinestro away. Oh, it had worked for a while. But the Qwardians had recreated him from the yellow ring that had transferred his entire being back to Qward.

The only chance they had of putting Sinestro away was to appeal to the Eddie inside. She knew he was in there. She could feel him. If she could show Eddie the record of the flight controller, what had really happened, they stood a chance.

Cautiously, she disentangled herself from the captain's seat, fearful that it would seize and hold her fast. The ship was still rising with that hideous scraping noise against the hull, and an unpleasant burning-rubber odor emanating from the control console. Jenny carefully hefted the flight box. It felt like it weighed a ton. Through the viewscreen, the green and yellow flashes increased in frequency and brightness.

The mists parted before a vast cumulus valley. Green Lantern on the left, planted on a table-sized asteroid like a Heroclix. A mile away, Sinestro straddling a buffalo-shaped rock hurling bolts like Nolan Ryan. Like a cosmic game of billiards they sent asteroids hurtling toward one another, or used bankshots to try and take advantage of the angles. The action was fast and furious with no let-up on either side. If they saw the ship they gave no sign.

"Kyle!" she beamed. No go. She would have to leave the ship.

"Okay, baby," she said to herself. "Let's do it."

Hefting the flight recorder like a football, she walked back amidships where an airlock bulged on the port side. "Let me out," she said.

No response. She placed her hand against a square plastic panel. The door to the airlock instantly irised open. She stepped through into a cubicle with rounded corners. Another iris appeared on the inside of the outer hull as a ceramic design. The inner door whizzed shut and air began to leave the chamber with an ominous hiss. In seconds she would be in a vacuum.

She hoped her powers hadn't deserted her on Qward. She didn't want to throw bolts or build worlds, she merely wanted to survive and get her message to Kyle. Nursing the bolus of life at her core, she tapped into the power of the Starheart, reflexively holding her breath while the atmosphere disappeared and the outer door opened up. A soap-bubble thin emerald forcefield protected her.

She was transfixed by the naked heavens. Rocks hurtled silently past in a raging river. Comets blazed, glowing exclamation points across the sky. Green and yellow reflected off the crazy clouds. The good ship *Sid* slid forward. Its vector put it directly between the combatants. Sinestro and Green Lantern stopped fighting.

"Jen!" Kyle's voice rang in her skull. The link was up!

"Stay there. Sinestro won't take a chance on hurting this ship. I have something I think will stop him." In a concentrated burst she told him what she had.

Sinestro looked confused. "Jenny?" he called in Eddie's voice.

Hope leaped in Jen's heart. Eddie was alive! Somewhere within the monstrosity, he was alive.

"Eddie, the Qwardians told you that the Green Lanterns destroyed this ship, but that's not true."

"Silence!" Sinestro raged, crushing Eddie like a cigarette butt. "How dare you bring the *Sid* into a battle zone? Haven't you done enough damage?"

"What have I done, Eddie?"

It was weird. The three of them talking like a love triangle at the coffee house while hovering over Saturn, kept alive by enormous energies channeled over vast distances.

"You tried to seduce him from his mission. You are a liar!"

"Him, Eddie? Or you? Can you still feel, Eddie? Are you still human?"

Careful babe, Kyle telewhispered in her ear.

"Who's the liar, Sinestro? You told me the Green Lanterns were responsible for the death of the *Sid*."

"They are."

"How can that be when the *Sid* entered our solar system five hundred million years ago, before humanity even existed?"

"The Green Lanterns are as capable of time travel as am I."

She had him now. She was no lawyer, but she was expert at debate. "Sinestro, you just admitted you could travel back in time." She held the dense black box over her head. "Look. The *Sid*'s flight recorder. It has recorded the *Sid*'s last minutes. Are you willing to hear the truth?"

Chromium spikes radiated from Sinestro's head as his subconscious raged. They flickered into the clouds where they radiated, fainter and fainter, sending back a low rumble. Kyle maneuvered so that he had a clear field of fire. He kept his fists clenched and his head down.

Is this going somewhere?

Yes! Sinestro caused the Sid *to crash.*

Kyle had the wisdom not to voice his apprehension.

"How do I know you haven't manipulated the flight recorder?" Sinestro said.

"How? It's alien technology. Watch the replay and judge for yourself whether I had anything to do with it."

Sinestro made a little motion with his hand. *Come on.*

Jade held it out and pushed the button. The buttons were intuitive, marked with vectors. In the middle of the triangle the flight box told its story in three-dimensional hologram. Theater in the round. It was as if they were there experiencing the moment.

Sinestro's chest filled with pride—until the first meteorite slammed into the ship.

"*Lies!*"

The telepathic cry nearly tore her skull off. She flinched, holding her head. Sinestro seized the flight recorder with a yellow beam and hurled it into the frozen storm. It clipped the prow of the *Sid*, breaking it off.

In an instant, Jenny was at Kyle's side and within his protective glow.

"Hey, dummy!" Kyle projected his thoughts into Sinestro's head. "You're doing it again."

Sinestro went berserk.

41

B lack Canary was glued to Dr. Phil when the doorbell rang. Setting aside her glass of Chardonnay, she got up from the sofa and padded to the front door in pedal-pushers and a sleeveless Tennessee Titans sweatshirt, long blond hair done up in a French braid. Her first impression when she opened the door was an indigent who thought he was Jesus.

"Dinah, may I come in?"

With a lurching sensation in the pit of her stomach, she realized it was Hal. Hard to believe the light-hearted test pilot had turned into this grim Spectre.

"Come in, Hal. Have some fresh-baked lemon bars."

Jordan followed her into the sunlit oak-finished foyer. "Smells great. Hope I didn't catch you at a bad time."

You might have phoned first, she thought. "Not at all. Just laying around watching Dr. Phil. What's up, Hal? You want to stay for dinner? You look like you could use a good meal."

"I don't eat. Sorry to bother you like this but a situation has come up that might require your assistance. Sinestro's back, have you heard?"

Dinah Lance's perfect face scrunched. "You know," she said quietly, "this doesn't come as a complete surprise. I had a feeling he'd be back."

"How are your ultrasonics?"

"I've been practicing. Want to see me shatter a glass? Why? You want to try that stunt we used back in '71?"

"That's what I had in mind. Slight problem. He's on Saturn."

"Saturn?"

"I can transport you there and keep you safe."

"How am I going to reach his ears in space?"

"I can do that."

"Why don't you just sing to him yourself? You know—the Lullaby of Birdland."

"I can't do that."

"Does Ollie know about this?"

"Of course."

Black Canary smiled wanly. She'd been looking forward to a home spa day. "Give me a minute to get in costume and pack a few things."

"I really appreciate this, Dinah."

"Hey. What's not to like about saving the human race? You mind answering a question, though?"

Jordan sighed. "I dress like this because I find it comfortable and I don't want to attract attention, okay?"

"No problem," said Dinah as she retreated to her bedroom. She pulled off the pedal-pushers and put on a pair of heavy, baggy cotton trousers. She pulled on a black turtleneck and an insulated vest over that. Dressed, she left the bedroom, set the alarms and followed Jordan out to the street. Parked in front was a '67 Volkswagen Microbus festooned with Grateful Dead stickers.

"You've got to be kidding. We're going to Saturn in that?"

Jordan shrugged. "First we're stopping by Kyle's apartment to pick up his battery. As for the vehicle, it can take any shape you please. Would you prefer something else?"

Dinah shrugged, grinning. "No, leave it. It's so you."

They got in the bus. Jordan sat behind the wheel but didn't touch a thing. Silently, the bus rose into the air. Weightless, gentle, like a balloon. Elm leaves brushed the window as it cleared the shaded street. It rose above the outskirts of Star City. Dinah could see the stadium, the federal courthouse, all the way to the coast. Soon the earth below had diminished to a crazy quilt of farmland and development then that faded beneath a layer of clouds.

Faster and faster it rose. Dinah could feel the acceleration now, in the passage of atmosphere over the hull. It sure didn't ride like a

Volkswagen. Aside from the eerie whistle, the interior was silent. Dinah had an urge to punch the eight-track, listen to the Dead. They'd only left behind four continuous years of recorded music. She was a little more country herself, wondered if the radio would pick up transmissions.

Then the light around them faded, and they were in space.

"Hal, why don't you just kill him? The last Spectre would have snuffed him in an instant."

Jordan drummed his fingers on the steering wheel. "I have a different set of marching orders. No direct interference."

"Back to that again," Dinah clucked. "But you bring me out there to zap him. Why don't *you* knock him out, Hal? Gently."

Jordan grimaced and gripped the wheel. Hard driving ahead. "I'm not too good at the finesse stuff. You are. I'll never forget the way you took him out that time in Colorado."

"I'll bet Sinestro never forgot it either. Certainly he's taken steps to guard against a recurrence."

"It's not the same Sinestro."

"Wouldn't he share the same memories?"

"Possibly. It's been a long time. He may have forgotten."

"This strikes me as a long shot."

Jordan issued a complex shrug. "I have a gut feeling it's the right thing to do."

"By all means, go with your gut." Dinah settled back in her seat. They were making tremendous progress now, Earth receding visibly. She reached out one long, elegant finger and pushed the radio. "Sugar Magnolia" poured from the tinny speakers.

CHAPTER

42

E ven in his fury, Sinestro had the wit to seal the *Sid* in a yellow envelope and shove it aside. Within the envelope, a bluish vapor leaked from the damaged prow.

"*You!*" the purple devil raged. "It's *your* fault I damaged the *Sid!*"

Kyle stood in a fighter's crouch, bobbing, ready to move in any direction. Jenny was the South Pole to Kyle's North, looking at Sinestro "upside down." Separated by six miles, they could see each other clearly through refracted vision, their positions constantly changing. Sinestro projected his face up close and personal like the Wizard of Oz, a psychological trick designed to unnerve them. Jenny still saw a little of Eddie and felt a smirk creep onto her lips even as her pulse redlined.

On the other side of the rock, "Eddie" never entered Green Lantern's mind. He faced Sinestro, the greatest threat to Earth in his lifetime. Would even Ion have the power to stop this berserker and close the gates? GL could feel them opening all over Earth, a faint echo of the cosmic consciousness he'd possessed as Ion. In his mind, he could see the JLA projection centering on Saturn.

Sinestro was somehow coordinating the gates.

A blazing line cracked the sky. Kyle couldn't look at the line directly. It was too bright. It stretched from Earth's moon to Saturn's core. Then came the crack of doom. It threatened to implode their skulls. It was the loudest sound Kyle ever heard. If the ring hadn't automatically thrown up a barrier, he would have gone deaf.

He *had* gone deaf. Sinestro's face hung within touching distance three yards high, twisted in a froth of hate. Kyle couldn't make out the words. His ears rang. The rock on which he stood plummeted away so fast he thought Sinestro had whacked it with a giant tennis racket. It was Jenny. She'd yanked them aside an instant before two purple hands slammed together where they'd just been. The twelve-foot hands shattered a rock the size of a Humvee into dust.

Kyle couldn't hear. He lay glued to the rock, staring up as they plummeted toward Saturn, purple glow receding in the sky. A green blur swept by him on a yellow strand. "Jenny!" he cried, reaching out for her with his mind.

I'm sorry, Kyle, reverberated in his skull. *He's got me.*

Kyle boiled in impotent rage. He willed himself in pursuit. He remained glued to the rock as it hurtled toward the center of the gas giant. What had happened to the charge he'd picked up on Qward? Spent already? He searched within himself for the glowing green nimbus. It was a faint smudge, a thumb print. He'd been using power like Manhattan during a heat wave. He felt in his bones that he'd caused a switcheroo coming back through the gate and that it had cost him enormous energy reserves.

A purple dot appeared overhead, grew rapidly into a hurtling face. The mask of Sinestro followed him into the depths like a dive bomber. Sinestro displayed his small perfect teeth.

"So it comes to this, ancient enemy. You are depleted and defeated. The energy you stole from Qward has a half-life of twenty-three minutes in your universe. I have your woman. I shall breed with her. Parthenogenesis be damned. I am not Qwardian. You'll plummet to the center and be incinerated. I wish I could tell you I respect you as a foe, but I don't. Farewell!"

The face receded in the sky. Green Lantern plummeted. All his energy had fled. He was helpless, glued to the damned rock like a bumper sticker. The rock rotated, and he faced down. He was into thick atmosphere now, unable to see because of the intense cloud cover. Tiny bits of solid matter struck his face. Grit. He was losing what little protection the ring offered. His air was leaking out. It was getting difficult to breath. The ring had stopped generating oxygen. His hand flopped to his side. He felt the other ring, the one Superman had made for him.

Too late. Too late.

I love you! He pinged, preparing himself for impact with the planet's rocky core. A tiny rectangle appeared far below and quickly grew in size.

Whump. He stopped. He'd landed on an air mattress. He looked around. Black Canary grinned at him over the back of her seat. He looked up. He'd fallen through the moonroof of. . . a Volkswagen Microbus?

"Hal!" he exploded, recognizing the driver. "What's going on?"

"Not much," Jordan replied. Kyle boosted himself to a kneeling position and looked through the windshield at the violent clouds of Saturn. The Grateful Dead played on bus's sound system. Kyle wondered if someone had slipped him a hallucinogen and he was back in Manhattan at some dumb model party. On the other hand, that was more Jordan's trip than his.

"Sinestro's got Jenny-Lynn. We've got to save her."

"That's why we're here," Jordan remarked, as if they were going to pick up some cinnamon buns.

"I need to recharge."

Black Canary reached under the dash, turned around and handed Kyle his battery. "Here."

Kyle thrust his ring to the lens. "Hal," he said, "in honor of your past incarnations—or at least one of them—it's my pleasure to say: In brightest day, in blackest night, no evil shall escape my sight . . ."

Jordan and Black Canary joined in. They all recited the oath together. The interior of the bus flashed chartreuse. Kyle was juiced. He was the Energizer Bunny, the Green Avenger. He soared into Saturn's stratosphere at Mach 5. Jordan joined him on the right, arms crossed, coat tails flapping, encased in a green nimbus—Hal had tapped into the power of Kyle's ring.

"Got a plan?"

"I'm gonna deconstruct the bastard."

They were standing on a rock, clouds swirling around them. What had happened to their upward momentum? Kyle looked at Jordan.

"Just a second, Kyle. This isn't the same Sinestro we fought thirty years ago."

"No kidding, Sherlock. That's what I've been trying to tell you!"

"No. What I mean is his cells still retain their genetic imprint of Eddie Rocheford."

"Well whoop-de-do! Hal, every second we delay could cost Jenny her life!"

"He's not going to kill her. If he does that he loses all touch with his humanity. *Besides.* You heard him."

"You heard that?"

Jordan nodded.

"You think he gives a damn about his humanity?"

"He does care, Kyle. The Qwardians think they can get around nature. They can't. The basic biological nature of each organism will eventually assert itself. Sinestro may look like an alien, but he was made to look that way by his masters. The ring knows."

"What does the ring know that I don't?"

"Use the power of the ring to bring Eddie back. On a cellular level. The ring remembers the man. Devolve him."

Kyle was restive. Jordan had picked the worst possible time to lecture. "I don't have time for this!" he hissed. *You old burn-out,* he nearly added. Jordan looked at him funny as if he'd read Kyle's thoughts. He pulled back a little and a wry smile settled on his thin lips.

"Sorry if I seem a little mysterious or didactic. In life as in comedy, timing is everything. Sinestro is much stronger than you know. You're going to need a distraction if you're going to get past his barriers."

"So give me a distraction!"

Jordan shook his head as if in amused bewilderment. He made a little brushing motion with his finger tips. "Go now. Go on."

Kyle blipped Jen, found her twelve thousand miles overhead. Instantly, GL was gonesville. Jordan shut his eyes to preserve Kyle's purple after-image against his retina. He prayed that he'd timed it right.

CHAPTER

43

At four in the morning, Eastern Standard Time, the White House chief of staff woke the president. Seventeen inter-dimensional portals had opened all over Earth, mostly in the Northern Hemisphere, and had effectively shut down all satellite and cellular communications. Land lines still worked.

At six, the president met with the joint chiefs of staff and the national security advisor in the Situations Room at the White House. A massive electronic flatscreen showed a Mercator projection of the globe and a series of small flashing red lights.

"We have nothing in the air," the secretary of defense said. "No one does. Whatever it is, it's playing hob with electrical transmissions. We can't even get a drone up. It's the same all over."

"How many gates are there in the United States?" the president asked.

"Six," replied the NSA. She was a petite woman with a voice like Betty Boop, but her words meant business. "One of them in downtown Gotham. The rest are scattered all over, mostly in rural areas. There are four gates in Russia, one in Kazakhstan three in China, two in Africa. There might be more but we wouldn't know. All our comsats are down."

The president looked down the long table at the somber faces of his staff. "Where's the Justice League representative?"

"Sir," the defense secretary said, "just before we lost all communications, I spoke to the sentinel on duty, Plastic Man."

There were several groans. The president slammed his palm on the table. "Go on."

"He said they were aware of the situation and were trying to reach other members, but only Green Lantern was actively involved in the current situation."

"Green Lantern," the president said. "Good man."

"He's a boy," said the defense secretary. "I wish I had more confidence. I wish we had some way of contacting Superman."

"From what I understand," said the NSA, "not even Superman can affect the situation. It appears as though the Qwardians are attempting to open a gate to our universe. Because of inter-dimensional physics, Saturn is the best place for that gate. All these beams emanating from Earth to the Moon to Saturn are an attempt to create a flashback channel."

"Flashback?" the president asked.

"Yes, sir. Instantaneous teleportation. It would be my guess they are mounting an invasion force on the other side of the gate. As soon as the gate opens, they will appear here on Earth. You might consider moving to the secure facility in Virginia, sir."

"What's the point of that?" the president asked. "A mass invasion would result in war. Do they think we won't resist? What do they get by destroying Earth?"

"Revenge. With the energies they hope to harvest, they'll terraform a new planet and occupy this spot."

"What energies do they hope to harvest?"

The NSA advisor looked up and down the table. "It's going to be a big bang."

The lights went out.

"Everybody stay calm," said the president. "The emergency generators should kick in any second."

A minute later the lights went back on, dimmer than before. The wall display did not light up.

On Qward, two hundred and fifty thousand Weaponers began filing into a hundred troop transports. Troops necessary to subdue Earth defense forces. The planet Earth would not blow up. The purpose of the beam extending from Earth to Saturn was to provide instant transport as soon as Qwardian forces crossed over. The matter/anti-matter collision would not take place because the new Sinestro had pioneered a complete cellular flip-flop. Only through the generation of a Qwardian Sinestro that included human tissue were they able to cross over without exploding. Now that Eddie-Sinestro had paved the way, they had obtained a sample of his DNA to inoculate every Qwardian.

The old method of controlling matter/anti-matter collision through electromagnetism had failed. The new method would succeed. The entire Qwardian invasion force would be transported to Earth in an instant, at which point the beam would collapse and all Earth-based communications systems would go back up. They would have a fight on their hands.

The Qwardians estimated that it would take seventy-two hours to subdue Earth, at which point Earth defenses would be so degraded they could bring over the rest of the Qwardians. Because Qward was not long for the anti-matter universe—the planet was days away from death by exhaustion. The ineffable element of life that had driven the Qwardians for eons had run its course. Only by transforming the entire race, by crossing over into the posimatter universe, could they renew their lease on life.

Sinestro waited on the other side of the gate to guide them through.

He appeared as a purple dot on the display aboard the JLA satellite.

Plastic Man slumped in his chair watching the dot, unable to communicate with Earth. All Earth communications, including land lines, were now frozen within a stasis sphere that extended from the Earth to the Moon to Saturn. Eel could see it through the heavily filtered window. A blinding beam circled the Moon like a lottery cage, forming up on the far side and shooting toward Saturn.

The JLA satellite lay outside the energy sphere encapsulating Earth. Eel had been searching for Kyle for forty-five minutes, since he'd abruptly disappeared off the screen. Eel was frightened. The way Green Lantern had simply blipped out could only indicate one thing—he was dead. Eel didn't want to think about that. So many strange energy fields surrounded him it was possible the equipment had simply malfunctioned, or Kyle had gone around to the other side of the planet and the equipment couldn't pick him up.

Alan Scott looked over Eel's shoulder. "I've half a mind to go up there."

"Don't do that, sir. You can do more good here."

"What good?"

"Someone's going to have to fight the Qwardians if they do make it through."

"My daughter's in the hands of a madman and you want me to fight a rearguard action?"

"Someone—someone with significant power—has got to be here . . . just in case, sir."

O'Brien felt like a worm. He slunk away from the furious CEO and glanced anxiously at the member monitor board. Nothing. He was so freaked out he'd even activated the Superman signal from Olsen's old watch. He hadn't told Kyle he had it. No one was supposed to know he had it. Superman had brought it to him months ago when he'd been cleared for satellite duty. The signal couldn't penetrate the energy sphere. Superman could be anywhere. His Fortress of Solitude spanned several dimensions. He might not even be in this universe. In any case Eel couldn't count on him, or any of the others apparently.

"Wonder Woman!" he yelled, listening to his voice echo down the long curving corridor until it faded from the ear completely.

"Why hast thou deserted me," he followed up in a conversational tone. "Hawkman, J'onn J'onz, Flash, where are you guys?" The silence was creeping him out.

"Shut up," Scott snapped without looking up. "I'm trying to find them."

"Sorry."

Ping!

Eel opened his eyes and glanced at the board. A bright green dot had appeared approaching the purple dot and its pale green satellite. Green Lantern was back.

"Sir!"

"I see him."

Heart in throat, Eel took his seat at the big board. "You go, boy," he said under his breath, searching the board for other JLA members. Two other readings, Hal Jordan and Black Canary.

"Where's my daughter?" Scott muttered in a threatening tone.

"Huh!" Eel exclaimed. The Spectre could go anywhere he liked, but Black Canary? What was she doing there?

"The Spectre! Yeah, boy!"

Minnie the space cat yowled and leaped into Eel's lap. He was happy to have the company. "Minnie! We're saved! The Spectre is on the case."

Eel stared hard at the monitor, waiting for the Spectre to make his move. The bright green and purple icon indicating the Spectre didn't move. The green and crimson dots jockeyed for position.

With a sinking sensation in his gut, Plastic Man realized the Spectre wasn't going to do anything.

CHAPTER

44

The gate began to open at 50,000 miles above Saturn. It began as a postage-stamp sized gleam, dazzling white. It reflected off Sinestro's eyes, nestled deeply beneath his brow like two badgers in a burrow. He arced his back in fierce exultation, watching the gate grow to the size of a door in the shape of a rhomboid. It was large enough for the dreadnaughts to insert their bows and force themselves through like an invasion from the womb. But they would wait on the other side until the gate stretched for many miles, then drive through a dozen abreast.

The distant Sun kicked up monumental flares, which would not reach Saturn for weeks. Sinestro had to keep the gate open and the Sun was the most potent source of nearby power.

The Earth blacked out, a victim of Sinestro's monstrous energy needs. Power fled the grid like water down a drain. Only independent emergency generators still functioned, lighting most hospitals and some private homes. Looking down from the JLA's lunar tower, Plastic Man was shocked to find Earth gone dark.

Sinestro savored the moment. The arrogant humans brought low, their champion crushed. The gate was the size of a football field and the intensity of the Sun. He could see through to the other side, the hazy outline of hundreds of dreadnaughts standing by. He could just make out the wavery shape of the control tower at the back of the field.

Sinestro held his arms wide in welcome. "Come!" he commanded. "Do not wait! Earth is ours for the taking!"

They saw him. The lead craft began to levitate.

A bolus of green entered his peripheral vision. Sinestro whirled and loosed a killing bolt. The jagged lightning shattered against a green umbrella.

"Not now," Sinestro snarled. "Not now you miserable little toad!" He sank into a kempo stance, leveled both arms at Green Lantern and channeled the power of the Sun. He struck Green Lantern like Tiger Woods teeing off. Green Lantern sailed eighteen thousand miles into the rough. Behind Sinestro, the green girl gasped.

Sinestro turned to regard her, bound in crimson coils. He smiled. She tried to send more spores his way but he'd installed a filter along the single strand connecting them. He turned back to watch the lead dreadnaught enter the posimatter universe, aware of everything around him for a parsec, everything but Black Canary and the Spectre, who had used his power to shield their approach.

"Go ahead," the Spectre urged, extending a filament between the bus and Sinestro.

Black Canary sang so softly Sinestro was not aware he was being serenaded until blinding pain erupted in his head.

"AAARGH!" he screamed so loudly he created a backwash that nearly drove Black Canary mad. The Spectre dropped his link. Sinestro's head cleared. The hairs on the back of his neck reached for the sky. Too late, he turned to see what object had come upon him in the void and gasped.

The green coffin struck him in the gut. Over nine feet long, it was sheathed in solid jade and bore his death mask in bas relief on the lid. As it bore him relentlessly toward the center of the planet he looked down and saw his own image staring back at him, upside down. The image Green Lantern had carved.

"EEYARGH!" he cried, shoving it away with all his might. He couldn't tolerate reminders of his own mortality. The casket tumbled toward a house-sized asteroid and split open. There was nothing inside.

Sinestro heard a dog barking. "Barkley?" he said in Eddie's voice. He turned, and the black-and-white mutt was all over him like a cheap suit. Green Lantern floated nearby, Jenny's hand on his shoulder, casting his ring over the eight-foot-tall alien. GL had recreated the dog from Jenny's memories, gleaned from her touch. As the Qwardian hit-man embraced his ghost dog, Kyle cast a green funnel searching for a morsel of humanity. The green glowed hot in Eddie's heart.

GL cushioned and surrounded Eddie's cellular memory, pouring everything he had into reversing the transformation. Sinestro stiffened, shoved the ghost dog away. It evaporated. Sinestro's window of vulnerability closed. But too late. Green Lantern had seized the handful of cells, strengthening their human DNA and causing them to multiply.

Each time he and Sinestro had clashed, their rings had exchanged information. Green Lantern had an advantage over Sinestro—he was still the same man, while Sinestro had evolved from a human being. GL's ring retained enough memory of Eddie to picture him, which stimulated regression. A sprinkling of flesh-colored freckles spread on Sinestro's scarlet cheek.

An enormous crack split the sky. All eyes turned toward the glowing rhomboid. Six dreadnaughts were coming through side by side. Sinestro turned from the gate to his ancient foe, tiny eyes strobing hate.

"You can't stop us . . . " he hissed, eyes rolling back into the top of his head.

Green Lantern played his cone of light over Sinestro like a hand-held hose. "We'll stop you every time."

The smattering of pink across Sinestro's face spread downward. His extremities wavered and shrank. As Sinestro lost his grip, the force binding the channels from Earth to Saturn wavered.

Jenny shifted her grip around Kyle's waist, pressing her cheek against his back. *It's faltering*, she thought.

The Sinestro program raged against erasure, twisting its host like a worried rosary. "Fight it!" Kyle exhorted Eddie.

"Fight it, Eddie!"

Half-human eyes turned from scarlet to brown. Boyish wonder bloomed on a resurrected face. Eddie Rocheford III, "Roach" to his pals, found himself inexplicably above Saturn witnessing a phenomenon. The rhomboid-shaped gate flexed and flickered like a bad television transmission. The dreadnaughts tried to reverse their forward progress but were caught in an energy flux.

The universe had a grip on their prows, which had transformed to positive matter while passing through the gate. The Qwardian universe seized their negative sterns with the force of gravity. The gate gyrated like bad neon.

Eddie gave a strangled cry. As he waved his hand, the ring slipped off. Kyle caught it and put it in his pocket. Next to the other ring. Making a gun with his hand, he enclosed the now human Eddie in a protective sphere. Eddie would see things most humans never dreamed of seeing. Green Lantern hoped it wouldn't drive the exterminator insane.

The gate snapped shut, severing the prows of the six dreadnaughts, spilling hundreds of Weaponers who disappeared in a sea of bloody explosions. An instant later the prows broke up, dissolving like marzipan in the rain, trailing glitter across thousands of miles of sky.

The beam from Earth blinked out.

The lights on Earth blinked on.

"What am I doing here?" Eddie asked in a frightened voice. Green Lantern had seen exposure to space destroy personalities. For some people the immensity was too much. It caused their minds to shut down. He was about to conjure up an enclosure, something to help Eddie feel more secure, when a Volkswagen Microbus nosed up with Hal at the wheel.

Jenny still had a grip on Kyle's waist. He looked down, tilted her head up. "Hey. Come up here a minute."

She slithered up so they were face to face. "Have I told you today that I love you?" Kyle said. Jenny grinned and planted a wet one on his face, pulled back and assumed a modest stance. She was not an exhibitionist despite her chosen profession. The bus pulled to a stop on their left. The rear door slid open. The Spectre used the borrowed power of the lantern to extend a protective energy conduit to Eddie. Black Canary helped a dazed and groping Eddie into the back, where he collapsed on the mattress face down.

"Man," he said. "Somebody must have slipped me some ecstasy or something." "You'll be all right, Eddie," Jenny told him. "We'll take care of you."

"Come on," the Spectre said. "Get in the car. We don't have all day."

Kyle and Jenny piled in and slammed the door shut rocking the plastic Buddha glued to the dash.

"Careful!" Jordan said. "This is a classic."

"But Hal—you conjured up this bus out of the whole cloth. It's *not* a genuine classic."

Jordan hunched over the wheel. "Doesn't matter. It's the principle."

With Kyle and Jade on cushions in the back, Jordan turned the bus around and headed back toward Earth. An excited voice overrode the endless Dead jam that had been playing on the speakers.

"Plas to Green Lantern! You did it! Boy howdy, Jim! We were beginning to get a little worried!"

"I had some help, but thanks."

"You were about to get a lot more. Everyone checked in. Everyone wants to know what happened."

Kyle felt exhaustion sweep him under. "They'll have to wait for my report, Plas. I'm bushed."

He lay his head in Jenny's lap. She put her hand on his head. With the Dead warbling he fell asleep, one hand resting on a *Have Gun Will Travel* lunch box.

CHAPTER

45

E ddie was admitted to a sanatorium on Long Island for observation. He was told he'd had a toxic reaction to some bug spray. Eddie asked who had admitted him. "Green Lantern," the nurse told him. GL had dropped Jenny-Lynn and the lantern off in Greenwich Village and gone to the JLA's lunar Watchtower. Alan Scott had returned to Earth to terrorize his employees and get the story out.

The yellow ring hung suspended between Green Lantern and the Spectre on the Watchtower's bridge. Plastic Man slumped in a chair playing with his keychain and staring at Sinestro's ring with a larcenous gleam in his eye. Both Kyle and Jordan turned to accuse him with silent stares.

"I'm just looking, all right? Can't a guy look?"

"What will we do with it?" Kyle asked.

"Give it to Superman. He'll put it in a safe place."

Kyle didn't doubt it. There was probably a door to Qward somewhere in the Fortress of Solitude.

"Will you do it?" Kyle said. "I really have to get back to Jen."

The Spectre smiled. "Sure. I've been meaning to take a look at that Fortress."

"What about Black Canary? Does she need a ride earthside?"

The Spectre made the little brushing motion with his fingers. "Go. I'll deliver Pretty Bird to Star City."

Jenny looked fresh as a spring crocus in tight jeans and loose Army surplus sweatshirt, lounging in an Eames chair sipping Kristol. Alan Scott sat on the sofa in a banker's pinstripe drinking Bushmills on the rocks. Father and daughter were laughing when Kyle opened the door, much to his relief. His eyes went at once to the lunch box open on the coffee table.

"Where'd you get that lunch box?"

"Hal gave it to me," Jade said. "He said he wanted us to have it. He baked fresh brownies! Have one."

Scott picked up a brownie.

Kyle was famished. He picked up a brownie and bit it in half.

"Jenny tells me you had quite a struggle. Congratulations, son. Looks like you've saved the universe. I wish we could run it on the six o'clock news but it would only cause panic and the stock market to plunge. I'm putting it all in my book, to be published after my death. Jenny, I'm counting on you."

"Oh Daddy! Stop it."

"Why can't you print it now?"

"Because you pulled the curtain on something best left unseen. Your average man in the street has enough to worry about without alien invaders. Now that I've seen for myself that my wayward daughter is alive and well, I'll leave you young people. I'm sure you have lots to talk about."

"You don't have to run off because of me, sir," Kyle said automatically.

Scott ignored him, gathered his things, kissed his daughter, shook Kyle's hand and left. Kyle turned around. Jen was holding up the Little Pink Pregnancy Test.

"Is this what all the frenzy was about?"

Kyle blushed. Finally caught. "Why wouldn't you tell me if you were pregnant?"

"Because it's not my pregnancy test. It belongs to Sonya. You know Sonya—the model from Czechoslovakia?"

Kyle pictured a wire-limbed beauty who occasionally stopped by. He turned a shade not dissimilar to Sinestro. "What's it doing here?"

"Never mind what you were doing in my closet, it's here because Sonya spent the night with me last month and was worried that she was pregnant so she brought the test over here. Only she forgot it. I jammed it back there because I didn't want you to find it and jump to the wrong conclusion."

"You mean you're not pregnant?"

"Noooo."

"I'm an idiot."

"That you are. But you're my idiot. Didn't you have something you wanted to show me?"

Kyle reached into his pocket and felt the ring. He pulled it out. He got down on his knees.

"Jen," he said.

She eyed the ring and smiled. "Kyle," she said, "we've got a lot to talk about."